D1150203

The Morrow Secrets

Trilogy

Book One

Sweet Cherry Publishing Limited
Unit E, Vulcan Business Complex
Vulcan Road
Leicester, LE5 3EB
United Kingdom

First published in Great Britain by Sweet Cherry Publishing 2013
This edition first published in the UK in 2015

Printed and bound by Thomson Press (India) Limited.

Title: The Morrow Secrets
© Susan McNally 2013

ISBN: 978-1-78226-245-9

The right of Susan McNally to be identified as the author of this work has been
asserted by them in accordance with the Copyright, Designs and Patents Act 1988.

All rights reserved.
You may not copy, store, distribute, transmit, reproduce or otherwise make available
this publication (or any part of it) in any form, or by any means (electronic, digital,
optical, mechanical, photocopying, recording or otherwise), without the prior
written permission of the author. Nor can this book be otherwise circulated in any
form of binding or cover other than that in which it is published without the prior
permission of the author. Any person who does any unauthorised act in relation to
this publication may be liable to criminal prosecution and civil claims for damages.

All the characters in this book are fictitious and any resemblance to actual persons
living or dead is purely coincidental.

Illustrations © Luke Spooner, Carrion House 2013

Find out more about the Morrow Secrets trilogy by visiting:
http://www.themorrowsecretstrilogy.com
www.facebook.com/morrowsecrets
www.twitter.com/morrowsecrets

To Christopher

For all his support, for keeping me on track
when I faltered, and for his playfulness,
which inspired me to get in touch with my own

To Hannah and Scarlet

For being the best daughters I could have wished for

Dead flies make the perfumer's ointment give off an evil odour;
So a little folly outweighs wisdom and honour

- Ecclesiastes, Chapter 10, verse 1

The Morrow Secrets

From Wycham Elva
To The Land Of Breedoor

To the
Northern Wolds

Hellstone Tors

Tear Drop
Tarns

Out-of-the-Way
Mountains

Hellscip
Pass

Starling
Caves

Wycham
Elva

Breedoor

Ragging Brows
Forest

Shivering
Water

Gulping
Mire

Wycham
Moor

Winderling
Spires

Wycham
Village

High Bedders
End

Dolly Moor
Fell

Sweet-Side
Pastures

Burnt
Heath

One

It was on that cold, wet miserable day that Tallitha Mouldson made the decision that was to change her life forever. Had she but known the momentous events that would unfold perhaps she would have taken a different course, but she didn't and Tallitha was nothing if not headstrong. Taking two steps at a time she raced up the staircase and darted down the dark corridor, hurriedly wiping away the tears that were streaming down her face. At last she reached the sanctuary of her room, slammed the door shut behind her and with a dramatic flop landed on the bed.

'I won't do it, they can't make me!' she wailed as she twisted her tangled hair in and out of her fingers, sulking about her predicament.

Those dreadful sisters had lied to her all these years, kept secrets from her, she was certain of that now.

'Damn them all,' she shouted and buried her face in the quilt.

Her sobbing came in fitful bursts until eventually she lay quite still in the tumble of blankets, scheming and plotting. Her mind flitted from one daring escape plan to another. She imagined leaving Winderling Spires, she imagined living somewhere else, having a completely different life. She would run away, that was it! But it was hopeless, where would she go? The impossibility of her plight made her cry all the more.

Tallitha was in many respects quite a cranky, sullen girl, at least with the grown-ups in her family. She was not plain and she was not pretty, just somewhere in the middle, with a small round face and an abundance of messy dark hair that rarely entertained a brush.

Sighing loudly she clambered off the bed, flung the quilt to the floor and stared longingly at the mountains in the distance. Hot tears of frustration trickled down her cheeks as she pressed her damp face against the cool glass and watched the rain sheeting down in waves across the pale washed-out skies.

She had to escape from her wretched family. Get away from them all.

'Far away from this dreadful house!' she cried, as her breath misted across the windowpane and obscured her view of freedom.

There were so many things she didn't understand about her eccentric relatives and the mysterious house they inhabited together.

Tallitha lived in a grand apartment in the East Wing of Winderling Spires, an enormous, sprawling house in the land of Wycham Elva. There were servants to do her bidding, row upon row of beautiful clothes and boxes of sparkling jewels but the trouble was Tallitha hated all of it. Some would say she had everything a girl could wish for but Tallitha did not agree with them, and now she was in a worse mess than ever.

Tallitha sniffed loudly and surveyed her untidy bedroom. In her distress she had thrown all the cushions off her bed and messed up the powders and perfumes on her dressing table, with one sweep of her hand.

'I hate her, and I hate it here!' she shouted to no one in particular, pacing the room and kicking a chair.

But the old house was eerily silent in response. Cissie, Tallitha's faithful nurse, heard the rumpus from her sitting room and came bustling in.

'There, there, my little Miss. You must stop frettin' and scowlin', she said lovingly, stroking Tallitha's hair.

Tallitha lifted her tear-stained face and began sobbing again.

'It's so unfair. She wants me to speak like a lady and spend all day doing boring things. She never listens to what I want,' she said, mimicking her Great Aunt Agatha's voice, 'I'm never allowed to do anything!'

'Now, calm yourself my dear'.

'I won't!' Tallitha shouted angrily, 'I'm even forbidden from going upstairs,' she cried, raising her eyes to the ceiling, 'there are floors up there I haven't ever seen!'

'Hush there. What are we to do with you? Makin' such a racket,' replied her indulgent nurse, clicking her tongue in dismay.

'Don't look at me like that,' said Tallitha petulantly, kicking her feet in annoyance.

'Well, what do you want to go upstairs for?' asked Cissie trying to take the heat out of the situation.

She was a small busy bundle of a woman with a kind disposition. Her plump frame was always covered in flowered aprons tied tightly round her generous middle.

'But I do, I do! I want to see what's up there. I want to explore this weird old house.'

'Eh, all those gloomy old rooms, most of them have been locked for years. Fusty and smelly, they 'aven't been slept in since I first came here. Anyhow 'alf the keys are missing,' said Cissie chuckling away to herself.

'It's not funny, you don't know how rotten I feel,' snapped Tallitha.

The trouble was Cissie had heard all of Tallitha's complaints before. But Tallitha was not about to give up that easily.

'I'm going to run away. I will! No one cares about me or Tyaas,' she cried, sneaking a sideways look at Cissie.

'You must stop speaking so. Tyaas is your little brother and looks up to you, now don't you be encouraging him in your naughty ways.'

'I will do as I please!' Tallitha said haughtily, 'stop treating me like a child.'

'But it's dangerous outside Winderling Spires. This house, well it may be odd in its way, but it's your home and you're safe here. There, there, stop cryin'. You must promise me, no more silliness about runnin' away.'

Tallitha folded her arms and scowled. She wouldn't promise Cissie any such thing.

'Besides,' Tallitha said, 'it doesn't have to be like this. Why can't Father be Aunt Agatha's heir?'

'Now, you know why not. Wycham Elva has always been ruled by the women of the family, goin' back for generations.'

Cissie felt put on the spot by Tallitha's questions, the girl had a habit of cornering her.

'Well, what about Mother? She likes all the grandeur.'

'There's no use kicking against it. Snowdroppe can't rule Wycham Elva. It was decided long ago,' said Cissie becoming exasperated.

'I'm not going to do what they want. They can't make me,' she said sharply.

'But they can, my dear. You know they can, and they will,' said Cissie in her softest voice.

Tallitha flung herself across her nurse's lap.

'Do stop now. 'Tis no use,' said Cissie, lovingly.

But Tallitha felt wretched. She was the wrong girl in the wrong life. Something was just not right and she knew it.

Of course the strange old house didn't help. Tallitha was certain that Winderling Spires, with its secrets and peculiarities, had somehow infected the personalities of all the occupants turning them into freakish, contrary beings. Each generation of the Morrow family had tried to outdo the last by building ever more extraordinary wings and adding bizarre turrets to the grand facade of the Spires. The ancient topsy-turvy house was a forbidding landmark as it towered loftily over the countryside, imposing its haunting presence over all it surveyed. The dark cluttered interior with its bewildering layout was no more welcoming. Abandoned rooms and dark lonely floors were linked by a labyrinth of corridors and twisting staircases where the family never ventured.

In the darkest corners of the Spires, complete wings had been locked for generations, their history lost to the collective memory of the Morrow family. Tallitha had once overheard the housekeeper, Mrs Armitage, complaining that she needed more staff, with over four hundred rooms to clean – and they were just the ones she knew about! The house had an ominous atmosphere. On every landing, high up in the corners of ornate ceilings and leaning earthward with lashing tongues and bulging eyes, malevolent gargoyles jutted out from dusty cornices and leered from old carvings encased in wooden staircases.

As Tallitha saw it, her predicament had become worse that very morning. She had been summoned by her great aunt to discuss her progress. Agatha Morrow had designed a programme of study for her great niece. She was determined to teach Tallitha the old-fashioned accomplishments of painting and needlework, and mastering Ennish, the ancient language of the Northern Wolds. Unfortunately, Tallitha was hopeless with needles and she found it hard to concentrate on unpronounce-able verbs from a language she had never heard spoken. Each week she did her best to please her great aunt, to paint pretty scenes and to keep the stitches in her sampler neat, but this went against her unruly nature. She tried to follow the stencil and use the colours in the correct order, but somehow she got into knots, terrible knots, and Agatha Morrow despised knots.

That morning, at the appointed hour, Tallitha sighed and straightened her dishevelled appearance. She meandered through the Spires, wasting time, hoping to avoid the meeting, until one of the Shroves came and found her in the conservatory. The Shroves, the strange old retainers who worked at the Spires, roamed the house from dawn to dusk. They knew every hiding place, and if they found Tallitha in the wrong place at the wrong time they would snitch on her to Great Aunt Agatha and she would get into more trouble. So there was nothing for it. She knocked on the door of her great aunt's sitting room and waited.

Great Aunt Agatha lived in the oldest part of the house, a ramshackle collection of ornate rooms with interconnecting staircases known as the Fedora Wing, named after her ancestor, the first Grand Morrow. Agatha's sitting room was filled with needlework and tapestries and Tallitha was convinced that her aunt laid these samplers out each week to make her feel even more inadequate.

'Enter!' shouted Agatha imperiously.

The Grand Morrow sat on a huge chair with a vexed expression on her face. Marlin, her great aunt's Shrove, had collected Tallitha's sewing earlier that morning and now Agatha was turning the sampler round in her hand and sighing.

'Oh there you are. Well Tallitha, this is poor. What have you to say for yourself?'

The Grand Morrow had a knack of making all those in her presence feel rather small and a little afraid. But Tallitha was a resourceful girl and had rehearsed her speech to achieve maximum charm, or so she thought.

'Dear, dear Aunt Agatha, please don't be cross with me, I have tried hard this week,' she said and feigned an exhausted expression. 'I've spent hours on these stitches. Look, how I've embroidered the pink sherbet flowers, the Persian indigo sky and the tea green hedges in that field!'

Tallitha pointed at the sampler and gasped. Her endeavours had become a fudgy mess of muddled threads. Yet the stitches had seemed so neat yesterday. Oh bother, what was she to do? Agatha Morrow repositioned the spectacles on the bridge of her thin nose and peered at the needlepoint, clicking her tongue and pulling out Tallitha's knotted stitches.

'Such sloppy embroidery!' she snapped.

'But the sewing was neat yesterday. Maybe Marlin dropped it, or trod on it,' said Tallitha shooting an acid look at the old Shrove.

'Nonsense girl, what am I to do with you?'

Tallitha twisted nervously from side to side, wishing she could disappear. Her Great Aunt Agatha was about to deliver her weekly lecture and Tallitha braced herself. Agatha Morrow leaned forward and peered right into Tallitha's face.

'The women of the Morrow family, and this includes you Tallitha, have important duties. The responsibility for all this will fall to you someday. Wycham Elva is a wild place with strange ways. There are some who would take our lands, if we let them,' she said darkly.

Agatha bit her lip and glanced towards the mountains in the distance. Tallitha noticed a look of sadness flit for a moment across her great aunt's face.

'What is it, Aunt? You look upset,' she ventured.

'Upset! Of course I'm upset, with your laziness,' she scowled, 'and why can't you look tidy? That dress is appalling,' she shrieked pulling Tallitha's clothes into place.

Tallitha wrenched away from her great aunt's grasping fingers.

'Why can't you let me be?' she shouted.

Agatha slammed her hand down on the table.

'Do not vex me further! We will try again, Tallitha, and this time you must pay attention. My fear is that you're not up to the responsibilities that will one day fall to you, but you must TRY!'

At that moment Tallitha thought she would explode. She hated Agatha Morrow and every one of her peculiar family, apart from Tyaas of course. Why couldn't her mother take on the family responsibilities? After all, she had nothing better to do.

'You're right. I'm hopeless at this. So why not let Mother take my place? She would love all the tea parties and ...,' persisted Tallitha.

'Snowdroppe, don't get me started on her! She's a vain creature. Besides she isn't my relation, she's married to that numbskull, your father, and he's a feckless wastrel and intoxicated half the time.'

Agatha stared hard at her great niece. She was undoubtedly a wilful child with little talent and scant regard for her duties. But the frustration of trying to unpick the tangle of knots became so upsetting that she momentarily forgot herself.

'These are terrible knots! I despair Tallitha. If only things had been different and my …' She stopped, put her hand to her brow and pressed her lips firmly together.

Tallitha was taken aback by her great aunt's momentary lapse. So there *was* something she didn't know.

'If what was different? What do you mean Great Aunt?'

Agatha shot her niece a withering glance and put the sewing in her lap.

'Absolutely nothing. I'm considering what to do with you!' she said changing the subject.

That girl would be the death of her. She raised her eyes to the ceiling. What was she to do?

'I have tried, week after week, giving you careful instruction. Either you're wilful or just plain stupid. I cannot decide which,' she snapped.

'But I can't see the point. Why do I have to sew and paint? Maybe learning Ennish is just too hard for me.'

'Don't disappoint me Tallitha. All the Morrow girls have had to learn these skills. As a child I too found them difficult, but I persevered, as did my sisters.' Agatha paused and her expression softened. Perhaps there was a solution after all. 'You require strict instruction. The time has come. I'm afraid there's only one solution.'

Agatha Morrow closed her eyes, sighed and summoned her Shrove to attend her.

'Marlin, ask my sisters to come to my sitting room this afternoon at four o'clock, in time for tea.'

Marlin, who had been half-snoozing whilst ear-wigging from his cosy nook, leapt at the sound of the Grand Morrow's voice and hurried to his mistress's side. Without speaking, he bowed and scraped, curled his lip at Tallitha and scurried from the room. The old Shrove was an expert listener-in on other people's conversations. He prided himself on knowing all the tittle-tattle in the Spires. There was nothing better, as far as Marlin was concerned, than poring over the misfortunes of others and gleaning what he could from their problems in order to further his own scheming ends. On this occasion, satisfied he wasn't missing any further tongue-lashing, he scampered up one of the many staircases to the sisters' suite of rooms.

All the while, plans of escape were forming in Tallitha's mind. Perhaps she could be ill. Or Tyaas could help devise a plan to release her from the clutches of her Great Aunt Sybilla Patch and her equally loathsome grandmother, Edwina Mouldson. Grim was not the word once these two vitriolic hags got their hands on her. They would bore her to death droning on about the family history, and her dear little fingers would be so sore from needles, thimbles and bodkins. Of course she could always run away. That was it! She had to escape.

'But Grandmamma will be cross at having me under her feet,' said Tallitha trying to wheedle away at her great aunt's resolve.

'Do be quiet. That will be all for now,' said Agatha losing patience, 'return to me a little after four o'clock, when my sisters will take you in hand.'

'But Great Aunt Sybilla isn't that keen on me either,' said Tallitha with a final attempt to extricate herself from the arrangement.

'Enough, do you hear?!' shouted Agatha thumping the chair, 'I have my reasons.' Agatha Morrow's fingers twitched nervously. 'These are circumstances beyond my control and unfortunately you are the only one left!' she said finally.

Agatha slumped back into her chair and reached for her smelling salts.

'You've upset me, you wicked child. Quiet now. Be off with you before I completely lose my temper!' she snapped.

In a dark fug of resentment Tallitha turned on her heel.

'You can't make me do anything I don't want to!' Tallitha shouted as she flounced out of the room.

'We'll see about that! I can do a great many things and taking you in hand, my girl, is one of them!' replied Agatha firmly.

That girl was the limit. If only things had been different, she thought sadly to herself as she wiped away a stray tear. Tallitha must learn to behave for the good of the family.

Outside, Tallitha slumped heavily against the banister, kicking her feet against the loose carpet.

What was she to do? Those sisters were impossibly difficult and would make her life even more miserable. Perhaps there was a way out after all. They were definitely keeping something from her. Her great aunt had nearly let something slip, she was sure of it. But what was it? She had to find out, but who would tell her? It was hopeless; no one in the family told her anything.

Tallitha ran back to her bedroom, pushed the servants out of the way, and burst into tears.

Two

When Marlin hurried from his mistress's presence he took the longer route up the meandering south staircase. He needed time to consider how to deliver the Grand Morrow's message. The old sisters hated being disturbed whilst they were working, to do so would incur their nasty remonstrations and these would pierce his delicate ears. Marlin muttered angrily to himself, wishing he could snooze in the Grand Morrow's sitting room instead of having to take messages.

Sybilla and Edwina's apartments were on the fourth and fifth floors of Winderling Spires in the heart of the Crewel Tower. There were two principal entrances and a number of secret staircases that only the Shroves and the Misses Edwina and Sybilla knew existed.

Marlin had served the Morrow family for many years and understood their curious ways. The Shrove was an odd spindly creature, bow-legged and skinny, with large bushy eyebrows and sticking-out ears. His clothes were shabby and much too small for him. They had shrunk over the years and the Shrove was much too mean to acquire any new ones.

Shroves were canny creatures, innately secretive and sly. They came from the wet marshland in the south-west of Wycham Elva and from the caves in the north-west of Breedoor. They were most at home in the nooky recesses of the Spires and were partial to snoozing when they got the chance. Tucked into their stone lairs they would take naps, sip their noggins of wild berry juice and keep themselves cool by curling up against the dry stone walls. But their half-sleeping state was a pretence, as their ever-sensitive ears were always alert to gossip and their heavy-lidded eyes constantly spied on the Spire's inhabitants.

The last flight was hard on Marlin's chest as he crawled to the top of the winding staircase. At last he reached the sisters' landing, clinging to the banister to get his breath.

'A curse on those sisters always up to summat and that wayward child,' he moaned in his wet, nasally voice. 'Makin' old Marlin do their biddin'. Well we'll soon see about that. They'll rue the day,' he chuckled wickedly.

Marlin smoothed down his greasy grey hair and prepared to enter the sisters' rooms. Tentatively, he pressed his ear to the crack in the door. He could hear the sisters' muffled conversation and wondered whether he should put a note under their door instead. Moisture slavered down his stubbly chin with the weight of indecision as he wrung his hands and hopped about. Oh dear, he was in such a quandary. What if they didn't notice the message? Then he would get into worse trouble. Biting his sinewy lips and grumbling away to himself at the sisters' impending crossness, he knocked softly and waited.

Inside the conversation stopped dead.

'Oh bother, who's that?' Sybilla moaned, screwing up her flustered face.

'Is someone there?' asked Edwina crossly, 'we are only just finishing our work,' she barked, trying to deter the intruder.

Marlin shuffled, knocked again, and the two sisters bristled with annoyance.

'Well, disturber of our peace. Speak to me. Who is it?' demanded Sybilla.

Marlin peered round the door and slithered into the sitting room, making his body as low as possible. In the circular tower room, eight full-length windows opened onto a balcony overgrown with purple-flowered creepers. Every surface of the sisters' apartment was covered with books and papers, fabrics and half-completed weaves which Marlin knew he must avoid touching at all costs. He hovered nervously, wringing his hands, prepared for the worst.

Sybilla Patch was precariously balanced on top of an extremely long ladder. She was transferring her fabrics from the hanging rack into the compartments in her material archive. The colours were incredible. Twilight lavender, sunglow orange, wild strawberry, peach puff and razzle-dazzle rose. Sybilla snapped her eyes at the Shrove, climbed down the ladder and knelt to meet Marlin at eye level.

'What do you want? Speak to me since you have troubled us so wickedly!' she said sharply into the Shrove's weaselly face.

'May it please you, my lady, the ...'

Edwina stamped her foot, and the Shrove jerked backwards.

'Spit it out, Shrove creature, spit it out!' hissed Edwina.

She snagged his collar and twisted him round to face her. 'Come here you wretched bug. Well what do you want?'

'Ooooooh errr,' squealed Marlin as he tried to protect his ears. 'Please my lady, the Grand Morrow wishes to see you for tea. At four o'clock. In her sitting room,' he cried, the words spluttering out of his wet, slimy mouth.

Edwina twisted his collar tight so that he struggled to catch his breath. 'Bother! What does SHE want? I suppose you know all the details. I bet you've been ear-wigging haven't you? Little spy! What do you know, Marlin? Tell us quickly, you verminous rat!' she hurled the words in his face.

But Marlin knew that worse treatment was to come. Maybe a tweaked ear or a nip from their sharp nails, and he was not waiting around for that. He had done as he was asked so he deftly wriggled out of Edwina's grasp and dodged backwards out of the room, past the rolled satins and damasks, and fled down the staircase with Edwina screaming after him.

'Get back here, worm, get back into my presence at once, do you HEAR ME?' she screamed, stamping her feet in quick succession like a petulant child.

But Marlin was by this time already two flights below. The sisters had a wicked temper, and Marlin needed a nip of berry juice and a rest by a cool wall in order to restore himself. Later as he snoozed in his lair he soothed himself with an abundance of wicked thoughts. They would all get their comeuppance in time, he would make certain of that.

*

To say that the sisters were peeved by Agatha's summons was a gross understatement. They sat on their balcony like two over-wrought hens, intermittently cluck-clucking at each other, trying to imagine what their elder sister wanted. It was an outrage! This was their sanctuary, their special place, and they despised visitors! The interruption had soured what had otherwise been a perfect day for the sisters. Each day they busied themselves with their archives, experimented with their perfumes and powders, dozed in the sun and ate their favourite food prepared by Florré, their Shrove. Now their routine had been disturbed. They were twitchy, put out by Agatha's enduring ability to unsettle them both. Although the three sisters lived in the same house, many months could go by without their meeting, and they preferred it that way. They twittered at each other, peck-pecking at the subject that had vexed them both.

Their balcony looked out over the ornate gardens of Winderling Spires to the steel-grey mountains in the north-west. Florré, their Shrove, brought the sisters' lunch of goose paté and melba toast, served with raspberry cordial, at precisely one o'clock. He had heard about Marlin's unfortunate encounter with his mistresses and was therefore particularly careful not to aggravate them further. His special skill was his almost noiseless invisibility, flitting in and out of the sisters' apartment without them quite noticing his presence.

Edwina stiffly dabbed her mouth. All her seething emotion was contained in her thin tortured lips.

'What do you think SHE wants?' enquired Sybilla of her sister.

Edwina pondered and fidgeted, stroking her fat white ermine, who snapped greedily at her greasy fingers, eating titbits from the lunch.

'Why? To bother us and make us attend to her wishes of course,' Edwina replied petulantly.

Edwina Mouldson was a fractious, peevish woman who was always cross at one thing or another. Her endless complaints were legendary with the servants. Her food was either too hot or too cold, or they failed to run her bath with the right amount of bubbles. She had an acute sense of her own self-importance. It was an observation well-rehearsed by all those who worked at Winderling Spires, that the three sisters tried to compete with each other in their superior mannerisms. This manifested itself in their ability, collective and individual, to stick their imperious noses high in the air whenever they walked the corridors of the grand house.

Edwina was a cold fish with stand-offish ways. She could not abide small children, despite having produced the almost always intoxicated Maximillian Mouldson when she had briefly been married to his bookish and very boring father, Lionel, Lord Mouldson of Dorne.

'She's always been the same, just because she's the eldest she thinks she can boss us about,' said Sybilla nervously playing with her embroidery.

She fanned herself in the languid heat of the warm afternoon. Sybilla, the younger sister, was a scatter-brained creature. She was often too hot because she wore many layers of clothing. Her cardigans and blouses were covered with samples of her sewing, randomly pinned to a sleeve or a bodice. She constantly mislaid her fabrics and their corresponding threads, and her patchwork of samples pinned to her clotheswas her particular way of keeping track of her needlework, albeit haphazardly. She looked like an absent-minded ragamuffin most of the time.

'It's most irritating of her!' said Edwina crossly.

Sybilla fiddled nervously with her pins. 'But, on the other hand dear, tea is rather good in Agatha's sitting room, so let us make the most of it and dress for the occasion,' she said, attempting to extricate herself from the muddle of threads that had become tangled in her buttons.

Edwina brightened momentarily, remembering that she was the prettiest of the sisters. Everyone had made a point of saying so when she was young. It had been such a long time since she had worn her fine clothes.

'I will wear my ostrich feathers and my pearls with my ruby-coloured dress. I think you should wear your turquoise skirt and your apricot silk blouse and remember to remove the sewing samples from your clothes, dearest,' said Edwina beginning to preen herself.

'What about my special pins? Can I perhaps wear some of those today – please?' whined Sybilla pathetically.

'No dear, not today,' insisted Edwina, who was by now engaged in painting her fingernails a lurid green colour.

The sisters were quite odd. Peculiar, many would say. Sybilla had an obsession for black-headed death-pins. They were her absolute favourite things in the whole world. She had an arrangement with the local undertaker to collect boxes of her special pins from his funeral parlour once a month. When he ran out, as he sometimes did, she secretly crept into his workroom and stole them from the shrouds of corpses. She did not care that the servants thought these pins an ill omen, their only function to be flung into the coffin with the corpse when the lid was sealed. Sybilla liked to upset the maids. They were silly creatures and she liked to play with her special pins because they were sharp and black, and she relished the satisfaction of sticking them into things.

Sybilla Patch had been a widow for many years. As a young woman she had also had a child, a strange and distant daughter called Esmerelda, or Essie as she was known in the family. Essie lived alone on the fifth floor of the Spires with her two cats, Licks and Lap, who were the colour of brown sugar with black smudges on their paws. Esmerelda kept her distance from the family, especially her mother and her Aunt Edwina. Sometimes she disappeared for many weeks at a time. Then she would suddenly turn up, either arriving late for some event or missing appointments altogether. Tallitha did not mind Essie, but she did not understand her. Sybilla seemed to forget she had a daughter most of the time, and Essie mostly did not remind her.

Edwina sat at her dressing table and began to apply her bright pink lipstick and touch up her cheeks with powder from her pot of caked rouge. Perfume was sprayed and dangly earrings chosen and the sisters nodded approvingly at each other's horribly mismatched outfits. In tandem, the powdered, highly fragrant pair tottered down the west staircase in unfamiliar high heels, arriving slightly out of breath at Agatha's sitting room, knocked, tittered nervously, and entered.

Afternoon tea was being served by the Shroves, Marlin and Florré, who hovered and fussed over the preparations. The tea trolley was covered with tiered plates of scones, a large sticky chocolate fudge cake, elderberry jam, muffins and a selection of delicately cut sandwiches, while the tea steamed away in the silver samovar on the sideboard. Edwina, still feeling irritated, shooed the Shroves away and sat down to wait for Agatha.

'Where is she? Agatha summons us and then makes us wait. I just …,' said Edwina tetchily.

At that moment Agatha entered the grand sitting room. Her billowing taffeta skirt noisily swept the parquet floor and, with her nose proudly in the air, she sat opposite her younger sisters. They surveyed each other making mental notes on each other's dress and how much each had aged in the intervening months. Not a single detail was lost on any of them. Did Agatha have more grey hair perhaps? Oh, Edwina did look gaunt and Sybilla really should do something about those whiskers protruding from her chin! Agatha forced a weak smile and summoned Marlin to pour the tea. She waited until the Shrove had finished, then began.

'It's been a while since we had tea together, a season or perhaps two? Would you prefer scones or muffins, Sybilla? And for you, Edwina, what would you like?' asked Agatha politely.

Edwina and Sybilla replied demurely to their elder sister as each took a plate of cake and scones, sipped their scented tea, and watched Agatha's expression, waiting for her to reveal the reason for their invitation. Agatha knew her sisters of old so she made them wait attendance on her as she sipped her tea and laboriously nibbled a delicate cucumber sandwich. Agatha regarded her sisters as a pair of nervous birds, preening and fussing in their circular room with only their books and needlework for company. The Grand Morrow dabbed her thin lips, waved for Marlin to replenish her tea, cleared her throat and decided to break the burdensome silence.

'Sisters,' Agatha began. She had their undivided attention which was just as she liked it. 'I'm sure you must be curious as to the reason for my invitation.'

Edwina cleared her throat. 'Well, we always enjoy seeing you, Agatha dear, don't we Sybilla?'

The fat lie tripped so easily off Edwina's tongue that Sybilla spluttered and choked whilst Edwina patted her sister firmly on the back. Agatha revelled in their insincerity, smiled inwardly at their flattery, and decided to continue in the same vein.

'I have asked you here today to assist me in a very delicate matter, and the subject of this matter will soon be joining us for tea. I refer to your granddaughter, Tallitha,' she said nodding at Edwina, who looked like someone had just given her a hard poke in the stomach. Her mouth gaped open and she looked quite gormless.

'Tallitha! What has she been up to now?' asked Edwina suspiciously. 'Do you know, Sybilla?'

'No dear, I don't know anything about that girl. Haven't seen her for ages.'

'Nor me, I'm really not that fond of her, Agatha. You know she can be quite vexing,' said Edwina in an off-hand manner.

Agatha stared at her younger sisters, sitting stiffly on the sofa. They were in for a shock, so she savoured the moment and continued sipping her tea.

'For some time, I have been trying to teach Tallitha the proper accomplishments, those necessary for a girl from a good family. We have started with the art of embroidery, studying languages and painting.'

'Have you dear? Well I shouldn't bother with all that, she won't be …' interrupted Edwina.

Agatha lowered her eyes and tried again. 'Her efforts are quite poor, I agree. But one day she will rule Wycham Elva, so, given that I have had little success with her, I have been considering what to do next.' Agatha paused and delivered her clever blow. 'I have decided to hand her over to you, for you to teach her, drum into her if necessary, the skills required to be a lady.

She must learn discipline,' said Agatha firmly.

The sisters were startled. Edwina's face looked as though a mouse had just run up her skirt. She grabbed her knees, leant forward and let out a strange pathetic mewing sound. Sybilla did not know what to do, alternately forcing a weak smile at Agatha and fidgeting, observing Edwina's reaction to the news.

'But sister, although she is my granddaughter, she is such a noisy child and she will disturb us in our work so dreadfully,' Edwina added quickly.

'We have no choice, I'm afraid. She has to learn,' insisted Agatha relishing their reaction.

'But how long must we endure her?' enquired Edwina, with a petulant face.

Sybilla copied her sister's expression, clicking her tongue and shaking her head to stress the point.

'Until she is cured of her gross tardiness and can demonstrate some skill in the areas I have mentioned, of course.'

Agatha caught Edwina's hateful glance and toyed with her like a fish on a hook, challenging her to disagree.

'After all, she is your granddaughter and she must be disciplined in our ways if she is to take over, well you know … after … later on … when I'm gone,' said Agatha irritated at having to allude to her own demise. 'Essie is not an option because of her unfortunate history.' Agatha pursed her lips and the sisters shuffled together on the sofa. 'Besides, Tallitha is young and I still believe she can be moulded, given time and the right amount of instruction.'

At that moment Marlin indicated that their guest had

arrived. Tallitha sat next to her grandmother and swiftly planted a half-hearted kiss on Edwina's proffered cheek. Cissie had prepared her for the ordeal and her words were still ringing in Tallitha's ears.

'Your great aunt will 'ave her way missy, so there's no use fightin' against her. Accept what she says and do her biddin'. It will work out in the long run, you mark my words. Now kiss old Cissie, take that scowl off your face, tie back your hair and be off with you.'

So when Tallitha met the sisters she was resolved to try her best.

'Ah, there you are. Tea is served. Now take a sandwich and some cake.'

Agatha indicated the tea trolley, meanwhile surveying her great niece disparagingly. Tallitha was, as usual, impossibly untidy. She looked crumpled and creased even when her clothes had just been pressed. She caught Agatha's critical appraisal and glared back at her, smoothing down the hopeless dress and pulling herself up straight. Normally she didn't care two figs about her appearance, but today she was resolved to try harder to make a good impression. At least, that's what Cissie had said.

Rather haphazardly, Tallitha helped herself to the squidgy layered chocolate cake. She took an enormous mouthful and the cake fell apart and landed in sticky lumps in her lap.

'Oops. Sorry about that,' she said, flushing pink.

Chocolate butter icing dripped down her chin and stuck to her fingers which she noisily sucked one by one to the sisters' absolute horror. Her great aunt shook her head in despair.

'Tallitha eat properly, can't you?'

'Sorry. It just fell apart,' explained Tallitha and started to wipe her hands on her dress.

'Not there! Be quick Marlin and give Miss Tallitha a napkin.'

Marlin hobbled over and pushed a napkin into Tallitha's ungrateful hand. She grabbed it and stuck her tongue out at the Shrove so that only Marlin could see.

'I've been explaining the situation to your grandmother and Great Aunt Sybilla and they have agreed to tutor you.' Agatha took her sisters' dumbfounded silence for agreement. 'You must spend the next two weeks under their direction. You must do as they instruct and don't be late. They will report your daily progress to me,' said Agatha pompously.

'Two weeks! But that's such a long time!' cried Tallitha, staring beseechingly at her great aunt and her grandmother.

The two sisters looked as depressed as she did about the arrangement.

'Shall we say ten o'clock each morning? You have my permission to go up to my sisters' apartments. Marlin will show you the way,' replied Agatha in the same pompous manner.

Marlin! Tallitha threw him a vicious glance and the Shrove hopped about and glared back at her. Tallitha noticed the smallest of evil smiles playing for a split-second at the corner of his thin, wet mouth. He was salivating, damn him!

'Can't I find my own way?' said Tallitha acidly, 'I don't need him!'

She eyed Marlin spitefully, looking disdainfully up and down his crooked little body.

'You're not wandering about the Spires alone. You're bound to get lost. Now do stop complaining, child.'

Tallitha grabbed another piece of chocolate cake and stuffed it into her mouth just to antagonise them further. Agatha stared in disbelief at her great niece's inability to eat anything properly, trying to ignore a piece of cake that had fallen on the floor with a splat.

'That's settled then. Finish your cake without slopping it all over my sofa. My sisters and I wish to discuss the arrangements,' said Agatha finally.

Tallitha bolted down her lemonade, wiped the back of her hand across her mouth, muttered something unseemly to the annoying trio and hurried from the sitting room. She made a bolt for the staircase, reached the top of the stairs and sat down on the landing with a tremendous thump. Those three sisters were definitely in cahoots with each other! They were trying to turn her into the kind of girl she was not, just because there was no one else to take her place in the family.

'Well, how did it go?' asked Cissie who had been waiting anxiously for Tallitha's return.

'It was as bad as could be expected,' said Tallitha putting her head in her hands.

'Did you behave yourself?' asked Cissie.

'Sort of ...'

But Tallitha's mind was elsewhere and Cissie might just be able to help her.

'What I don't understand,' she said, watching Cissie's reaction, 'is why that old witch is bothering with me. I'm clumsy and I'm careless. She doesn't think I'm suitable.'

'You're the heir to the Morrow family and this old house,' replied Cissie.

'Perhaps I'm not,' said Tallitha, 'maybe there's someone else who could take my place?'

Cissie stiffened and began fidgeting with the laundry.

'Well, is there someone?' asked Tallitha staring at her nurse.

'How should I know, Miss? And you mustn't call the Grand Morrow names. Now I must be about my work. I can't stand here chatting to you all day or Mrs Armitage will be after me.'

With that, Cissie picked up the laundry basket and hurried down the corridor.

Tallitha stared after her. Then there *was* someone. Cissie was hiding something. It wasn't just her imagination after all. Cissie was definitely uncomfortable. But what about?

Her great aunt had said, 'Due to circumstances beyond my control,' 'and reasons ...' What reasons? What had she meant by that?

There must be a family secret! Something so big that they were all in on it, even Cissie!

Tallitha hugged herself and smiled a very naughty smile.
She had to find out what the secret was!
Now she had to find her brother.

Three

The children's apartments were on the second floor of Winderling Spires, at the far end of the East Wing, down a long winding corridor and off to the right. Tallitha knew every inch of their corridor, each nooky recess and dark spidery corner. This was the best part of the house, where the grown-ups, apart from Cissie and their servants, never ventured. Tyaas was probably hiding in one of his secret dens. He was particularly fond of piracy and his adventures involved shipwrecked sailors marooned on mythical desert islands. Tallitha searched his encampments, hidden under four-poster beds and in musty dressing rooms, tucked away at the back behind the trunks, but all his makeshift camps were empty.

'Bother Tyaas, where is he?' she asked herself as she peered under his messy bed.

As Tallitha sat on the floor wondering what to do next, she

remembered Cissie's holed stones. The children had a secret way of locating one another when one of them went exploring on their own. It had been Cissie's idea. She said the stones should be placed in a particular order to indicate where the other one had gone to in the big house. Cissie had some strange country ways. '*My magic methods*,' she called them and these included her holed stones, which she insisted would protect the children from evil spirits.

Cissie's grandmother had told her folk tales, about village children being taken away at the dead of night, disappearing from their beds, never to be seen again. Cissie was a superstitious woman and swore on the power of the 'holed stones' which she placed outside the children's apartment to protect them from the *Dooerlins*, or evil spirits, who were said to wander Wycham Elva at night.

Tallitha stepped into the corridor and stared down at the uneven row of roughly hewn stones. The smallest stone had been moved, placed out in front of the others. It was a sign that Tyaas was outside, somewhere in the grounds.

'Got him!' she said, feeling pleased with her detective work.

The children's corridor was unusually quiet on that warm afternoon. As Tallitha stood in the shadows she began to experience an uncomfortable feeling in the pit of her stomach. Then she heard a shuffling noise behind her. Perhaps she had been followed by a Shrove. Damn them! Tallitha's heart began thumping as she turned around and peered down the corridor.

'Who's there?' she asked, her voice trembling slightly.

She inched forward, screwed up her eyes and stared into the patchy darkness.

'Come out at once!' she demanded trying to sound braver than she felt.

Tallitha held her breath as a tall figure stepped out from a doorway. It was Benedict, their slightly older distant cousin. Behind him, just for a fleeting second, Tallitha thought she saw a Shrove slipping away into the gloom. She put her hand to her mouth and gasped.

'Benedict, you gave me such a fright!'

Benedict, or Bumps as they called him, was a swot, much too clever for his own good. Benedict hovered uneasily with his messy fringe falling into his eyes. He pushed it out of the way and it flopped back down again.

'Are you following me? Was that Marlin with you?' she ventured, her courage returning.

'Marlin? No ...,' he said looking quickly behind him, 'I just wondered what you were doing?'

There was something furtive about Benedict. He was a clumsy boy, always bumping into things, hence his nickname. He wore sloppy jackets with deep pockets so he could carry around lots of books.

'Weren't you going home after class?' asked Tallitha eyeing him curiously.

Bother Benedict, what did he want? He knew far too much for any normal boy. He wasn't too bad in small doses, but she must get rid of him so she could find her brother.

Benedict's home was in a remote part of the country and he had begun to visit Winderling Spires so he could practice his chemistry experiments with Miss Raisethorne, their teacher. It was something he looked forward to immensely. Fumbling awkwardly he pulled a notebook from one of his pockets.

'I forgot my experiment write-ups. I wanted to work on them later,' he said shaking the book for effect and blushing, realising how his studiousness would come across to Tallitha. 'I know what you think, but I like science,' Benedict stammered.

'Never mind Bumps, I suppose we all like different things but I must be off, too many things to do.' With that she hurried past him.

Benedict felt foolish. His cousins always made him feel that way. He never knew how to be their friend as well as their cousin. He stood, watching Tallitha, wishing he had a brother or a sister to share secrets with and to take his side against the grown-ups.

As Tallitha ran along the corridor she wondered why Benedict had been following her. She hastily looked over her shoulder. In the gloomy recess of the hallway, he was still standing there, watching her.

*

The gardens at Winderling Spires were a mixture of formal lawns, extravagant shrubbery and colourful flower beds with acres of unkempt grasslands full of wild flowers and clumps of woodland. The grounds were tended by a team of Skinks, willowy creatures who lived in the gardens, camping in tree houses whilst working at the Spires. In winter they returned to their forest home, only coming back to Winderling Spires when the spring came and they needed work.

Tallitha guessed where Tyaas would be. They had taken over an abandoned tree house where they kept their secret possessions. It was hidden above the lower branches and the children were certain no one in the family knew of its existence. It was a mess. Tyaas had been there earlier, rummaging in their boxes. They were usually meticulous about hiding their treasures so something must have made him leave in a hurry. As Tallitha began clearing away, she noticed a chalk mark, pointing in the direction of the house.

'What is he up to?' she whispered as she moved the boxes to one side.

There, scribbled on the floor was a message.

'*I'M UP ON THE ROOF.*'

Tallitha parted the overhanging branches to get a better view of Winderling Spires. She scanned the roofline and the turrets for any sign of movement. Then she saw something. There it was again, high up on the roof, just behind the battlements. From the distance of the tree house she could see something moving about on the roof. It was someone's head, bobbing up and down behind the battlements. Tallitha needed no further encouragement. If Tyaas could break the rules so could she!

*

The hall was empty when Tallitha crept beside the grandfather clock, tick-tocking its deep melodic sounds in the stillness of the warm day. She hid in the shadows then tiptoed quickly across the parquet floor and flew up the grand central staircase.

'Goodness,' she said, out of breath, stepping on the bottom stair tread and gazing wistfully at the unexplored world high above her.

The staircase twisted like the branches of a gnarled old tree, disappearing into the shadows of the enormous house. But the main staircase was always busy and Tallitha knew she would have to discover another way up to the roof. She slipped past the schoolroom and down a series of corridors until she came to one of the enclosed wooden staircases, which were a feature of the Spires. Quick as a flash she stepped inside the dark closet, closed the door behind her and ran up the next two flights of stairs trying to suppress the rising excitement bubbling away inside her.

There, she had done it at last! She had made it to one of the forbidden floors.

On the dark landing, faded velvet curtains draped the many archways and dusty chandeliers hung from ornate painted ceilings. At the head of the stairs, a large stuffed raven sat proudly on a stone plinth, its cold beady eyes dark and alert following her every step.

Stupid dead bird, it's watching me, thought Tallitha as she shivered and brushed past it.

The house meandered on through a maze of dingy corridors offering tantalising possibilities for exploration yet always tinged with an atmosphere of gloom. Long shadows leached out from the darkened stairwells, each one holding the spectre of a Shrove, waiting to leap out and apprehend her. Tallitha kept to the centre of the corridors, avoiding the darkest recesses and piecing together the layout of the house from Cissie's bedtime stories. Despite Cissie's repeated warnings, Tallitha knew just where she was headed, to the west side of the house, to one of the least used parts and one of the most isolated.

At last, there before her was the gloomy entrance to the Raven's Wing, built by one of her Morrow ancestors. The heavy wooden door creaked open to reveal an entrance hall bathed in shadow and populated with lonely statues covered in dust sheets. Weak shreds of daylight poked through dirty windows and layers of ancient cobwebs floated like ghostly gossamer in the draughty hallway, becoming entangled in Tallitha's hair.

'Ugh, disgusting!' she cried as she frantically tried to free herself from the clinging webs.

The wing wore a shade of worn-out grey, as though the colour had been washed out of the long flowing curtains and sucked from the huge tapestries, turning them into a ghostly hue. Tallitha crept up the stone staircases and explored ice-cold tower rooms, peeking into the dark past of the people who had once occupied the mysterious wing. Closets were filled with ancient garments and dismal bedchambers led on to enormous salons laid out for long forgotten banquets. It was a place frozen in time and Tallitha felt like an intruder, poking around in the murky past of the Morrow clan.

Suddenly, a door banged in the wind and strange wailing sounds began to seep through the corridors as if the house had begun to moan and sing for her.

'Who's there?' she gasped, 'please, come out and let me see you.' But her small voice disappeared into the vast, unwelcoming space.

Unearthly melodies moaned round every corner, getting louder and louder.

'Please! Stop!' she screamed, trying to block out the eerie chorus.

Tallitha fled up the next staircase, trailing her fingers along the banister, leaving a snail-trail pattern in the dust and trying to disentangle herself from the clawing, grasping cobwebs that hung down all around her. The fine threads stuck to her fingers and as she brushed them away, they turned into a discoloured stain. They clung to her hands and lodged in her hair and the more she rubbed at the stains the darker and the redder they became. Suddenly a rippling, tingling sensation began flooding through her body. A surge of energy filled every part of her, snapping away. The corridor began to whirl before her eyes throwing up spectral ghostly faces from the past. Time and space altered before her eyes, the light flickered uncontrollably. Then she entered another world.

When Tallitha opened her eyes everything seemed much brighter. She could smell the woody aroma of fires burning in the grates and hear laughter filtering up from empty rooms. She clutched her head, remembering her dream-like state and the ghostly apparitions that had appeared before her. Now the Raven's Wing looked strangely familiar as though she had slipped into another time when it had been inhabited by the ancestral Morrow family. Her imagination must be playing tricks on her! She had to get out of there! She had to find Tyaas!

Tallitha ran to door, leaving the eeriness of the Raven's Wing behind her. Cissie had been right. She shouldn't have gone there. The wing was possessed by something unspeakable. Cissie had warned her again and again. But even in that moment, something compelled her to turn around and take one final peek. There in the shadows she saw the wizened face of a Shrove, his twisted lips smirking and his blackened fingers gripping the edge of the door, then banging it with a resounding thud behind her.

'Ohh no,' she gasped, turning to flee from the evil place.

It was Marlin – he was following her! She had to get away from him.

Tallitha ran further up into the shadows of the enormous house until at last she found herself at the very top of Winderling Spires.

Four

The house was spookily silent on the uppermost floor of the Spires. Tallitha caught her breath and peered over the banister past all the twists and turns of the staircase, making a zigzag pattern into the distance. At the top of the house the grand landings and corridors were replaced with narrow passageways, which Tallitha followed until she found what she was looking for, a small wooden door to one of the hexagonal turrets. She stepped inside and forced open the stiff outer door to the roof. Cool fresh air rushed into her lungs and savagely whipped her clothes in all directions.

'Mountains!' she cried as she steadied herself against the stone ramparts.

The view was incredible. Way over the rolling countryside of Wycham Elva was a picturesque scene of sludgy browns and humming greens. A group of black crows circled the Spires, screeching and soaring on the strong thermals, spying on their intruder with territorial beady eyes, then landing to stake their claim. The roof was an uneven expanse of crumbling roof tiles, dirty skylights and stacks of twisting chimney pots.

Tallitha peered round the first stack of chimney pots. Tyaas had been up here, the little stinker, not even bothering to wait for her. By the skylight were the remains of his half-eaten sandwich. Something had disturbed him. The turret on the far side of the roof was a mirror image of the one she had just passed through. Tallitha crawled across the roofscape as the wind howled, stinging her ears. She opened the turret door.

Inside it smelled of stale air and it was pitch-black. As she stepped over the uneven doorframe she tripped, falling on top of something soft and warm, and making an awful noise. In the mess of arms and legs shouting and pushing, Tallitha realised she had fallen on top of a squirming, squealing Tyaas.

'Stop shouting Tyaas, it's me you're kicking!' gasped Tallitha.

Tyaas grinned at his sister. His dark hair stuck out at odd angles and he had smudges of dirt all over his face, but Tyaas often looked like he had just been down a muddy hole.

'Phew, I thought you were a Shrove.' he said sounding relieved and lighting a candle.

'I didn't mean to frighten you. But you came without me,' said Tallitha slightly miffed.

'Sorry it happened so quickly. I was in the tree house and I saw someone on the roof waving in my direction.'

'I saw someone too,' whispered Tallitha, 'maybe it was you?'

Tyaas shrugged. 'I got hopelessly lost and climbed onto the

49

roof through a trapdoor at the back of the house.'

'But if it wasn't you, then who was it?' asked Tallitha, looking anxiously at her brother. Perhaps the Shroves were watching them. 'Have you found anything?'

'Just this old book, it was by that trunk,' he said, passing it to his sister.

In the meagre light she could just make out the spidery handwriting.

'*This book belongs to Asenathe Morrow.*'

'But who's she? I've never heard of her!' exclaimed Tallitha.

Tyaas hushed his sister, 'Some relation of the sisters, I suppose. But whoever was here this morning may be back. I thought I saw Marlin creeping around.'

'Me too, he scared me! Let's take the book and get out of here.' whispered Tallitha.

They held hands on the ramparts, steadying each other in the wind as they climbed into the small turret and back down into the main house.

'Come on,' said Tallitha, disappearing down the nearest staircase.

Tyaas caught up with her many floors later.

'Wait, can't you?' he whispered as he bumped into her.

The walls were painted in pale gold and the chandeliers cast a creamy glow in the dim hallway.

'I know this place,' said Tallitha staring around, 'Mother brought me up here on my seventh birthday.'

Before them was a large oak door, ornately carved with bird motifs.

'Come on,' said Tallitha, 'let's take a peek, this is the Jewel Room.'

The door creaked open to reveal an ornate state room.

'Wow,' said Tyaas, 'I've never seen so many precious stones.'

The walls were lined with glass cases filled with sparkling jewels graded in order of their size. There were diamonds, sapphires, rubies and emeralds all glinting in the bright sunlight.

'Who do they belong to?' asked Tyaas, in awe of the dazzling stones, 'there are hundreds of them!'

Tallitha shrugged, 'Great Aunt Agatha I suppose.'

They would be hers one day. They were pretty enough but not worth wasting her life over. In the centre of the room were two jewel boxes and Tallitha opened the smallest box. As the dazzling sunlight struck the magnificent gemstone, a kaleidoscope of sparkling colours sliced the room, one after another. There was aquamarine, emerald, cerulean blue, rose quartz, diamond white and viridian. Tallitha was awestruck by the brilliant lights and entranced by their intensity. She shaded her eyes from the piercing brilliance of the jewels but her head began to swim. Tyaas opened the second box.

'What's this old thing?'

Inside was a dull green stone with ruby thread markings. Tallitha banged down the lid.

'What's wrong?' asked Tyaas.

Tallitha looked pale and clutched her forehead.

'I feel dizzy.'

She couldn't look at the gemstones any longer.

'Come on, let's go,' she said, 'someone may come.'

The room felt stuffy. Something was wrong with her, had been all day. She closed the door behind them and stroked her aching head as the colours continued to dance before her eyes.

'This way,' said Tallitha, beckoning to Tyaas to follow her.

'Where are we?' asked Tyaas, peering down the darkened passageway.

'We're on the fourth floor,' she said, trying to sound convincing, but in reality the house was a complete mystery to her.

'Can you hear that?' he asked suddenly.

The sound of muffled voices could be heard across the landing.

'Quick, in here,' she whispered as she dragged Tyaas behind her.

The bedroom smelled of mothballs. As Tallitha put her ear to the door, she heard the unmistakable sound of Shroveling wending its way down the corridor. Marlin and Florré were inspecting the rooms and were heading in their direction. In a heartbeat they dived onto a huge poster bed, hiding behind the heavy curtains and burying as neatly as possible beneath the quilts. They lay in the darkness trying to quieten their rapid breathing.

'What do you think they're up to?' asked Tyaas.

'Shhhhhhh, don't speak,' said Tallitha, 'keep absolutely still.'

Within a few minutes the Shroves entered the chamber. They gabbled to each other whilst snooping into the chests of drawers. There was a sudden clang of metal hooks as the velvet bed curtains were roughly pulled apart. Tallitha clamped her hand over her brother's mouth in the suffocating darkness.

'Ne ne kempora dernal canlera del ae nan trath. Spirrrnthndas al na durnath nem kemporan.'

One of the Shroves spoke sharply. Tallitha wished she had paid more attention in her language classes.

'Encrremblan dur na clerna ni fenran. Nan trath an doorn ken lam naen, spirrrnthndas al na durnath.'

They had wedged themselves underneath a lumpy bolster that smelled of old mouse droppings. Tallitha decided that if they were discovered they would pretend to be playing hide-and-seek. It would never work though, she would be taken before the Grand Morrow to explain herself and would get into more trouble. But fortunately for Tallitha, she did not have to tell her lie. The Shroves were also being followed. From beneath the bedcovers Tallitha heard the sound of high heels click-clacking on the parquet floor.

'What are you two doing in here? Come out before someone

sees you. Grintley needs your help downstairs,' ordered Snowdroppe, snapping her fingers at the Shroves.

Tallitha heard the sound of scampering feet as the Shroves obeyed her mother and scurried down the corridor. Then Snowdroppe roughly pulled the velvet curtains back into position and closed the door behind her.

When Tallitha's heart had stopped pounding she popped her nose out from under the smelly bedclothes, slipped from beneath the bolster and sat on the edge of the bed, dangling her feet over the edge. Within a second Tyaas was sitting next to her.

'What's Mother doing up here?' whispered Tyaas.

'And what's she doing with the Shroves?' added Tallitha, perplexed.

She chewed her fingernails, thinking over their mother's possible motives. Snowdroppe was notoriously idle and never bothered with anyone who could not further her own scheming ends.

'Something's definitely going on,' she said as she crept out of the door. 'Come on, the coast is clear, let's get back to our rooms and take a look at the book.'

*

Unfortunately it wasn't as easy as all that.

When Tallitha started down the next staircase she spied Grintley, their mother's Shrove, below them on the landing. Tallitha had always despised Grintley. They waited for him to carry Snowdroppe's trunks into her suite as he snivelled away to himself. He was larger than Marlin, with sprouts of ginger hair sticking up above his ears, but he still had the unmistakeable shrunken appearance of a Shrove. His misshapen hands gripped one of the heavy jewel boxes as he minced awkwardly on his skinny legs into Snowdroppe's sitting room. If only they could get past Grintley without him noticing.

'When he's gone we'll make a dash for it,' whispered Tyaas.

But the plan did not work. Their mother chose that same moment to leave her suite. Snowdroppe appeared in a violet dress, gesticulating to her Shrove to quicken his duties. She held her amber-coloured fennec fox, Stiggy, in her arms, petting and adoring it.

'What are you two doing on the third floor?' she asked suspiciously.

Grintley licked his salivating mouth, waiting for the opportunity to apprehend the children.

'Are you trying to sneak away without saying hello?' asked Snowdroppe in an accusatory manner.

Stiggy barked her weak yapping noises in the children's direction.

'Yes, yes, Stiggy darling, they are wicked children,' said Snowdroppe burying her nose deep into the fox's fur. 'Did Great Aunt Agatha not tell you I was coming home today? You may kiss me.'

Snowdroppe bent down and a waft of exotic perfume enveloped them as they pulled ever so slightly away from her embrace. Then their mother's ever watchful eyes spied Tallitha's hand and she slowly traced her finger along the dark red stain. She stared into her daughter's eyes and a strange look crossed her beautiful face. Tallitha wrenched her hand away but it was impossible to keep anything from Snowdroppe.

'You two are up to something. Have you been somewhere you shouldn't?' she asked.

Stiggy yapped as if trying to echo his mistress. Snowdroppe roughly grabbed hold of Tyaas and smelt his clothes.

'Ouch you're hurting me, get off!' he shouted as Stiggy tried to join in and bite him. 'Get that rodent off me!'

'Tyaas, you're filthy and you're humming like an old stoat. Where have you been?' insisted Snowdroppe, pulling a disgusted face.

'Leave me alone and get that excuse for an animal off me,' said Tyaas, 'I've been …'

Tallitha quickly interrupted.

'Of course we knew you were coming. We wanted to surprise you, that's all. We were on our way to get your gift!' she said, pretending to pet the small fox.

Snowdroppe softened at the mention of a present and purred appreciatively at her children. She had an abundance of clothes and jewels and never tired of receiving more. Tallitha understood her mother very well even if she did not always like her.

'A gift, my pets? Well go and get it. But that doesn't explain wandering around upstairs, now does it?'

'We were just playing hide-and-seek,' said Tallitha cautiously.

Snowdroppe looked down her nose at her daughter, 'Ummmph – really?' she yawned.

Snowdroppe flicked Tyaas away like a nasty bug then turned on her heel. She waltzed down the corridor, admiring her violet-painted fingernails as though nothing else in the world mattered.

Once back in their apartment Tallitha fished out an unused birthday present.

'We'll placate Mother with this, then after dinner we can study the book. Quick, hide it under the mattress,' said Tallitha.

She rubbed at the stubborn stain that was still visible on her fingers. Perhaps the old house had made its mark on her.

Snowdroppe was sitting at her dressing table surrounded by bowls of her favourite flowers when Tallitha entered. Hundreds of snowdrops filled the room with their delicate white-green petals and unmistakable smell. Miss Brindle, her lady's maid, was brushing Snowdroppe's long red hair, which fell in waves down her back. Tallitha stroked her mother's beautiful hair and daintily handed her the gift. Snowdroppe gasped in pleasure and seemed to forget the earlier incident. They were safe, she hoped, this time.

Tallitha sat on the window seat wishing her mother would hurry up, but smiling amiably and chatting to her. All the while she could hear her father singing in the bath in his adjoining rooms. She would see him later.

*

After dinner, which was a laborious event, Tallitha and Tyaas yawned a great deal, excused themselves and went up to their rooms.

'Let me see, let me see,' demanded Tallitha impatiently.

Tyaas took the book from under the mattress and they sat hunched together over the pages. It was a small story book and some of the pages had been scribbled on. As Tallitha turned the last page she saw something that made her gasp.

'Look, there!' Tallitha read out the words

'This book belongs to Asenathe Morrow,
Daughter of Agatha Morrow and Machin Dreer
Winderling Spires.'

'But who is she? I've never heard of Asenathe or her father,' exclaimed Tyaas.

'I didn't know Great Aunt Agatha even had a daughter, or a husband,' whispered Tallitha.

Tyaas poked her for a response.

'Sis, what IS the matter? You look pale.'

The implication of the written words had begun to sink in.

'Do you realise what this means?' asked Tallitha.

But, as usual, Tyaas didn't have a clue.

'It means Great Aunt Agatha has a daughter of her own. That means she's the heir! Not me! But where is she?'

'How should I know? Maybe she's dead,' said Tyaas.

'No she can't be. We would have known about that. We have to find her.'

Tallitha hugged herself. She was happy for the first time in ages.

'Ok,' said Tyaas, 'but first we must hide the book somewhere safe.'

Tyaas placed it at the bottom of his trunk and turned to his sister.

'I wonder who knows about Asenathe,' he asked.

'All of them,' said Tallitha angrily, 'as usual they're keeping it from us.'

'Tomorrow we can look in the library and ...'

But Tallitha pouted. 'I have to spend the next two weeks with the dreadful sisters so they can teach me boring stuff. I was going to tell you. Then we found the book.'

'You could have a nose around,' he ventured. 'Those old bats are bound to have some interesting things hidden away. While you're doing that, I'll go to the library and have a root about!'

Tallitha kissed her brother goodnight.

She was determined to unearth the secret about Asenathe Morrow.

There was no stopping her now.

At last her life was becoming exciting.

Five

Tallitha woke early the next morning from a dream-filled sleep about the mysterious girl. She snuggled down under the soft quilt. This was her favourite time of day. Outside she could hear the clamour of rooks, caw-cawing high above the Spires and the rain pitter-pattering against the window. Alone in her room she could imagine all kinds of 'what ifs' and 'what nexts'. She picked up her mirror and studied her small face. A fairly ordinary girl looked back at her and she liked what she saw. She wished it could always be like this, with no one telling her what to do and how to behave.

Cissie brought Tallitha breakfast in bed as a treat. The tea and muffins tasted wonderful and as she savoured the hot melting butter and licked her fingers one by one, Tallitha invented details about Agatha's daughter. She imagined the colour of her hair and the sound of her voice, what sort of things she liked to do and whether they would be friends. Tallitha could smell adventure in the air. Secrets were so irresistible. If only she could find the missing girl, then she would be free. The day ahead was beckoning and she leapt out of bed.

Marlin called for Tallitha at precisely half-past nine, grumbling away in her sitting room. She could see the black-hearted snake nosing around and picking up her things. Despicable toad! She coughed loudly and slammed the door to warn him off.

'What's he come so early for?' she whispered to Cissie, spying on the Shrove from behind her bedroom door.

'Knowing 'im, he's probably going to try and confuse you so you won't remember the way to the sisters' apartment.'

'Well, we'll see about that. How can I mark my way, without him noticing?'

They found a box of coloured pins and some tailor's chalk.

'Look these should do,' whispered Cissie, 'chances are the servants won't notice them. Drop 'em by the staircases and mark the walls when His Nibs isn't watching.'

So Tallitha put the chalk and the pins in her pocket and left with the old Shrove. Cissie was right, Marlin was an odious worm. He led her down a maze of corridors and staircases, charging ahead bad-temperedly, scratching his chin, as if to feign confusion. But when he wasn't looking, Tallitha dropped her pins and marked the walls with a small cross. Eventually she realised the devious Shrove had doubled back. They had returned to the corridor with the bluebell wallpaper.

'We've been here before, Marlin. I thought you were

supposed to know the way,' said Tallitha sarcastically.

Marlin hopped about salivating and sniffing at her in his devilish fashion, flinging back a cursory look every now and then. After a steep climb up two of the enclosed staircases, Marlin began fumbling about with his precious keys and unlocked a door to an abandoned apartment. Inside, the room was bare apart from stacks of towering papers. Marlin opened a small door to reveal a spiral staircase. The Shrove scampered inside and up into the dusty darkness. At the top was another door, a series of steps and more corridors. Although Tallitha kept dropping her pins and marking the way, the Shrove had outwitted her. How would she ever retrace her steps to the Crewel Tower?

After more devious twists and turns they eventually arrived at the sisters' apartment. The Shrove smiled victoriously and bowed with an insincere flourish. Tallitha pulled a face, pushed him out of the way and barged through the sisters' door.

'You're late!' grumbled her grandmother.

Edwina Mouldson's vexation oozed out of every pore as she stiffly turned and coldly eyed her tardy granddaughter. Tallitha knew the evil Shrove had made her late on purpose.

'Sorry, but Marlin took me on a very complicated and unnecessarily long route.'

'Fiddlesticks! Leave earlier tomorrow. We won't be kept waiting!' exclaimed Edwina pompously. 'Here's the sampler – now copy it if you can,' she sneered.

Tallitha pulled a face behind her grandmother's skinny

back and pretended to settle to her needlework. But the sisters' enormous sitting room was much too interesting, especially as Tallitha had things she wanted to discover about the Morrow family. The room was designed like a spider's web, with corridors leading to spinning rooms and manuscript vaults. One half of the room was festooned with fabrics and the other was full of books. The sisters used two long ladders on steel runners to whizz backwards and forwards past all their treasures. As Tallitha watched her grandmother climb the library steps she wondered how she could get rid of the interfering sisters and start exploring on her own.

Tallitha was drawn to the colourful stacks of material and mesmerised by the shimmering hues neatly organised in descending shade order. There were tens upon tens of hot reds, crazy pinks, iridescent yellows and fizzing greens, each one individually sorted and neatly labelled. The kaleidoscope of brightly snapping colours made her head spin as if she had drunk a bewitching potion. Tallitha was so absorbed that she didn't hear her Great Aunt Sybilla creep up behind her.

'You're distracted little girl. Daydreaming rather than sewing!' she hissed nastily in her ear. 'If we have to waste time with you, then your needle must be busy!'

Tallitha hated her aunt but decided to turn on her charm.

'I'm admiring Grandmother's wonderful library,' she said sweetly.

Sybilla was taken aback and studied Tallitha more closely. She was an odd child.

'Sister, she's being annoying,' Sybilla shouted to Edwina.

Then she turned on Tallitha. 'They're our things little girl, not yours!' she said sounding extremely spoilt.

'Is this Great Aunt Agatha as a girl?' asked Tallitha picking up a miniature portrait, 'or maybe someone else?' she ventured, gauging Sybilla's reaction.

Tallitha's fingers tingled as she held the portrait and she experienced a powerful urge to find Asenathe, much stronger than before.

'That's our mother,' Sybilla replied tartly, snatching the portrait out of Tallitha's hand.

Tallitha knew her Great Aunt was lying. The two old crones were as tight as a clam. They would never reveal anything.

'May I look at your books?' asked Tallitha, desperate to begin her search.

'No of course you can't, wretched child. You're here to ...'

But Edwina's train of vitriol was disturbed by an unexpected visitor. In a flurry of silks and perfume, Esmerelda entered and waved a bumbling Florré out of her way. She rarely visited her mother and the two sisters glanced at each other with irritation all over their faces.

'Why Essie, what an unexpected pleasure,' said Sybilla un-truthfully.

They both knew it was a lie but proceeded nonetheless with the slippery veneer of politeness.

'You should have made an appointment. Well, what brings you here today?' asked Sybilla fiddling with her pins and eyeing her daughter suspiciously.

Esmerelda was dressed in a long silky purple and pink dress that fluttered tantalisingly behind her as she walked. Her demeanour created the impression that she was constantly on the move, a restless woman who would not stay for long. Her long auburn hair hung like a mane about her shoulders. She looked more like a Romany gypsy than the daughter of a wealthy family. Esmerelda threw her mother a look that perfectly captured the lack of affection between them.

'I came to borrow some samplers and a couple of stitching books,' said Esmerelda coldly rummaging in an old needlework box.

'Very well, but don't mess up the materials,' said Sybilla crisply.

'We're in the middle of our work so don't disturb us,' added Edwina cantankerously.

The sisters exchanged under-their-breath complaints and sauntered off, hag-like, into the depths of their archives. As Esmerelda watched them disappear her face twitched and she turned on her heel to face Tallitha.

'I hear you're being tutored by my mother and Aunt Edwina. How's it going?' she asked, watching her young cousin carefully.

'They're too strict and I'm hopeless at this,' she grumbled showing the knotted sampler to Esmerelda.

Esmerelda winked at Tallitha and took the sampler. The girl was interesting and definitely ready. She was at her peak, she was certain of that.

'Let me help you, just a little improvement here and there, and it will be beautiful,' she whispered enticingly.

The needle flashed before Tallitha's eyes, transforming the bargello stitches in moonstone and jade into an intricate pattern. Esmerelda's touch was magical and Tallitha became aware of the hypnotic way Essie chanted to herself whilst she expertly manipulated the stitches, adding some and removing others.

'*Canya, canya-fe, canya, canya-fe,*' she said hauntingly, over and over again.

Esmerelda lips twisted into a knowing smile and her eyes shone brightly.

'What are you doing?' asked Tallitha.

Esmerelda stared into Tallitha's eyes and she began to feel drowsy.

'Essie, what's happening to me?' she sighed.

A sickly odour filled the air and Tallitha pulled at the neck of her dress, trying desperately to breathe more easily. Esmerelda took a shiny bauble from her pocket and dangled it in front of Tallitha's face, making the light sparkle in all directions. Tallitha could hear Essie's voice as it ebbed and flowed, lulling her deeper into a trance.

'Just relax. Stay with the sensation and let yourself be drawn in by the shimmering light,' said Esmerelda bewitchingly.

Tallitha felt herself falling and the sensation of being stretched away from her body. She was powerless to resist Esmerelda's hypnotic control and the repetitive, humming sounds.

'I can't breathe, Essie,' she said trembling, 'everything feels so tight.'

'Tallitha, stop resisting me,' demanded Esmerelda, hauntingly.

Tallitha was transfixed by Esmerelda's eyes that hexed her

like a bobbing owl. Her deep eye sockets held circles of swirling dark green, blue, and purple whirlpools that pulled her further in. Tallitha felt the last vestige of her will slipping away. She was falling into an unknown place which was bottomless, timeless and endless. She was slipping away from her body … then there was an enormous *whoosh!* and she entered another realm.

The noise from the sisters' room stopped abruptly and Tallitha found herself floating, surrounded by a foggy grey light. Everything was slow and dream-like and as Tallitha turned she could see her own body lying motionless, connected by a fine translucent silver cord that shimmered in the soft light. Then a strange force pulled her from above and she began to move upwards through a narrow tunnel, the twisting motion elevating her until she was floating free with the cool air rushing past her.

Tallitha found herself flying over the mountains with the rivers and forests spread out beneath her. Then out of the mist she saw the jagged outline of a castle with many towers, and she began to feel afraid. Suddenly she found herself pressed up against a window and saw a girl … the vaguest outline of a face … a girl in a black dress. Tallitha looked back at the flimsy silver cord, it seemed insubstantial … Then she panicked. Immediately there was a snapping sound and the vision disappeared.

Esmerelda clicked her fingers and Tallitha returned with an enormous *whoosh!* – sucked back into her still body. She felt as though she had fallen and had bumped down a long tunnel, ending at the bottom with a thump, although she wasn't hurt in anyway. Esmerelda threw her head back and laughed.

'Did you have an interesting journey?' she asked menacingly. 'Whom did you see?'

Tallitha's tongue felt oversized in her dry mouth and her head felt grainy as though she hadn't slept for many hours. Her body tingled, and her hands and feet were numb. Esmerelda lifted Tallitha's face and smiled.

'No matter, you can tell me later.'

Perhaps Esmerelda was a devil, a crazy woman who had possessed her.

Esmerelda clicked her fingers one last time, and as quickly as she arrived, she collected her samplers and floated from the room.

The sisters, who had been busy in their archives, ambled back into the circular room. Tallitha felt heavy from the trance and looked down at her needlework – it was perfect!

Had Essie done that? She couldn't remember and she felt decidedly odd. Esmerelda was weird, thought Tallitha.

'Has Essie gone?' asked Sybilla with relief.

Tallitha nodded. 'Here's the sampler, it's finished.'

Sybilla took the sewing and turned to her sister. 'Yes, quite good. That will be all for today,' she said ushering Tallitha out of the room.

Tallitha hesitated by the towers of bright fabrics.

'Grandmamma,' said Tallitha tentatively, 'tomorrow, will you tell me about the Morrow family?'

'What do you mean?' asked Edwina suspiciously.

'What did she say?' asked Sybilla stiffly.

'Nothing dear,' shouted Edwina to her sister.

'I just wondered about the family and its past.'

Sybilla stared at her great niece. She was a handful and no mistake, Agatha had been right about that.

'Now run along. Stop asking questions. You'll wear us out,' and with that, Sybilla shooed Tallitha out of their apartment and closed the door.

It was useless. They wouldn't tell her anything. They were as tight as ticks, the pair of them. Damn them all!

She would find out about the missing girl without their help.

Now Tallitha was more determined than ever to discover the secret about Asenathe Morrow!

Six

As it turned out Tallitha didn't have long to wait. Every morning she returned to the sisters' apartment accompanied by Marlin and each day he took her on a slightly different route, meandering through the grand house in order to confuse her. But Tallitha had begun to notice how the wallpaper patterns followed on from each other and piece together a route of her own, which she was determined to try out at the first opportunity. She had also decided to make the best of the situation with the sisters – to use it to her advantage, and so the days took on a certain rhythm. Bit by bit she teased information from Edwina and Sybilla about the Morrow family and when she returned at the end of her lessons, Tallitha reported these snippets to Tyaas.

'Today Great Aunt Sybilla told me Great Aunt Agatha had been briefly married, but that the marriage hadn't 'properly taken', whatever that means. She said the husband, Machin

Dreer, upped and left a few months after the wedding, vowing never to return to his horrible wife, and from that day forward he has been as good as his word! Isn't that odd? All the sisters seem to have misplaced their husbands, one way or another.' But Tyaas was quiet. Tallitha poked her brother for a response, 'Tyaas, are you listening?'

Her brother sat with his head in his hands.

'It's all very well for you but I'm left here to play with the Cotters' and Minkles' children from Wycham village. Hattie and Maisie are fine, but when the girls aren't looking, the boys punch me! It doesn't hurt but it isn't fun,' he grumbled.

Tallitha knew how to cheer Tyaas up. 'But I have a plan,' she said encouragingly, putting her arm round her brother's shoulders.

Whilst Tallitha had been whiling away her mornings in the sisters' apartment, it occurred to her that Asenathe must have had a suite of rooms somewhere in Winderling Spires. If only they could find these rooms they may hold clues as to where she had gone, and Tyaas could help her find them.

The Spires had two floors below ground level which housed all the workings of the enormous house. On the lower floor were located the vast array of storerooms and the cold inhospitable cellars, and the floor above contained the enormous kitchens and the housekeeper's office. Tallitha knew that was a good place to start. She suspected that a complete set of plans must be kept in Mrs Armitage's office so she could organise the servants' rotas for all the cleaning and household maintenance.

The problem was that the children had never been allowed down to the lower floors. Tallitha knew something about the layout because Cissie often amused them with stories about the 'goings-on' downstairs. There were boiler rooms, coal stores, pickling and jam stores, laundry and drying rooms, a number of wine cellars, plus crockery rooms, three kitchens and an array of sculleries. All they had to do was to locate Mrs Armitage's office and parlour.

'I've been thinking,' she said, 'if we can find Asenathe's apartment, we may find out what happened to her.'

Tyaas turned to his sister and his eyes lit up with excitement. 'Do you mean we're really going to explore the house?'

'Yes I do. But first we must find the floor plans. Mrs Armitage must have a set in her office. The problem is, we've never been down to the lower floors and we certainly can't go during the day, it's much too risky, so we'll have to go at night,' she said eyeing Tyaas from under her messy hair.

'Wow! Exploring the Spires in the dark! When shall we go? What about tonight?'

Tallitha shook her head. 'We'll go the day after tomorrow when Mrs Armitage is visiting her daughter. Cissie said she sometimes sleeps in her parlour when she has an early start, so we can't take the risk. Best try when she's away.'

'What about the Shroves?'

'They're so tricky,' replied Tallitha. 'They mostly sleep in the cellars, but Cissie said they have Shrove holes all over the house, so we must be careful.'

Tyaas needed no more persuasion. 'The servant's staircase by the hall clock is hardly used except by Mrs Armitage, so I guess it leads down to her rooms. Tomorrow morning I'll watch to see who uses it.'

Tallitha nodded. It was an excellent plan but she had also been developing one of her own. Whilst building her knowledge of the intricate passageways and staircases over the intervening days, she had decided to find her own way to the sisters' apartment without Marlin. He was a hindrance, spying on her every move and preventing her from exploring the Spires alone. So when the next morning arrived, Tallitha left early to avoid the old Shrove.

She followed the pins and the marks she had made on the walls, and after going up the wrong staircase a couple of times she found herself at the foot of the Crewel Tower. The sisters had certainly chosen one of the most outlandish settings of Winderling Spires for their retreat. The north staircase was carved, with panels of ornate birds and spiders set into the banisters and newel posts. Wooden falcons, eagles and ravens sprouted from the railings along with leggy arachnids and their nests of grotesque spiderlings. Tallitha thought they were curious and wonderful. Even if she disliked the sisters, she admired their ornate taste.

As she wandered up the staircase counting the spiders and trying to name all the different species of birds, she came face to face with Marlin, coming from the opposite direction, bumbling along on his spindly legs. This was her opportunity to dismiss him from his role as chaperone. If he didn't like it he could take it up with Great Aunt Agatha, but by then it would be too late. She ran up the stairs to greet him.

'Good morning Marlin,' she said sarcastically.

The Shrove hopped about when he saw Tallitha.

'Well as you can see, from now on, there's no need for your guidance. I can find my own way to my grandmother's apartment.'

Marlin screwed up his beady eyes and shrunk back against the banister as Tallitha elbowed him to one side. She could hear his oaths and mutterings all the way up the crooked staircase.

'I'll be back for ye,' he squawked and shook his fist, determined not to let Tallitha get the better of him.

'Who cares?' shouted Tallitha and stuck out her tongue at the nasty creature as she raced ahead to the Crewel Tower.

That morning there was an unusual amount of activity coming from the sisters' dressing rooms. As Tallitha entered the apartment she could hear their animated chatter and the creaking of wardrobe doors while their maid servant, Dora, ran between the dressing rooms, flustered by their incessant demands. Eventually the sisters emerged in their finest and strangest day outfits. Edwina wore an otter-brown velvet suit with bright green gloves and a yellow feather boa. Sybilla wore a dress of dogwood-rose with blue gloves and a purple feathered hat. The sisters were extremely pleased with their appearance and were obviously dressed to go out. Tallitha tried to keep a straight face.

'You'll have to occupy yourself today. There's a sampler for you to copy, over on that dresser' said Sybilla, waving her gloves dismissively.

'The organising committee of Wycham Fair have asked us to judge the needlework competition and we're going to choose the prizes. Florré will bring your elderflower cordial at eleven o'clock. We should be back in time for lunch,' said Edwina excitedly.

Tallitha had never seen her grandmother look so animated and cheerful.

'Do hurry up sister,' snapped Sybilla, 'or we'll be late.'

With a swirl of cloaks and pungent lavender perfume, the sisters kissed Tallitha on each cheek and departed. Kisses from those beasts!

'Eurgh!' thought Tallitha, 'how ghastly!' as she wiped away the traces of their sticky lipstick.

Tallitha could not believe her good fortune. For days she had been trying to engineer a reason for the sisters to leave their apartment so she could snoop about and just when she was not expecting it and was absorbed with plans about the night time exploration, off they went!

Tallitha wasted no time. She hurriedly climbed the library ladder, using the lever to guide her along on the squeaky rail. She flew past poetry and geography, flora and fauna, gazetteers of the world, maps and travelogues. But nothing looked remotely interesting as a source of information about Asenathe. She went up and down the shelves getting ever more dusty, tired and hot.

There were thousands of books and Tallitha realised the search would take much longer than a couple of hours. She needed days! Feeling disheartened she climbed down again.

It was almost eleven o'clock so she sighed and picked up the sampler. It was a complicated monogram of interwoven stitching in old script. As she looked more closely she could just make out the letters as an 'A' and an 'M' and her heart almost missed a beat. Perhaps this was Asenathe's sampler and if so what did the other lettering say? But she couldn't translate the words. Old Ennish was difficult enough to speak and she had never seen any of these words written down before. The stitches had an unusual twist to them too. She thought they might be milanese or goblin, but they were unlike any other examples she had seen. The colours were striking, turkish rose, wild blue yonder and candy apple red on a rich vanilla background. Tallitha was stumped! If the sampler was Asenathe's and the sisters knew it was hers, why had they left it for her to copy? Maybe they didn't know it was hers? Maybe it wasn't hers? Maybe it had been left by someone else? So many questions, she thought, without any answers!

Later, after Florré had delivered her drink, she climbed the ladder once again, but this time she knew what she was looking for, the reference books on the ancient tongues of the Northern Wolds' people. She spun round the circular library and located the books on one of the top shelves. There were three volumes and after making sure she had the correct edition, she hid the copy in the deepest pocket of her dress and clambered down the ladder. Hardly pausing for breath, Tallitha took up her needle and began to copy some of the glorious stitches from the mysterious sampler and waited for the sisters to return.

They were an age, and time seemed to stand still in the warm drowsiness of the late morning. Tallitha was bored and fanned herself in the heat, letting her mind wander to Great Aunt Agatha's daughter and the mystery that surrounded her disappearance. Hours drifted by and, unusually, the spiteful sisters missed their lunch. Tallitha was impatient to do her research so she picked up her sewing, including the sampler, and wrote a note to that effect. Marlin could go hang himself! She would find her own way back without him. That would teach the nasty little Shrove and Great Aunt Agatha too.

As Tallitha left the apartment she noticed a movement on the landing. It was Florré curled up in the gloomy recess just outside the sitting room door. He unfurled himself like a cat when he heard the door open, poised, ready to pounce. Tallitha raced past the Shrove, averting her face, but as she sped down the passageway she could feel his eyes boring deep into her back. Had he heard her sneaking about? Had he been spying on her? She shivered momentarily and picked up pace, moving more assiduously down the inky-blackness of the corridor. The Shroves were always lurking, lying in wait for her. If ever she had any real power in Winderling Spires she would dismiss them all at once.

Then out of the darkness she heard Florré's wicked laughter echoing down the empty passageways. The Shrove was stalking her, slinking along, always just a shadow out of sight. Tallitha followed the small pins and the marks on the walls, dashing headlong down the unfamiliar corridors and staircases until eventually, sometime later, she found the East Wing. Breathless she raced towards the safety of her apartment and banged the door tightly shut behind her. Panting and scared, she kept her body firmly wedged against the door.

'Oh my word girl, what a fright you gave me! What on earth's goin' on? You scared me 'alf to death!' exclaimed Cissie, sitting down on the bed and clutching the washing to her chest. She was red in the face from bending down, sorting piles of laundry.

'Oh Cissie,' cried Tallitha, the panic rising in her voice, 'that was awful!'

'Whatever is the matter? You look like you've seen a ghost.'

'I'm sorry I scared you,' she exclaimed catching her breath, 'but it was so dark and scary outside the sisters' apartment and Florré was behaving oddly. Then I thought … oh I don't know what I thought, it was all so peculiar,' spluttered Tallitha.

'You should 'ave waited for Marlin to bring you back. You'll get into trouble, Miss,' said Cissie shaking her head.

'I wanted to find my own way back. But something's wrong, he scared me.'

'Oh those damned Shroves. Take no notice Miss. They're all cut from the same strange block. Them Shroves have a shifty way about 'em. Always have, always will. But you know that don't you Miss? Don't pay no mind,' replied Cissie, folding the laundry into neat piles.

'But there was something different about Florré today,

something menacing. The way he followed me, it was creepy,' said Tallitha chewing her fingers.

'Followed you, Miss? Surely not. You're imaginin' things.'

'I'm not!' insisted Tallitha, her eyes glued to the door expecting the evil Shrove to burst in at any second.

Cissie continued folding the children's clothes whilst keeping an eye on Tallitha. The girl seemed oddly preoccupied and she was clutching some needlework in her hand. It was true she looked shaken, but then she could be dramatic when she wanted to be. Cissie decided that it served Tallitha right. She shouldn't be going off on her own, exploring the upstairs passageways, after all the Grand Morrow had forbidden it.

'What you got there then?' asked Cissie.

Tallitha smoothed the sampler between her fingers. She wanted to ask Cissie about Asenathe so she sat quietly, deciding how to frame her question. Cissie knew Tallitha of old and could tell she was up to something.

'You look like you've got summat else on your mind.'

Tallitha knew she had to be careful. Cissie might tell Great Aunt Agatha.

'I want to ask you something important,' she said, cautiously peering out from under her messy hair. 'Is there a secret in our family?'

Cissie stopped sorting the linen. She had always dreaded this question and suddenly here it was. She would have to be careful.

'Well, all families 'ave their secrets, Miss. Now what shall

I do with these clothes? They're much too small for you,' said Cissie, trying to change the subject.

'Yes I know they do. But this is a big secret Cissie. B.I.G,' said Tallitha, spelling out the letters with emphasis.

'How should I know, Miss?' said Cissie abruptly.

Tallitha knew she could wheedle it out of her. Her methods were tried and tested.

'This 'secret' has something to do with someone very important, who isn't here anymore.'

She studied Cissie for any flicker of reaction. Her nurse had stopped fussing with the clothes and was now standing quite still, staring out of the window.

'This … *girl* … may have left the family for some reason,' suggested Tallitha, twisting her hair in and out of her fingers.

The very mention of *this girl* made Cissie jolt slightly.

'I don't know anything about that, Miss. It was before my time here. There are rumours. I'm not sure I can say …'

'Oh Cissie, you do know something, I can tell,' said Tallitha excitedly, jumping up and down on the bed. So she was on the right track, she just had to prod and poke a bit more.

'You see, Tyaas and I found an old book with a girl's name in it,' said Tallitha coming up behind her nurse. 'The name was … Asenathe Morrow.'

Cissie went bright red in the face and turned quickly to face Tallitha.

'Have you been upstairs? You know you shouldn't 'ave. The Grand Morrow will be very cross,' exclaimed Cissie.

'Then don't tell her. Come on Cissie, I want to know the truth,' demanded Tallitha.

'Oh Miss, I don't know.'

But Tallitha would not stop. 'I must know who she is! And today I found this sampler with the initials 'A' and 'M' embroidered on it. You have to tell me,' insisted Tallitha.

Cissie sat down on the bed next to Tallitha and gently stroked her arm.

'Some things are best left unsaid, my pet. The family have thought best not to tell you. Happen they will in their own good time.'

'But maybe they won't ever tell me. So you have to!'

Tallitha squeezed Cissie's hand.

'Oh you could never be a patient child. Always headstrong, it'll get you into trouble and me too, no doubt,' said Cissie shaking her head.

'It won't, come on, tell me,' said Tallitha refusing to give up.

Cissie continued sorting the linen and sighed. 'Well, your Great Aunt Agatha did have a daughter. Oh I shouldn't be telling you this …'

Tallitha just kept mouthing the words '*please, please*' to Cissie in a desperate way.

'I don't know Miss. If the Grand Morrow should find out I said anything …'

'Tell me Cissie, come on.'

'Promise me you won't tell where you 'eard it from,' she said finally.

'I promise – cross my heart and hope to die!' she said dramatically.

Cissie shook her head at Tallitha's antics and continued.

'This … *girl* was called Asenathe, and she disappeared some time ago. Went off, or maybe she was taken, one night it was. No one knows for sure.'

Tallitha grabbed hold of Cissie's hand.

'*Asenathe*, what a strange name! But there must be more. How old was she? What was she like? Was she pretty? What did she like doing? Tell me,' pleaded Tallitha.

Cissie held up her hands for Tallitha to stop her barrage of questions. 'Oh Miss, do stop goin' on so. No one talks about it downstairs anymore. Mrs Armitage has given strict instructions not to gossip about the family.'

'But this isn't gossiping, is it Cissie? It's what really happened,' replied Tallitha looking pleased with herself.

'Eh Miss, if you're not fishing for summat, you're mending your nets, plotting and planning, you've always been the same. You don't let a body rest.'

Tallitha just kept mouthing '*please*' at her exasperated nurse. Cissie shook her head, sighed and eventually gave in.

'I think, but mind, I don't know for sure, that she was about your age; fourteen or fifteen. Maybe a bit older, but not by that much.'

'What else do you know?'

'Now this is it, 'tis all I know. I don't know no more, Miss, so you 'ave to stop pestering me if I tell you, promise me now,' insisted Cissie at the end of her tether.

'Okay, if you're sure this is all you know. When you've told me I'll stop, I promise.'

Cissie folded her arms and looked out of the window, taking a moment to consider what to tell Tallitha and what not to tell her. She was a persistent child and no mistake. But Cissie knew she would have to tell her something to shut her up. She smoothed her apron and folded her hands in her lap.

'I 'eard tell that before Miss Asenathe went missing, there was trouble. Things weren't right between the girl and her mother. Some fallin' out I think, but it's probably just a rumour. People like to make up stories if they don't know the truth so don't put too much store by it, and for goodness sake don't tell any of the sisters or your mother what I told you, or I'll be for the high jump and no mistake.'

Tallitha let out an excited scream and pummelled the bed.

'I promise Cissie, I've already said I won't tell, and thank you!'

Tallitha kissed her nurse on her warm plump cheek. It was true then. There was a daughter and *she* was the heir to the Morrow family, not her. Now Tallitha just had to find the missing girl.

'Perhaps you were right about the holed stones protecting us at night. Is that because of Asenathe going missing?'

Cissie bit her lip and looked sadly towards the dark mountains. Then she rallied and patted Tallitha's hand reassuringly. 'Well, you may laugh at old Cissie, but I know a thing or two. The holed stones are special and will keep you safe from the *Dooerlins*.'

Tallitha flopped back on the bed and let out a huge sigh. She was satisfied for the moment but she could tell there were more secrets to be unearthed.

She waited for Cissie to finish her chores then she went into her study and picked up the small leather book from the sisters' library. It had curious lettering unlike any alphabet she had ever seen before and the twisted shapes were strangely like the stitches in the sampler.

Tallitha had to find out what all the clues meant.

Strange things about her peculiar family were beginning to fall into place.

Seven

The next morning Tyaas gobbled down his breakfast. He would begin by searching the library on the ground floor. Miss Raisethorne was always badgering him to do more reading, so he had a ready excuse if he was disturbed. Unfortunately the library was quite useless. What was the point of all these books if you couldn't find what you wanted? So he started skulking around the grandfather clock to see if any of the servants came out of the green door. After what seemed like hours no one had emerged, which convinced Tyaas that he was correct. He paced the distance from the bottom of the stairs to the old clock. '*Twenty-one, twenty-two steps*,' he said to himself. They must make absolutely certain no one was around when they came down after dark. He couldn't wait!

Happy with his contribution to the forthcoming adventure, Tyaas decided to reward himself with a glistening toad. The sun parlour was just the place to find one and he tootled along at a jaunty pace, whistling and looking forward to telling Tallitha the news about the entrance to the lower floors. The sun parlour was a glorious room bursting with exotic plants that reached all the way to the glass ceiling. Tyaas bent down by one of the small pools to examine a fat toad whose back legs were peeping out from the lapping water.

Toads were endlessly fascinating and Tyaas often carried one in his pocket, croaking away at meal times, much to his delight and the horror of his sister. But just as he was about to bag another unsuspecting specimen he was distracted by a noise. Someone else was in the conservatory. There, behind one of the huge leafy banana plants, Tyaas spied two Shroves huddled together in conversation. He carefully released the toad back into the warm pool with a plop and moved on all fours across the tiled floor, keeping his body low and ending up behind the enormous plant. The Shroves were whispering together.

'*Spirrrnthndas al na durnath nem kemporan. Encrremblan dur na clerna ni fenran.*'

'*Nan trath an doorn ken lam naen. Ne ne kemporan derna canlera del ae nan trath.*'

Tyaas peered through the leaves, watching the Shroves as they snitched and gossiped. They were up to some skulduggery, he was certain of that. Grintley bent towards Florré and pointed towards the old house, his mouth salivating while the other

Shrove rubbed his hands together and hopped about. Whatever the infernal pair were up to, it was some wickedness. Tyaas inched stealthily towards the conservatory door.

But nothing much got past a Shrove and they smelt the boy before they saw him. Florré and Grintley were Shrove-cousins and their bond was unbreakable. They disliked Tyaas as much as his sister: nasty children who could not keep to their rooms, constantly on the move, poking their noses into things that didn't concern them. But the sneaky Shroves continued muttering to each other and pretended they hadn't seen the boy.

Tyaas slid out of the conservatory and ran into the nearest greenhouse, nearly colliding with a gardener, one of the Skinks, carrying a bundle of sacks.

'Whoa there!' she shouted, 'watch it!'

'Sorry,' shouted Tyaas as he slipped, then sped out of the rear door.

The Skink watched Tyaas disappear as a Shrove scampered past her and began spying on the boy. Then Florré turned and hissed at the Skink and she bristled. They hated one another. The enmity between them went back for generations, but in Winderling Spires the Shroves held the upper hand and the tall Skink let the matter pass.

Panting and dirty, Tyaas raced up the main staircase and bumped into Cissie who was ambling along with a load of ironing.

'Where're you rushing off to? It's unlucky to pass on't stairs. There'll be a consequence and no mistake. Both you and your sister 'ave been flying round like mad ferrets all mornin'. What's gotten into you?' Cissie clicked her tongue.

'Sorry Cissie. Is Tallitha in her room?' asked Tyaas, breathless.

'She is, and you know what …' said Cissie, but Tyaas didn't stop to hear the rest.

He flew up the next staircase and burst into the sitting room, calling Tallitha's name.

'In here, quick! I have something to tell you,' she shouted from her bedroom.

Tallitha was sitting at her desk surrounded by sheets of paper and the old book.

'The Shroves,' he shouted breathlessly, 'I heard them plotting.'

'What? Me too! But never mind them for a moment. Look at this sampler. It's got the initials 'A' and 'M' on it. Perhaps it belonged to Asenathe. What do you think?'

But the lettering was too complicated for Tyaas.

'I've been trying to decipher the script from one of the sisters' books but it's so difficult. I think it's the name of someone, or something.'

'Oh, heck Tallitha, I have no idea. Maybe you should ask Grandmamma?'

'Actually, I did ask someone about *the girl*,' she said, watching his reaction.

'Tell me, come on!' he shouted excitedly.

'I can tell you, I suppose,' she said teasing. 'Only I promised not to tell the ancient ones and Mother! I asked Cissie about it, but you mustn't let her know you know … when you know … If you know what I mean!' spluttered Tallitha.

Tyaas had no idea what she was talking about but listened just the same.

'Well go on then, what did she say?'

Tallitha savoured the moment, twisting her hair round her fingers.

'Come on!' exclaimed Tyaas, 'it's too exciting.'

'Well she was reticent at first. But I got it out of her. She said that Asenathe is Agatha's daughter but she doesn't know where she is. No one does. She thinks there was a falling out, and then Asenathe left the Spires, or was taken away at night.'

'Wow that's incredible! I can't believe you asked her, Sis, and I can't believe she told you. How did it happen?'

Tallitha explained about finding the sampler and the book, and how Florré had stalked her down the corridors.

'You see, I was so scared I raced into my bedroom and banged the door behind me. I must have looked frightful. Cissie would not let me be, and it all came out. And now I'm trying to decipher the words in the sampler.'

Tyaas looked away nervously. 'The Shroves scared me too today. Isn't that odd? I was in the sun parlour and I overheard them plotting together. They're up to no good,' he said quietly.

Brother and sister exchanged worried glances. Never before had they been scared of the Shroves. They had never liked their insidious, grovelling ways, but what had just happened to them both was quite different. They were wary and a little scared, and in their own house too. Something was afoot. There was a new sense of danger in Winderling Spires they had never experienced before. It was sinister and it had to do with Shroves. They would have to be extra vigilant when they went in search of the house plans.

*

Nightfall came soundlessly, falling swiftly over Wycham Moor until it swallowed up the Spires in its dark heavy jaws. Shards of moonlight glinted through the trees casting jagged shadows across the extensive lawns and meadows. When the house was finally asleep and silence had descended, Tallitha crept from her bed and tiptoed into her brother's bedroom. Tyaas was wide awake, lying fully dressed beneath the covers, impatiently waiting for their midnight adventure to begin.

The journey downstairs was one they had made many times before, just not at the dead of night. They crept along the shrouded corridors, anticipating all the creaks that awaited them on the dark staircase as they watched the moonlight flickering through the trees, dancing wildly with the shadows on the wooden floor of the grand hallway.

Tyaas took Tallitha's hand and whispered to her, 'Twenty-two paces, remember, quickly now.'

They darted from the bottom of the staircase, counting each step until they reached the safety of the shadows, hiding breathlessly behind the old clock. The house was eerily silent apart from the tick-tocking of the grandfather clock as they entered the narrow space at the top of the servants' staircase. Tyaas hurriedly lit one of the lanterns, shading it with his hand as the flame spluttered in the upward, howling draughts. The stairway was cold as a knife as they pressed their bodies against the stone wall and moved slowly down into the heavy darkness. The passageways were narrower in the servants' quarters than in the rest of the Spires and the light from their lantern licked up the dark stone walls, drawing haunting shadows all about them. They made their way to the door at the end of the passageway and stepped gingerly into the largest of the three kitchens.

'Come on, let's go this way,' whispered Tallitha, creeping under the kitchen implements hanging from racks above them, shining dagger-like in the candlelight.

Cissie had mentioned that the kitchen staff could never take a break from their chores because Mrs Armitage watched them through the glass panel outside her office. Tallitha noticed the glass corridor and, keeping a sharp look out, they moved towards it. There before them was the nameplate for the house-keeper's office on the last door but one. Tallitha turned the handle and by the light of their lantern, the cosy room took shape. In one corner there was a desk and chair, a little day-bed and a small fireplace with a hob to make tea. On the wall above the desk were the staff rotas detailing the servants' shifts, and the cleaning and laundry duties over the coming weeks. Tallitha began searching the desk while Tyaas studied the work rotas on the noticeboard. The world of the sleeping servants was gradually being revealed to them.

'I'm glad we aren't servants,' said Tyaas sadly.

He was a sweet boy but, completely unaware how his clothes got washed or his trousers were miraculously mended. They just ended up back in his drawers, clean and pressed.

'Did you know that we have six scullery maids and they have to clean the kitchen floors twice a day and scrub all the stoves?' he said incredulously. 'I feel sorry for them.'

Tallitha smiled indulgently at her younger brother. He would be giving the servants extra holidays next.

'Shhh, let's get on,' she said, sifting through piles of receipts and endless lists.

Tyaas gasped at just how little the servants were paid and giggled at their first names.

'Did you know that the footman, the one with the red curly hair, is called Archibald,' he laughed. 'He's married to Nora, one of the downstairs parlour maids from Wycham village.'

'Shh! I can't believe you didn't know that,' answered Tallitha in hushed tones.

Almost at once Tyaas tugged on his sister's sleeve. There, on the inside of the cupboard door was a floor plan. Tallitha opened the other cupboard doors and more plans were displayed. They stared in wonder as the enormity of Winderling Spires was laid out before them as they had never seen it before.

'The South Wing has eight, nine, ten floors, and more half-floors with so many staircases,' said Tyaas incredulously, attempting to count them all.

They each took one of the plans in turn and searched every floor meticulously.

'It's the same problem all over the house. You think you've found the staircase up to the next floor, but when you look again it doesn't make sense,' said Tyaas, scratching his head.

The interconnection of floors, half-floors and landings was bewildering.

'This wing's been shut up for years,' said Tallitha sadly.

Tallitha and Tyaas were fascinated by the picture of the Spires staring back at them, where whole sections of the old house had been closed up and forgotten.

'Look, *Sir Humphrey's Apartment, study, sitting room, gun room, valet's room*. I wonder who he is?' asked Tyaas.

'Whoever he is, the South Wing is abandoned. Keep looking for Asenathe's name,' whispered Tallitha.

Tyaas eventually located the plan they had been searching for.

'Up on the fifth floor – a suite of rooms with *Miss Morrow's bedchamber, Miss Morrow's study, dressing room, receiving sitting room, bathroom suite and library*,' said Tallitha excitedly.

'That's not fair, she gets an enormous sitting room and a library and we don't!' complained Tyaas.

Tallitha pushed him. 'Shhh, it doesn't matter, and don't make a noise. Bother, we forgot to bring a pen and paper. We'll just have to memorise the location,' she whispered.

'But where's her apartment in relation to the rest of the house?' asked Tyaas blankly.

No matter how much they studied the floor plans they couldn't work out how each floor was connected to the one above.

'Remember what you can and we'll make it up as we go along,' said Tallitha finally, 'at least we know it's somewhere on the fifth floor.'

They closed the cupboard doors, doused the lantern and tiptoed out of the housekeeper's parlour. But as Tyaas stepped into the corridor he stiffened. There was a noise coming from the kitchen. Tyaas spied two Shroves through the glass panel. They were moving boxes about in the large kitchen. Tyaas grabbed Tallitha and pulled her to the floor.

'Shhhh, get down. Marlin and Grintley are out there,' he whispered feverishly.

They listened to crates being scraped across the floor. After a while, Tallitha poked her head just far enough over the wooden panel so she could watch the Shroves through the glass panel. They were heaving wooden boxes out of one of the large pantries. Then they quickly slipped inside the pantry and closed the door behind them. Tyaas tugged on her jumper.

'What's happening?'

'They've disappeared inside the pantry. Come on, let's spy on them for a change,' she said impishly.

They crept to the pantry door and listened. It was ominously quiet and they tentatively stepped inside. It was an ordinary kitchen pantry filled with jams, pickles and cold meats resting on a wooden bench that ran along both walls. But underneath the bench, at the back next to the wall, was a trapdoor, and it was open. The hole was steely-black.

'Come on,' said Tallitha, tugging on Tyaas's jacket.

They held onto each other tightly as they inched down into the dark hole. At the bottom of the stairs they stopped and the hair stood up on the back of Tyaas's neck. It was pitch-black under the Spires, cold as the grave and deadly silent.

'Either we have to go back, or we light the lantern. You choose,' whispered Tallitha apprehensively into her brother's ear.

Tyaas immediately struck a match and the strong smell of sulphur laced the stale air. As their eyes became accustomed to the spluttering light, a strange world opened up in front of them. It was a messy hole littered with the remnants of half-eaten meals, flagons of berry juice and wooden crates piled high in one corner. There were six small burrows carved from the rock, filled with tattered blankets and bits of old pillow shaped into nesting material.

'It's one of the Shrove lairs,' whispered Tallitha peering into a smelly burrow.

The place stank of old Shrove, of too many of the fetid creatures living together in one confined space. The lingering tang of unwashed clothes and greasy food sat heavily in each burrow. Tallitha pinched her nose, reeling back from the stench.

'But where are they?' asked Tyaas bewildered.

'Beats me,' said Tallitha. 'There must be another way out, way down there,' she said, pointing towards a tunnel which smelled of soaked leaves in the rain, peaty and dank.

The dingy tunnel narrowed and sloped away into the flat darkness. They could hear the distant sound of water, drip-dropping away under the big house into the cold, damp ground.

'Where do you think it leads?' asked Tyaas nervously.

Tallitha bit her lip and shook her head. 'The Shroves mean to keep this a secret. Let's get out of here before they come back.'

They retraced their steps back to their apartment, edging uneasily through the dark shadows of the great house.

Eight

Over the days that followed it proved impossible to explore the Spires. Snowdroppe demanded their presence and, what with Tallitha's duties and their schoolwork, there was no time to slip away. Deciphering the sampler was uppermost in Tallitha's mind, and she carried it with her always. On the third morning after they had discovered the floor plans, Tallitha sat in the schoolroom waiting for her teacher and brother. She had a few minutes to spare and could not resist taking out the sampler and the book of old scripts. She hoped that buried somewhere within the pages would be the clue to interpret the stitches. But the book required a basic knowledge of the ancient language and Tallitha was stumped.

'I'll never be able to do this,' she said, slamming the book shut with annoyance.

Then she stiffened. Tallitha sensed she was no longer alone.

A noise at the back of the schoolroom confirmed her fear. It was Benedict who had just tripped over the leg of a chair.

'What can't you do?' he asked, extricating himself.

He must have snuck in without her noticing. Tallitha stood up too quickly, knocked the desk and everything fell on the floor.

'Oh! Bumps, you gave me a fright. Why are you always sneaking about?' she asked, throwing him a vexed look.

Benedict looked hurt. Tallitha thought he resembled a helpless puppy that had lost its mother.

'I'm not sneaking about,' he said pathetically.

'Well what are you doing?' Tallitha snapped.

'I'm here for lessons, like you. What's that?'

Benedict bent down and picked up the sampler.

'That's my needlework, give it to me!' Tallitha shouted, trying to grab it back.

But it was too late. Benedict was already taking in all the details.

'Where did you get this from?' he asked, studying the lettering.

'That's for me to know and you to find out.'

'There's no need to be like that. Do you have any idea what it says?'

'It's in Embric script and before you interrupted me I was just about to translate it,' she said petulantly.

Benedict stared at Tallitha. She really hadn't a clue what the sampler said. Perhaps this was his opportunity to get closer to his cousins. He pushed his hair out of his eyes.

'It's not Embric, this is old Ennish script and it's the name of a place,' he said guardedly.

'Oh really,' said Tallitha sarcastically, 'and what do you know anyway?'

'Well I know it says Hellstone Tors,' said Benedict giving Tallitha a sidelong glance.

Benedict was such a swot. Of course he would know how to translate the script! She grabbed the sampler back from him and tried to sound uninterested.

'Thanks a lot, but where is that anyway?'

'You're telling me you've never heard of Hellstone Tors!' he said in amazement.

Tallitha shook her head. She was cross that Benedict knew something she didn't.

'It's over the mountains, far away from Wycham Elva, to the north-west,' he explained.

'Where's that?' asked Tallitha, becoming curious.

'It's in Breedoor, a wild, strange sort of place,' he said, observing her reaction.

But Tallitha had no idea what he was talking about.

At that moment Tyaas came bounding into the schoolroom, flinging the door wide open.

'Amazing, guess what? Old Raisethorne has a sore throat. So, no school today, or tomorrow! Oh hi Bumps, how's things?'

Tyaas looked from one to the other. Something was definitely going on so he pulled up a chair and sat down.

'I was explaining what these words mean.'

Benedict pointed to the sampler and repeated what he had said to Tallitha.

'You mean this weird place called Hellstone Tors is somehow connected to us?' said Tyaas.

'Of course. Didn't you know either?' Benedict asked incredulously.

Tyaas shook his head. Now Benedict had their complete attention.

'So come on, Bumps, if you know so much, why don't you tell us?' said Tallitha, becoming irritated.

Benedict blushed slightly. Tallitha could sense he was in two minds about what to say to them.

'Come on,' said Tyaas, poking Benedict. 'You can't leave us in the dark.'

Benedict pushed his hair out of his eyes, bit his lip and thought for a moment.

'Okay, you asked, don't ever forget that. There's an old story and it isn't a happy one,' Benedict shifted in his seat. 'Many years ago there was a terrible feud in the Morrow family. On their mother's death, Fedora and her half-brother Edwyn quarrelled over who should rule Wycham Elva. Fedora demanded her birthright as the woman, but Edwyn had always been jealous of his half sister and insisted that he should inherit and they fought bitterly. Edwyn's hatred ate away at him and he arranged for his sister and her husband to be poisoned.'

'Wow,' said Tyaas, 'some family! Why have we never heard this stuff before?'

Tallitha shrugged her shoulders. 'What happened next?' she asked.

'Fedora survived but her husband, Rufus, died. The people of Wycham Elva rose up against Edwyn and they installed Fedora as the Grand Morrow. Edwyn called upon dark forces to execute his escape, fleeing with his gruesome entourage to the northern lands. Now his descendants rule Breedoor.'

'Are they related to us?' asked Tyaas.

'Distantly,' replied Benedict.

'What sort of dark forces?'

'Edwyn made a secret pact in return for his freedom and the lands of Breedoor. He had to give up something precious …'

'Who to?' asked Tyaas.

'What did he give up?' asked Tallitha excitedly.

'I don't know everything,' Benedict replied, smiling. 'Anyway it's supposed to be a secret pact, so maybe no one knows.'

'What about Asenathe, Great Aunt Agatha's daughter?' demanded Tallitha, 'where is she?'

'Asenathe?' asked Benedict, colouring slightly.

Maybe Benedict didn't know everything after all. So Tallitha told him what they had discovered about Great Aunt Agatha's daughter.

'So you see, we have to find her. She may be in Hellstone Tors. This is the first real piece of information we've had,' she said excitedly.

'So what are you going to do?' asked Benedict.

'Well, we have a plan, haven't we?' she said smiling at Tyaas. 'First we'll find her old apartment in Winderling Spires. It's somewhere on the fifth floor. There may be more clues there. Then we're going to Hellstone Tors,' said Tallitha excitedly.

Benedict shifted uncomfortably, kicking his feet on the underside of the chair. 'That won't be as easy as you think,' he said fidgeting.

'Why not?' asked Tallitha, 'what do you mean?'

Benedict was proving more interesting than she had imagined. 'It may be the reason she never returned.'

'Well …?' asked Tallitha impatiently.

'There's no known route to Hellstone Tors, at least over the top of the Out-Of-The –Way Mountains.' His cousins were hanging on to his every word. 'It's impassable.'

'So why did she start out,' asked Tyaas, 'if no one knows the way?'

'Maybe she went through the caves. But that's dangerous; full of creatures you wouldn't want to meet,' explained Benedict, observing their reaction.

'Wow!' said Tyaas. 'Amazing!'

This was his idea of bliss. Already in his mind's eye, he was climbing down dangerous caverns, fighting wild creatures and winning heroically. 'But that sounds great,' he said, completely gripped.

'There's no map. If Asenathe reached Hellstone Tors she must have been taken there by someone. Breedoor is a dark place,' said Benedict mysteriously.

'That's what makes it so exciting. We have to pursue this mystery to the end!' exclaimed Tyaas, banging the table.

'So many strange things have happened to us. First we discovered Asenathe's book and then the sampler,' said Tallitha lowering her voice.

'And the Shroves have been behaving oddly. I don't know how they fit in, only that they scared us both,' said Tyaas.

'Perhaps someone is leaving these clues so we'll find them,' said Tallitha thoughtfully.

'But there may be no way back,' said Benedict, shifting uneasily.

'We can't let that stop us. Everything that has happened so far is pointing us in the direction of Breedoor,' exclaimed Tyaas.

'It's an inhospitable place. I've heard people talking and if I was to go with you …' suggested Benedict.

'Who says you're coming with us?' snapped Tyaas, looking at Tallitha. 'Well he isn't, is he, Sis?'

They didn't know Benedict that well. But perhaps he could be useful.

'Maybe we need Benedict's help,' Tallitha replied.

Tyaas raised his eyebrows at his sister but there was no stopping her.

'Without his help I wouldn't have understood the script, and he knows a lot of stuff we don't. We've hardly been outside Winderling Spires, and never on our own.'

Tyaas mouthed the word '*NO*' to Tallitha, but as usual she wouldn't take the hint.

'We can do it by ourselves,' insisted Tyaas, staring hard at his sister.

'But can we? Let's be honest. Without him, we would have missed this clue,' she said, waving the sampler in Tyaas's face. 'Granted he isn't much good at anything that doesn't involve books, like climbing – sorry Bumps,' she said turning to their cousin, 'but he knows too much now to leave him behind,' she said firmly.

For some reason, Tyaas was uncertain about Benedict. 'I'm not sure,' he replied.

'He must come with us, he can help us. Come on Tyaas, don't be a stick in the mud,' said Tallitha sighing.

Tyaas felt put on the spot. Benedict knew their plans and if they didn't include him he might tell one of the grown-ups, and Tallitha always had to have her own way.

'Okay, I suppose so, but it will be dangerous and you'll have to learn to climb and stuff,' he said reluctantly to Benedict.

But Benedict wanted something in return. 'I'll come with you, but on one condition, and it isn't negotiable. I hate the name Bumps. It's a nickname you came up with. I want you to call me Benedict from now on.'

Poor Bumps, they hadn't really meant to upset him. Had they?

'Okay, sure,' said Tallitha.

Tyaas shrugged his shoulders.

All three took a vow to discover the way to Hellstone Tors and shook hands on it. Whatever danger lay ahead, they were all in it together – Tallitha, Tyaas and Benedict. But Tallitha secretly thought he would always be Bumps to her.

*

After lunch they met in Tallitha's study before setting off in search of Asenathe's apartment. Tallitha and Tyaas had copied down what they could remember of the floor plans.

'It'll be tricky,' said Tyaas, 'the house has so many floors. Some wings have seven floors, some up to ten. The staircases lead all over the place and never end up where you'd expect.'

'We'll have to discover the house we as we go along. Some of the plans could be out of date anyway. Mrs Armitage and the servants know more about the house than we do, and perhaps some of the abandoned wings aren't written down at all.'

They set off, passing Snowdroppe's rooms on the third floor and retraced their steps up the staircase where they had seen Grintley. This led them to the rear of the house. There was a large central staircase and a landing with eight main corridors leading from it: two to the North-West Wing, two to the South-West Wing, and so on.

'Let's go down there,' said Tallitha, pointing down a long purple corridor, 'from the floor plan it should lead us directly under Asenathe's rooms.'

They crept down a series of dark corridors before hearing a noise coming from one of the bedrooms. It sounded like the servants chatting to one another.

'Quick,' said Tallitha, 'in here!'

In the corner of the room by the side of the fireplace was a small wooden staircase.

'By my reckoning we should be somewhere below Asenathe's suite,' said Tallitha making her way to the staircase. 'Come on, let's try up here.'

They followed Tallitha up the dusty steps, trying to avoid the cobwebs and the scuttling mice. The staircase kept going up and up, twisting into the darkness way above them.

'Where are we?' asked Benedict, sulking. 'This hasn't been used for years. Eurgh, there are so many spiders' webs,' he cried, flicking away a long-legged spider that had lodged in his hair.

His clothes were covered in dirt and he was hot and sweaty.

'Shhh!' said Tallitha sounding irritated. 'Have you any better ideas? Let's just see where it leads and stop complaining.'

But Benedict continued to moan, much to Tallitha's annoyance.

At the top of the staircase was a metal door that had rusted on its hinges. Tallitha could smell the fresh air and sunlight shone through the cracks.

'Come on, push really hard,' said Tyaas.

All three put their combined weight against the door and it finally scraped open. They tumbled out onto a balcony covered in creepers. The smell of honeysuckle filled their nostrils as they clambered towards the edge and took in the view of the rolling countryside.

'It's so far down!' exclaimed Tyaas.

The walls were covered in creepers, which cascaded onto the balcony floor and trailed down the house like twisting snakes. Benedict wobbled and covered his eyes.

'Ohhh, I feel sick,' he whined.

'Then come away from the edge and help!' shouted Tallitha covered in leaf litter as she frantically pulled vegetation from the wall. 'Look – here's another door.'

Hiding behind the thickly tangled creepers was a dirty glass door covered in sticky creeper ooze that had trickled down and encrusted the window in sap. Tallitha leant hard on the door, gave it three hard pushes and it crunched open.

'It's so dark in here,' she said as she stepped into the circular room.

Inside there were boxes and trunks haphazardly piled in heaps.

'Where are we?' asked Tyaas picking his way past the trunks and sitting down on a shabby four-poster bed.

'In the north-eastern corner, under one of the turrets,' said Tallitha peering into the shadows.

They crept through an archway into a windowless library, piled high with bookcases and rolls of dusty yellowing manuscripts. Tallitha hesitated and put her finger to her lips.

'Sssh, did you hear something?'

She pointed back into the darkness of the circular room, then retraced her steps, stood for a moment and listened. It was ominously still. She felt her skin prickle and sweat began to run down her neck. Whatever was lurking nearby was not going to reveal itself. She shuddered and went back to join the others.

'I suppose I must have imagined it,' she said glancing back into the gloom.

Benedict was busily poking about, inspecting the wooden panels and peering behind the bookcases.

'What you doing?' asked Tyaas, coming up behind him.

'Looking for the secret panel, it's bound to be in here somewhere. They're all over the house.'

'How do you know?' asked Tallitha, sounding impressed. 'We've never seen any.'

'I've been doing some of my own research,' he said mysteriously.

Benedict pressed a section of the panelling and it slid to one side to reveal a cramped dusty cavity.

'Wow! See Tyaas, I told you he was helpful,' said Tallitha.

Benedict stepped inside the gap and the others followed in single file. Their clothes and hair were soon full of dust and webs.

'This is grim,' said Tyaas shining the lantern into the cold, grimy space. 'It seems to go on a long way.'

They slid along the rough wall feeling the surface for any change in its contours. Then the cavity came to an abrupt end. There was solid wall in front of them.

'It's a dead end. We must have missed an exit further back,' said Benedict.

'Wait, look at the wall. Is there anything unusual?' asked Tallitha.

Benedict inspected the stone wall and shook his head.

'There's nothing there.'

'Wait. Let me look,' she insisted. Tallitha took the lantern and climbed over her brother.

'There has to be a way out. We just can't see it yet. Keep looking, Benedict.'

Tallitha moved the lantern higher and noticed a square stone jutting out at least a head height above her. 'Lift me up, Benedict!'

As Tallitha touched the stone it moved and other stones began jumping out of the wall, making a series of sudden popping noises. The stones created a stepping stone effect leading upwards and slanting to the left.

'It's a small staircase. Let me go first,' said Tyaas excitedly.

'I'm not sure we should go up there,' said Benedict looking alarmed.

'We have to find out where it leads,' said Tallitha. 'We can't stop now.'

Tallitha and Tyaas climbed up the stones while Benedict waited at the bottom holding the flickering lantern. They scrambled over the last step and pulled themselves over the edge. There before them was a long wooden ladder.

'Come on Benedict, it's easy. Climb up and pass the lantern,' said Tallitha.

'But I can't see,' he complained pathetically. His face looked forlorn and miserable in the gloom. 'It's too hard,' he said like a spoilt child.

'Stop moaning. You wanted to come with us,' said Tyaas, 'this is only the beginning.'

Benedict eventually reached the top of the ladder, but there before him was another narrow staircase.

'Come on, hurry up Benedict,' said Tyaas as he disappeared up the stairs.

Benedict's legs ached and he was filthy. Yet up and up they clambered, way up into the leaden darkness that seemed to go on forever.

*

Tallitha had been right. There behind them, in the gloom, sat a sneaky Shrove with his head cocked to one side, listening. Marlin lurked, watching and waiting, sniffing the air for their scents and smelling them in all the dark musty places. He grizzled, pleased with his artful deception. Marlin knew every nooky recess in Winderling Spires. There was no one who knew the house better than him. Over the years Marlin had explored every floor, mapping the mysterious twists and turns of the Spires in his devious mind. He was the cleverest of all the Shroves. When the children climbed up to the balcony he had followed them, lying low on the staircase like a coiled snake. He hid noiselessly in the seeping darkness of the circular room. Tallitha had sensed something lurking behind them as his malevolence leached out. Marlin waited until they found the secret passageway but he didn't need to follow them up the stone steps. He knew they would find Asenathe's rooms. Silently he crept back to his Shrove lair to plan his next move.

Nine

Tyaas was first to reach the top of the winding staircase. He stood on a tiny platform, took a few seconds to get his breath and called down to the others in the darkness.

'Nearly there, come on, you two. Hurry up.'

He pushed open a small wooden door and stepped out onto a high gallery and into the dust-spangled light. Tallitha followed closely behind, shading her eyes, blinded by the brilliant sunlight streaming through the arched windows.

'Wow! Look at this! We're so high up,' exclaimed Tyaas, holding onto the balustrade and peering down at the palatial room below.

'It's amazing. No wonder we were forbidden from coming up here. This has got to be it. These must be Asenathe's rooms,' said Tallitha, her face full of wonder.

They found themselves on a balcony that ran the whole

length of the glass wall and projected out over the space below. It caught the sunlight from every angle and was the finest sun terrace they had ever seen.

'Where are we?' asked Benedict shading his eyes. Then he froze. 'Get me out of here. I can't stand heights!' he yelled.

Tyaas grabbed his cousin and pulled him to the floor. 'Stop it, toughen up can't you? You're being a real pain. Stay here, we're going down.'

'Don't leave me alone,' he wailed pathetically.

But Tyaas ignored him.

'Oh do stop being a ninny. Who knows what we'll find down there?' replied Tallitha excitedly.

This wasn't Benedict's sort of thing after all, but he would have to play his part if his cousins were to trust him. Nervously he helped them tether the rope to the gallery struts. Tallitha stepped over the edge and began to abseil down, using one of the window columns to bounce off. Benedict could not bear to watch her rapid descent. Tyaas quickly followed, laughing as he bounced down the column.

'Wow! That was almost as good as abseiling from my bedroom window. Just look at this room, it's like a palace, it's incredible. Where shall we start?' he shouted, landing with a thud in the enormous chamber.

They began searching the drawers and cupboards, under the beds and in the closets. There were girls' clothes, beautiful velvets and silks, storybooks and sweet-scented bathing gels. This had to be Asenathe's apartment, but curiously the room appeared to be lived in, as though someone was carefully looking after all the wonderful things in it.

'Benedict, open your eyes! Tell us what you can see from up there!'

Benedict moved a couple of inches and made a mewing noise. 'Oh, no – I feel dizzy.'

'Stop being a baby or we'll call you by that name again!' said Tyaas, teasing.

'There's a metal rail in front of you, so hang on to it,' said Tallitha, sounding frustrated.

Benedict made the same pathetic noise, unscrewed his eyes and briefly looked down. Tyaas and Tallitha were looking up at him with an exasperated expression on their faces.

'Come on!' they shouted in unison.

Benedict moved slightly, gripping hold of the balustrade.

'On the top of that wardrobe, there's something there,' he said pointing a shaking finger towards the far corner of the room. 'A box, I think, and a roll of something, like wallpaper. That's it. I'm closing my eyes now. How will I ever get out of here?' he cried pathetically.

'That's a good point,' said Tallitha laughing at him. 'We aren't climbing back up to get you, so you'll have to go back the way we came.'

Benedict looked green and tucked his head between his knees. Tyaas pulled a chair over to the wardrobe, climbed up and began poking around on top.

'Anything?' asked Tallitha excitedly.

'Some boxes. Eurgh, it's filthy up here.'

Tyaas felt about in the dust until he found a long cardboard roll and a couple of wooden boxes which he passed to his sister. Tallitha pulled the map from the cardboard roll.

'It's unlike any map I've ever seen,' she said in amazement, spreading it out on the floor, 'Look at the writing in this corner. Tyaas! Quickly! It says the name of that place – *Hellstone Tors*.'

Tyaas leapt from the chair and crouched next to her, placing the two boxes on either side on the crumpled map to weight it down. The faded map was a curious collection of scribbled writing and signs.

'It has strange writing and illustrations. But I can't read it. Is it in Ennish?' asked Tyaas.

But Tallitha didn't know.

Benedict half-opened his eyes at the interesting news floating up from below, mewed pathetically and quickly closed them again. Tallitha tried to open the smaller box but it was locked. She blew the dust from the larger box to reveal a mother-of-pearl lid which clicked open easily. Inside was a handwritten note and Tallitha read it aloud:

'*Through my window you will find what you are looking for.*'

'Quick!' she shouted.

They climbed on to the window seat and began scouring the landscape of Wycham Elva. There had to be a sign, but what was it?

'What are we looking for?' asked Tyaas, scratching his head.

'Whatever it is, it has to be out there, just like the stone steps in the secret passageway, but we just can't see it yet,' said Tallitha sighing. She pointed towards different landmarks, but nothing made sense. 'Think this through logically. There have to be other windows in here. The plans in Mrs Armitage's cupboard showed more rooms, so let's find them.'

Tallitha leapt from the window seat, quickly followed by Tyaas.

'Through here,' she said, making for a door in the corner of the room.

First they looked through the study window. Then they ran into the next room and looked through the sitting room window. But both rooms had the same view from a slightly different perspective. The library was next. It was a cosy room and Tallitha could have spent many happy hours leafing through books and studying the paraphernalia displayed on the shelves. The view from the window however proved to be the same as all the others. Tallitha sat down on the swivel chair and spun round, mulling things over.

'We're missing something,' said Tyaas.

'What you doing?' a distant voice called from the gallery.

'He's an idiot,' said Tyaas to Tallitha, then shouted up to him, 'you'll have to come down and see for yourself! – That should shut him up.'

'There's something curious about these rooms,' said Tallitha, spinning round on the chair. She closed her eyes and allowed the sensation to develop. She felt too big in the room and a little bit claustrophobic. She looked up at the ceiling – it was much lower than the great room. There must be another floor above this one, but where was the entrance?

'That's it! We have to find a ladder or a staircase.'

Tallitha ran back into the great room and called up to Benedict. 'Can you see an entrance to another floor, by that wall?'

Benedict shook his head. There was only a large painting hanging over a dresser. All three looked at the painting at the same time. It was of a girl sitting in a room with the sun shining through a lattice window whilst she did her needlework. Tyaas shrieked.

'There's the window. Look, in that painting!' he shouted, jumping onto the dresser and pushing the painting to one side.

There it was, hidden beneath the painting, a hatch to the secret floor, just waiting for them to find it.

'Come on!' shouted Tyaas excitedly.

They climbed through the hatch door and into a dark little room. Tyaas lit the lantern and the room took shape before their eyes. It was a wonderful hidey-hole with a sofa and a desk. Tallitha noticed a wall ladder in the corner which went up to a trapdoor in the ceiling. She stuck her head out of the hatch and called to Benedict.

'Move along the gallery, there's a ladder at the far end which you can climb down.'

Benedict didn't fancy finding his own way back alone so he did as he was told. He edged along the gallery trying to keep his nerves under control. *Don't look down, don't look down*, he kept saying to himself. The next thing Tallitha saw were the soles of his shoes coming shakily down the ladder.

'There must be more clues in here, perhaps the key to that box,' Tallitha said excitedly as Benedict stepped from the ladder. 'Here take a look at this.'

Benedict squidged onto the sofa next to Tallitha and began poring over the map.

'This is in Ennish,' he said authoritatively, 'but it's bewildering. I only know a few of the words.'

'Does the map make any sense?' asked Tyaas. 'Does it tell us where to start?'

Benedict shook his head. Tallitha walked to the hatch door and peered out.

'The light's fading. We can't miss dinner. Let's pack up, we can search tomorrow. Raisethorne's sick so there's no school.'

They took the map and everything they had found, climbed out of the trapdoor, scrambled over the gallery and back down the dark staircase. It took less time than they thought and soon they were back in Tallitha's study.

'Are you staying tonight?' asked Tyaas.

He was getting used to having old Benedict around, even if he could be annoying at times.

'Yes, I guess so, but I need to do my schoolwork. You go to dinner, and I'll have something sent to my room.'

As Benedict settled to his work an unfamiliar feeling began welling up inside him. He felt decidedly odd, as though he belonged somewhere for the first time in his life.

*

Tallitha and Tyaas hid their precious discoveries, cleaned themselves up and were ready just in time for the dinner gong. When they reached the dining hall, Great Aunt Agatha and the sisters were sitting at the enormous table but there was scant conversation. Tallitha hated the formal dinners and couldn't understand why they had to endure them when they would all rather eat in their own sitting rooms. On this occasion it was because Great Aunt Agatha had acquired a new cook and the family had gathered to taste her cooking.

Snowdroppe arrived looking elegant in an indigo-blue gown with deep sapphire earrings, her hair perfectly coiffed in coils and braids. Maximillian, on the other hand, looked even fatter, with shiny red cheeks as though someone had just scraped them with a cheese grater. He guffawed loudly, cuffed Tyaas cordially on the head and went back to his large glass of burgundy. Snowdroppe gave her corpulent husband an acid look, then indicated with a flourish that Tallitha should sit next to her.

'What have you been up to my pets?' she murmured.

Tallitha was on her guard. Why was their mother interested in them all of a sudden? Snowdroppe only cared about herself and the amber ball of fox fur with the sticky-out ears. The dreadful creature had his very own place setting and was eating food at their table!

Tallitha mouthed to Tyaas to be quiet. She would deal with their mother.

'Why, nothing much, sewing and schoolwork,' replied Tallitha, trying to look innocent.

Snowdroppe's mouth twisted into a bitter smile and she clicked her tongue at Tallitha, who stiffened as her mother drew closer. Her mother's wicked laugh started prettily in her throat and ended rattling snake-like in Tallitha's ear.

'But a little bird has been telling me you have been somewhat distracted from your studies of late,' she murmured nastily.

Tallitha edged away from her mother's unsettling proximity and tried to eat her melon. She was cornered by her appalling family. Sitting opposite was her ridiculous grandmother and Great Aunt Sybilla. Had they been snitching on her behind her back? She flashed a hateful glance in their direction, sitting like two overindulged peacocks, pick-pecking away at their food, analysing every minute mouthful before tasting it. They smiled at Tallitha, a little too sweetly, and carried on dissecting their first course with relish.

'I don't know what you mean. Grandmamma and Great Aunt Sybilla seem pleased with my progress,' implored Tallitha, looking at the sisters for confirmation.

The snivelling pair kept their eyes averted, fixed compulsively on their food as though their plates were about to be removed at any moment. Snowdroppe laughed wickedly at her daughter, gave her leg a nasty pinch under the table and summoned Grintley to pour more wine.

'Do stop telling fibs dear, you can't carry it off,' said Snowdroppe caustically.

Tallitha's cheeks began to burn with rage. By this time Maximillian was tiddly, and Snowdroppe was bored with his foolishness. She moved her chair closer to Tallitha, all the while smiling sweetly at the rest of the family seated around the table.

'Don't think I don't know what you're up to, my adventurous one. My spies are everywhere. Never forget that Tallitha!'

She dug her pointed nails into the soft skin on Tallitha's leg and the girl let out a yelp. Snowdroppe's words fell like poisonous droplets from her vicious red lips as she turned from her daughter and began snapping at Maximillian. Tallitha's eyes pricked with hot tears, partly from her mother's nails, but also from her cruel, unloving words. *Their mother was onto them.*

Ten

The next afternoon they retraced their steps to Asenathe's apartment. At the top of the winding staircase Tallitha stepped out onto the sunlit gallery and stopped dead. There was someone below, staring up at her. They had been discovered.

'Come down Tallitha, and whoever it is lurking behind you. I've been expecting you,' exclaimed Esmerelda.

One by one they climbed out of the secret hatch. Esmerelda stood, her long silky dress floating behind her, with Licks circling her legs and purring loudly.

'What you doing sneaking around? You're not supposed to be up here,' she snapped.

'We were exploring,' said Tallitha, 'playing hide-and-seek.'

'Don't try that old trick. I used that one before you were born,' said Esmerelda coldly. 'Who gave you permission to be up here? Or is Aunt Agatha oblivious to all this?' Esmerelda's dark eyes flashed

as she moved towards them. 'She will be cross when I tell her,' she teased.

'Please don't, Essie, we weren't doing any harm,' pleaded Tallitha.

'No, we were …,' said Benedict, but Esmerelda put her finger to her lips.

She was only interested in the girl. Esmerelda circled them holding their gaze with her smouldering eyes. She began to hum in a strange repetitive way, the sound coming from deep within her throat. They were easy prey and fell quickly under her powerful spell. She encircled them, once, twice, three times wrapping her long scarves around their faces and smothering them in strong heady perfume. Tallitha tried to keep her focus but the boys were entranced and went to mush.

'Please don't tell her, Essie.' Her voice tailed off. 'We can explain. We were just exploring and came across this room.'

'Well you paint such an innocent picture. But I don't believe you,' she snapped. 'Benedict, you for one, look guilty', she said, holding his drooping face in her hands. Benedict's eyes rolled back in his head. 'I know why you came here,' said Esmerelda, turning to Tallitha. 'You were searching for my cousin Asenathe's rooms, weren't you?'

Esmerelda spun round with her scarves flying wildly behind her. Then she began twisting an amulet before Tallitha's face, moving it backwards and forwards, emitting a foul-smelling odour. Tallitha could not resist the smell, the awful sweet heady smell, lulling her, making her drift and lose her senses.

'Essie! What are you doing? Leave me alone,' pleaded Tallitha.

But she was slipping, sliding away from her body. Esmerelda

made the strange bauble dance erratically before Tallitha's eyes. It shimmered and flashed, throwing a thousand sparkles across the room.

'Relax. Breathe deeply and listen to what I tell you,' she said bewitchingly.

Esmerelda's haunting voice penetrated Tallitha's mind.

'I can't breathe, Essie. I'm so hot,' she said pulling at her face and hair, 'I'm falling.'

'Then fall, Tallitha. Let go, don't resist me!' demanded Esmerelda.

Tallitha felt herself slipping into the infinite space that stretched before her, squeezed out from her body and taken beyond her world. Coloured whirlpools, deep and alluring, green, blue and violet pulled her in. They dragged her down through the ever-increasing spirals of colour, green, turquoise, blue, violet. Her will vanished and *whoosh!* – she entered a separate reality where all was silent.

Tallitha slipped easily into the foggy light. Flashing images cascaded, randomly flicking before her eyes. She was trudging through a dream, her feet like leaden weights. Then she heard the rich lilting sounds of Ennish, dark and repetitive, flooding her senses.

'*Snenathe ne certhe merl can an le ner*
Cerna la bernatha ne tor na lam, berche berche ne cer
Snenathe ne certhe merl can an le ner.'

What awful fantasy was this? Suddenly she felt her body become weightless and she was whipped up a long tunnel with a silver cord floating behind her. At the top, the cool rushing air transported her amongst the images, which kept rippling, forming, blurring and disappearing again. One image was just out of her reach and she put out her hand. It was the vaguest outline of a girl, sitting with her back to Tallitha and looking out of a window.

Then Esmerelda spoke. 'Tallitha - where are you? What can you see?' she whispered.

But the vision blurred. It kept coming into view then receding as if Tallitha was looking down a telescopic lens.

'A girl in a black dress, her hair is in spirals down her back. I can't see her face.'

Tallitha's voice was flat. Then she heard Ennish.

'Canyer ta serna fe la der, certhe merla canya fe-canya fe-canya fe.'

Tallitha reached out to touch the vision and the outline began to fade like ripples in a muddy puddle.

Suddenly a desperate, wailing scream filled the room.

'Essie, Esmerelda, stop this at once. Tallitha! Oh Tallitha. Essie, you must do something. Bring her back. Do you hear me? What foul loathsome trickery are you up to now?' cried Cissie, running towards Esmerelda and pushing her to one side.

Esmerelda snapped her eyes shut in annoyance and touched

Tallitha just once. Then Tallitha felt herself falling down a bumpy tunnel, lights flashed before her eyes and there was an enormous *whoosh!* flooding into her whole body. There was a thud and a tremendous thump, and Tallitha woke with a start. The air was rushing back into her lungs with huge searing gulps. Someone was shaking her, shaking her awake. It was Cissie.

Then she passed out into the darkness.

*

Some time later, when Tallitha came round, she was resting on Asenathe's bed covered in rugs. Cissie was stroking her hand and whispering fondly to her.

'There now you'll be fine, just drink this.'

She handed Tallitha a black-coloured drink that tasted of salt and liquorice. Tallitha gulped at the strange liquid and it began to revive her.

'What happened to me? Where's Esmerelda?'

Cissie shook her head, 'She went off in a bit of a blither, saying I'd spoiled everythin'. But she'll be back. She's found what she was looking for and she won't let that go, not after all this time,' said Cissie angrily.

'What's she found, Cissie?' asked Tallitha apprehensively.

'You, Miss, she's found you. She knows you're a channel, you can see things for her. Things she can't see on her own.'

It was true then. It had really happened.

'Where are the others?'

'She let them go. They went into the hidey-hole to get away from Esmerelda's strange goings-on. Lookin' for summat they said. Wait, I'll call them. Benedict, Tyaas!'

But there was no response.

'They've prob'ly found the other rooms by now. They were a bit unnerved by what 'appened.'

Tallitha rubbed her throbbing head.

'I don't understand. I went to a strange place.'

Cissie frowned. 'She shouldn't 'ave done that.'

'I left my body and it was misty all around me. Did Essie do that to me?'

'She hypnotised all of you, Miss, to try you out, so to speak. With you she found her channel, and that's what she's been searching for. You're part of her bloodline, aren't you?'

Cissie put her arm round the trembling girl and gave her a hug.

'She's probably tried before, if you think on.'

Tallitha remembered her strange experience in the sisters' apartment when Essie had completed her needlework.

'Yes I remember. So maybe it was Essie that left the sampler for me to find, and perhaps she led us to the turret where we found Asenathe's book?'

'I don't know about all that. There's queer goings-on in this old house, that's for sure,' exclaimed Cissie.

'What do you mean?' asked Tallitha.

'There's thems that would do bad things, if they could, to the family,' explained Cissie, 'I don't mean Essie. She's just after finding Asenathe, but there's others.' Cissie's voice trailed off.

'But who are they?'

'I don't know Miss, so no use quizzing me like you always do. There's summat unsettling about the Spires these days, something I can't quite put my finger on.'

Cissie smoothed down her apron and sighed.

'She'll want to try again. 'Tis only with practising that you'll see things clearer and she'll find what she wants to see. But is that what you want too? She's been searching for Asenathe for many a long year – since she went missin'. The Grand Morrow has no truck with it. She thinks Asenathe is never comin' home and that Miss Esmerelda's wastin' her time.'

'I think it's what I want, but I never imagined it would turn out like this.'

Tallitha paused and took Cissie's hand.

'You won't get into trouble, will you? With Essie, I mean?'

'Not likely. Her and me go back a long way. She knows I'm lookin' out for you. Her ways are strange though. She'll stop at nothin' to get Asenathe back, you mark my words.'

Tallitha looked out of the window, over to the mountains in the north. 'Asenathe's somewhere out there,' she whispered.

Cissie shuddered. She felt like someone had just walked over her grave.

''Appen she is,' she said quickly. 'There's evil goings-on. 'Tis a fearsome place, out beyond Wycham Elva, and especially not safe for the likes of you.'

They lapsed into silence and Tallitha sipped the liquorice drink. She had always known there was something nudging her in another direction, making her yearn for a different life, and now she was beginning to find out what that life might be like.

'I'm going to look for the others,' she said, 'I'll be back in time for dinner.'

Tallitha kissed her nurse, scrambled off the bed and climbed into the hidey-hole.

Cissie watched Tallitha disappear through the hatch. She sat for a while on Asenathe's bed and absent-mindedly played with a chain around her neck, hidden under her dress. It had a small silver key on the end which she twisted and turned, turned and twisted.

*

It was dark in the secret room and Tallitha saw candlelight flickering behind a curtain. Tyaas and Benedict were sitting cross-legged on the floor studying the map. They both looked up when she pulled the curtain to one side.

'Sorry we went off. You okay?' asked Tyaas.

Tallitha nodded and sat next to them.

'That was the weirdest thing ever,' said Tyaas, looking spooked.

'We left when Cissie arrived and Essie's power wore off. Hope you don't mind? She gives me the creeps,' said Benedict, pushing the hair out of his eyes.

Tallitha understood only too well. 'She put me in a trance. I saw strange things, people ...' said Tallitha mysteriously.

'Wow, what happened?' asked Tyaas.

'I went to another place outside my body. It was weird. I think I saw Asenathe.'

Tyaas thought the whole episode was bizarre. It gave him the collywobbles.

'What do you think Asenathe and Essie used to do in here?' asked Tallitha, surveying the room by candlelight.

There was a circular glass table in the middle of the room with large cushions positioned around it.

'Practise the black arts. It's a bit sinister if you ask me,' said Tyaas looking warily around him.

The boys had discovered a book of translations in the bookcase. Benedict was leafing through the pages.

'I'm sure this is what we were supposed to find, it's the cipher to the map.'

'It's too dark in here, let's move to the glass table,' suggested Tallitha.

They pressed the map firmly down on to the table so that the candlelight from below shone through. The heat began to affect the map, and slowly more of the brown spidery handwriting began to take shape on the yellow paper.

'Look, there are more place names showing up,' exclaimed Tyaas.

'It's the ink that's special. It's invisible until you warm it up. Then it reveals all the hidden words,' explained Benedict.

'Take a look at the cipher. These Ennish names translate as Smear-Seat Knells, Ragging Brows Forest and Weeping Holes.'

'There!' shouted Tyaas, pointing at the book, 'this translation means "Through water, or by the water".

The map was a curious collection of names and places written in Ennish. It was a disjointed pattern of small drawings without any obvious destination. What leapt out at them was Shivering Water, a cold bottomless lake in the north of Wycham Elva.

It had the drawing of a silver key next to it. They stared at each other in the candlelight.

That had to be the start of their journey to Breedoor.

Eleven

Cissie sat by the fire, staring into the flames as she twisted the threads of her needlework in and out of her fingers. She must tell them the truth. She had lied to Tallitha. Not a vicious nasty lie to hurt her but a good lie, if such a thing existed, to protect her. But it was no use pretending any more, they were sure to notice the silver key in the corner of the map. If only she'd got rid of that dreadful map, but Esmerelda had stopped her and made her promise. So she sat, full of trepidation, and waited for them to return after supper. At last she heard their voices chattering on the landing. The door opened and the three of them came in.

'What are you doing?' Tyaas asked, regarding her curiously.

'Sit down, all three of you, here next to me.'

She patted the sofa and they sat by the fire, each giving

the other a conspiratorial glance.

'I need to tell you somethin'. I can't tell another lie, and I can't pretend I've been meaning to tell you, 'cos I 'aven't.'

'What do you mean?' asked Tallitha warily.

'I wanted to protect you, so that's why I didn't tell you, Miss Tallitha, when you first asked me.'

The fire crackled on and Cissie began her story.

'When I was a young girl, I knew Miss Asenathe, before she disappeared.'

'But Cissie, you said you didn't,' blurted out Tallitha.

'I know what I said, but I'm tellin' you now, so hush and let me get on with it.'

Cissie stroked her apron and looked apprehensively at their young faces, gripped by the anticipation of what she was about to reveal.

'Miss Asenathe and I were about the same age. Maybe I was a bit older, I can't remember now. Anyway I used to come to the Spires when they needed an extra pair of hands. After a while I became maid to both Esmerelda and Asenathe. I grew very fond of them and they trusted me. My mother wasn't keen on me coming up 'ere though. It was an unhappy place, so she said. The Grand Morrow had her mind set on a marriage between Asenathe and an older man called Cornelius Pew, from an important family in Wycham Elva. She was only fifteen and the betrothal would last until she married him at sixteen. But Asenathe was a romantic girl and she didn't like, let alone love, this man. He was a widower and he showed

Asenathe no affection. It was just an arrangement between two wealthy families.'

'Great Aunt Agatha did that? How terrible, what happened then?' demanded Tallitha.

Cissie stared into the fire. It was no use; she knew she had to tell them the whole story.

'Esmerelda was as close as could be to her cousin. They were inseparable as children, like two little peas in a pod, their pretty heads always nestled together over a game or a book. They even shared a bedroom together. You can guess which one, the great room, where they added their secret hidey-holes. They were happy as larks until the Grand Morrow revealed her marriage plans. The worst of it was that Asenathe would have to leave Winderling Spires to live with her new husband. I remember the day they found out as if it was yesterday. They refused to be separated. Ranted and raved they did, and planned their escape together. I was upset of course.'

'You knew about it!' interrupted Tyaas, amazed that Cissie was involved but even more surprised that she had had a life before looking after them.

She nodded. 'They made me keep their secret. I shouldn't 'ave but I was young myself and wanted to help them, I didn't know the dangers that awaited ...' Her voice trailed off and her face became sorrowful in the flickering firelight. 'Somewhere they'd 'eard the old story of Edwyn Morrow so they planned to run away to Breedoor where no one would ever find them. Poor lasses, they didn't know they were jumpin' from the frying pan into the fire. So one night they escaped from the Spires through the old tunnel in the basement. They managed to get away before they were caught, but somewhere, somehow, they were separated.'

Cissie's voice cracked. She wiped away the tears that were running down her cheeks.

'Cissie, please don't cry,' said Tallitha stroking her nurse's hand. 'What happened then?'

'Now I don't know the whole story, so there's no need for badgering and quizzing me, Miss Tallitha,' stressed Cissie. She took a few moments to compose herself. 'Esmerelda came home months later. She was much changed. She'd developed some … well, I would say, some very odd ways and she'd lost her youthfulness. She was distracted and would never talk of it, except to say that Asenathe was alive and she swore to everyone, including the Grand Morrow, that she would bring her home. That's the long and the short of it.'

Cissie wiped her tears away and blew her nose.

'Cissie, please don't cry. It's all starting to make sense now,' murmured Tallitha.

Tallitha put her arms round her nurse and cuddled her.

'I'm not crying because of that. Thinking about them bad times wears me out. Both girls were lost to us in different ways. You mustn't go after Asenathe. It's so dangerous out there, beyond Wycham Elva.'

But the story had only succeeded in confirming Tallitha's resolve to head for Hellstone Tors to find the lost heir of Winderling Spires.

'There're evil goings-on out there in the wild places. Who knows what you'll find? Whatever became of Miss Asenathe might well befall you too,' she cried.

'You can't stop us now,' said Tallitha flatly.

'Now Miss, you mustn't put me in such a bind. I shall 'ave to tell the Grand Morrow if you're so set on going.'

Tallitha stiffened. 'Then I'll tell her you knew about her daughter running away and never lifted a finger to stop her!' cried Tallitha vehemently.

'Eh Miss, you wouldn't.'

But Cissie knew that she would.

'Then you have to help us and that's an end to it.'

Cissie's face crumpled. She knew that Tallitha had won.

'There's a drawing of a silver key on the map. Is that the key to the locked box we found on top of the wardrobe?' asked Tallitha, taking charge.

Cissie stood warming herself by the fire.

'I don't know about … about a key, Miss,' she faltered.

'But you must, Cissie. You've seen the map before and the key is next to Shivering Water. That lake is the only place we've heard of on the map, and maybe it was the only place that Esmerelda and Asenathe had heard of too. That's where they headed for, isn't it?'

Cissie shook her head and buried her face in her apron.

'Either you or Essie have that key! Don't lie to us anymore.'

Cissie dabbed her tears and pulled the chain from under her dress, holding it tightly in her hand.

'Asenathe gave me both keys for safe keeping, the day she went into that tunnel,' she said sadly. 'It was the last time I held her hand or saw her dear face.' She sighed, looking into the flames. 'Later I kept the silver key next to my heart. It opens the box that holds the key to the tunnel in the basement. It's an old escape route, in case those that we're afraid of,' she faltered and lowered her voice, 'should break into the house at night.'

'But who are they?' asked Tallitha, anxiously.

'Those that would take Winderling Spires from the Grand Morrow, if they could. The evil ones – the *Dooerlins*,' she whispered.

They stared at each other in the firelight. Perhaps Cissie was imagining things. Surely the power of the holed stones was just a country superstition?

'But it's no use. Don't you understand? The mountains are impassable even with the map. Esmerelda has tried many times to find Asenathe, to retrace the underground route they took all those years ago. She disappears, sometimes for weeks on end, but she always returns alone. Each time she's more changed.'

'We'll take good care, I promise,' said Tyaas.

Tallitha noticed how quiet Benedict had become. His face looked sullen.

'You okay?' she asked him but he flinched at her question.

'I don't think you realise how dangerous this will be,' he said to them.

'He's right, you don't understand. There are no directions, the map may give clues but there will be false paths ahead of you. A wrong turning will take you into danger, and there are strange folk out there with wicked intent. Maybe it will change you too, and I'll never see you again!' gasped Cissie.

'We'll take our chances out there. We'll be fine, won't we, Tyaas?'

He nodded. They would go, with or without Cissie's help.

'But what happened to Essie? You must know more than you've told us,' Tallitha persisted.

'Eh Miss, you do badger a soul', she said, biting hard on her lip. 'The last time she came home it was frightening. She was a wild creature. She had devils in her head. Each night she was tormented with terrors, raving mad she was. Her mind was full of the ghouls and demons she had seen underground.' Cissie played with the key, twisting it in her fingers. 'That was the last time I gave her the key. I've always kept it hidden for fear that I'll lose her completely if she tries again.'

Cissie turned away and stared into the flames. The strain of telling her story was becoming too much.

'So is the start of the journey from Shivering Water?' asked Tallitha.

'I think so, Miss, but I don't know for sure, and from there I cannot tell you.'

'Then Esmerelda must tell us about the places she has been to. We'll be able to learn from her mistakes,' said Tyaas.

'But she'll want to go with you. This constant searching for Miss Asenathe has affected her so!' she cried.

Tyaas took Cissie's hand and spoke gently to her, 'I promise you, we'll be careful.'

Cissie smiled at him and patted his hand. 'I believe you have goodness in your heart, Master Tyaas. As much as it upsets me, I know I can't stop you now.' She handed the key to Tallitha. 'Keep it safe. But remember, I'm giving you this key with a heavy heart and it's on condition that I know what's happening,' she said looking from one to the other. 'Well … you'll need provisions and I can help with that.'

They sat round the fire with the map spread out in front of them, poring over the strange names and curious symbols. Tyaas lifted the map nearer to the flames so the heat was behind it. The key stood out, the bright silver lettering glowing fiercely in the dark.

'Let's try the key now,' said Tallitha, excitedly.

The boys nodded and Tallitha reached for the small box. It clicked open and she lifted out a large rusty key, wrapped in a soft cloth.

'This will get us out of Winderling Spires,' she announced, turning the key in the firelight.

But as Tallitha wrapped the key back in the cloth she noticed some embroidery in the corner. She held the cloth up to the light and read out the words:

'*This is my key. Now all ye who dare, Follow the dark route in sequence.*'

'What does it mean – *follow the dark route in sequence*?' asked Tallitha looking at the others for inspiration. 'What sequence?'

''Tis a mystery,' replied Cissie. 'Essie embroidered it on her return. She kept sayin' the words about the sequence over and over to herself, when she was ill, ravin' like. But I 'aven't a clue what it means'.

They pored over the map, trying to interpret the Ennish words but despite the book of translations, the map revealed nothing more about the sequence.

'There must be a way to interpret the map that we don't yet understand,' said Tyaas.

But this time they were all stumped. As the flames spluttered, throwing shadows onto the walls, the curious names on the map became ever more intriguing. They had never heard of Burnt Heath, Sour Pits or the Ruby Falls.

'Esmerelda must have visited these places,' said Tyaas, the names becoming ever more fascinating.

'But she's taken the wrong turning many times, so we don't want to follow her route,' said Benedict cautiously.

'Better to know the mistakes Essie made, if she will tell us about them,' said Tyaas.

'Then we will just have to ask her,' said Tallitha finally.

Tired, excited, and with their heads full of plans for the perilous journey, they headed off to bed.

Twelve

The next day Tallitha left early for the sisters' apartment without the tiresome Shrove. She was preoccupied with Cissie's story and how to make sense of the map that wasn't really a map. Climbing the north staircase she became aware of an uncomfortable feeling. Someone was watching her. At the top of the staircase a cold hand went over Tallitha's mouth.

'Get off me,' she yelled, struggling to get free, 'how dare you!'

She could smell the greasy aroma of old Shrove. Tallitha bit the gnarled hand but it was hopeless, the thick leathery skin tasted vile.

'Eurgh,' she shouted, spitting out the taste of Shrove flesh.

It was Florré. She could smell the greasy lotion he used to keep his wiry hair flat.

'I know it's you, Florré!' she shouted struggling to get free. 'Let me go!'

'Hush you, girl,' he growled into the base of her neck.

He sniffed her body, moisture salivating down his chin as though he was going to bite her.

'Stop this at once!' she screamed and spat at him.

But there was no one around to hear her cries. He bundled her into an abandoned apartment and closed the door behind him. She saw his eyes glinting in the half-light as he twisted her arm and pushed her through a heavy velvet curtain. Tallitha stumbled to the floor as the Shrove leaned over her.

'Get away from me,' she gasped, turning to peer into the darkened room, 'W-Who's there?' she whispered, sensing someone else. The room beyond the curtain smelled sweetly familiar. Tallitha kept very still, 'I know someone's there,' she said, her voice rising in panic.

A familiar sickly odour hung in the air. Suddenly the room filled with the smell of sulphur and there was a flash of bright blue light. Death-black shredded drapes hung like widow's weeds from a high canopy, framing Esmerelda in the murky darkness. As the candle spluttered, Tallitha stared round at the eerie séance room. Along each wall were glass specimen cases containing bizarre exotic plants and fantastic fungi. Esmerelda was sitting at a round mirrored table painted with black, purple and silver symbols. In the centre were pointed coloured crystals, surrounded by a pool of rising vapour. The cats, Licks and Lap, leapt from the shadows and circled Esmerelda's feet, meowing loudly. Tallitha tried to escape but Florré barred her way. His brown broken teeth and rancid breath making her reel as he stepped towards her, smiling wickedly. Tallitha stumbled back into the room, and she felt Esmerelda grab her wrist.

'You're not going anywhere,' she hissed.

'How dare you order that Shrove to bring me here?' shouted Tallitha angrily.

Esmerelda pulled Tallitha close and stared deep into her eyes. She was dressed in a long purple robe and her eyes were painted with violet sweeps of colour. Tallitha thought she looked like a fortune teller.

'We must finish what we started yesterday. You can see things others can't,' said Esmerelda, 'you have the precious gift and you saw someone, didn't you? You spoke of her, wearing a black dress.'

'Let me go, Essie! You can't keep me here.'

Tallitha tried to push past Florré but he stood in her way, his cold heartless eyes fixed on her, daring her to escape.

'Come here, the Shrove won't let you pass,' Esmerelda said beguilingly. 'We both want the same thing.'

Esmerelda held Tallitha's gaze with her dark eyes and slowly her desire to escape evaporated. She was overcome by Esmerelda's haunting voice and blazing, hypnotic eyes. The ancient words of Ennish tripped off her tongue,

'*Snenathe ne certhe merl can an le ner*
Cerna la bernatha ne tor na lam, berche berche ne cer
Snenathe ne certhe merl can an le ner.'

Silky, violet-blue vapour trails drifted from the pool of liquid and Tallitha recognised the pungent odour from Esmerelda's amulet. The heady sweet-foul fumes made her drowsy. She tried to keep focussed but her eyelids drooped and she slumped to the table. Esmerelda lifted her head and stared deep into her sleepy eyes.

'Listen to me and do exactly what I tell you. Clear your mind of all thoughts. Now imagine you're a free spirit and there are no constraints on your human form.'

Tallitha felt a popping sensation as she was stretched outside her body. She moved through the coloured whirlpools and ascended the bright tunnel, away from her physical body. Up and up she went, and as she looked back she saw the silver cord float in the rush of air behind her. Her will vanished and *whoosh!* – she glided into another sphere where all was still.

'You are flying high over Winderling Spires, away over Shivering Water and beyond to the northern lands. Tell me what you see,' said Esmerelda, her voice sounding distant.

Bright images appeared, flashing before her. When Tallitha spoke, her voice had a flat, hollow sound.

'There are forests and mountains below me, and the grey expanse of sea and rocks. It's silvery.'

'What else can you see, Tallitha?' asked Esmerelda softly.

'There's a dark castle built into jagged rocks. It's becoming cloudy again. Please let me come home, Essie, let me come home.'

Tallitha was frightened and cold. Her body jerked in the chair as Esmerelda held her.

'Concentrate, Tallitha, and focus your mind on finding Asenathe. She is waiting for you. Can you see her?'

Tallitha moved through the grey light. She could hear the faint sound of Ennish coming through the fog.

'Canyer ta serna fe la der, certhe merla canya fe –
canya fe-canya fe-canya fe-canya fe.'

She flew towards the castle. Then through a tower window Tallitha saw the girl sitting alone. She wore a black velvet dress with a high collar and she had a talisman round her neck with a deep earth-green and blood-red stone.

'I can see her,' said Tallitha in her deadened voice, 'but the image keeps fading.'

Esmerelda spoke in Ennish, putting the tips of her fingers on each side of Tallitha's head and pressing down, chanting all the time:

'Snenathe ne certhe merl can an le ner
Snenathe ne certhe merl can an le ner.'

'Come Tallitha, breathe deeply and stop resisting your power.'

As Esmerelda pressed down, Tallitha felt another enormous surge *whoosh!* – and she slipped further into the tower room and stood beside the girl.

'What do you see?' Esmerelda whispered into Tallitha's ear.

'She's pointing at something. But I can't read the words.'

'Reach out and touch her, Tallitha, let her know you're there,' insisted Esmerelda.

Tallitha tentatively touched the girl's hair. As she did so, the vision let out a small cry of recognition and touched Tallitha's hand, stroking her fingers. Then her face changed, and she gripped Tallitha's hand, dragging her towards a door. All at once Tallitha recoiled as though she had been scalded. Esmerelda saw Tallitha's body jolt then *whoosh!* – Tallitha tumbled down the long bumpy tunnel and came back into her body.

'Tell me what happened!' demanded Esmerelda.

'I saw her,' said Tallitha, breathless, 'but she tried to keep me there. There was something strange about her.'

'What did she look like?' asked Esmerelda her face wild with emotion.

'I couldn't see her face clearly. She had dark curls hanging down her back. Is that Asenathe?'

'Did she have anything round her neck?' asked Esmerelda excitedly.

Tallitha nodded drowsily. 'A talisman, a bloodstone.'

'Yes, that's Asenathe. You've found her. At last!' cried Esmerelda and she slumped back into her chair.

'She seemed strange. Perhaps it wasn't her.'

'It's her, I can sense it. In time you'll learn how to handle your power. Only then, will the shadow-flight get easier.'

'Shadow-flight?' asked Tallitha.

'The transition from your physical body to your dream body,' explained Esmerelda. 'Soon the flight will be just like breathing and it will let you travel through time.'

Esmerelda called out to Florré. 'Show Miss Tallitha back to my mother's apartment.'

'No, not yet Essie, I must know how to read the map. I must know about the sequence and what happened when you …'

Esmerelda grabbed Tallitha's arm, twisting it viciously.

'How did you get the map? Did Cissie give it to you?' she shouted angrily.

Esmerelda pulled Tallitha's hair, yanking her head back.

'Ouch that hurts. Get off me, Essie!' shouted Tallitha as she struggled to get free. 'We found the map yesterday. If we're to find Asenathe we need to know everything!'

Esmerelda pushed Tallitha away. 'I will be the one to find her, not you. Besides you'll never succeed, even with the Shapeless Map. The sequence, I'm afraid, is beyond us all.'

Tallitha didn't know the map had a name. If Esmerelda was going to be uncooperative then she could play that game too, and she certainly wasn't leaving without knowing everything. She picked up one of the crystals, holding it behind her back ready to smash Esmerelda's cabinets. Florré moved towards her with a devilish look on his face, waiting for Esmerelda's command to strike Tallitha.

'Put that down, do you hear me?' shouted Esmerelda.

'Not until I get some answers, and keep that damned Shrove off me,' she spat the words in Florré's direction, holding the crystal over his head.

The Shrove hissed and hopped about but kept his distance.

'Leave us, Florré. Wait outside until I call for you.'

The Shrove slunk into one of the Shrove holes on the other side of the curtain.

Esmerelda turned on Tallitha. 'Why should I tell you anything? You're just a meddlesome child!'

'Because you need me. I'm the one who can see Asenathe. You were the one who said I have special powers. Besides, someone wants me to find her, whoever it was left all the clues,' said Tallitha hoping to elicit a confession from Esmerelda.

But Esmerelda was silent. She picked up Licks and began stroking her butterscotch fur. The cat purred loudly and Esmerelda closed her eyes.

'So tell me about what happened to you, when you first left Winderling Spires,' asked Tallitha, sitting next to her cousin.

It took Esmerelda a long time to respond. 'It was such a long time ago,' she said sadly. 'Asenathe left some clues and I left others, in case something happened to us, so perhaps they are the ones you found. But whatever you've heard is probably a muddle of half-truths and lies.' She stopped and bit her lip. 'It still causes me so much pain to know she's out there, alone and lost.' Esmerelda winced as she uttered the words.

'But why did you choose me?' asked Tallitha.

'You chose yourself,' she said enigmatically. 'I suspected you had the gift of seeing, that you were a channel and could help find Asenathe. You're my bloodline and female, so as the only one left in this family, it was bound to be you. Besides you had the telltale sign.'

'What do you mean? asked Tallitha, suspiciously.

'That day in my mother's sitting room, a soft glow surrounded you. I could only just make it out, but I knew you were ready. A fuzzy vibration appeared when I began to hypnotise you.'

Tallitha had often sensed when something bad was about to happen, a warning feeling that started deep inside her.

'As you develop your abilities, the vibration will become clearer to me and others like me. You will be able to control it and it will change colour depending on your mood.'

It was all true then, amazing and unbelievable, but true.

'Please tell me about what happened when you and Asenathe ran away,' begged Tallitha.

Esmerelda knew it was time. She had to tell Tallitha some of her story if she was to gain the girl's cooperation.

'No map existed when we started out. We had no idea where we were going but we knew we had to make for the lake. The journey to Shivering Water was easier than we imagined and we managed to outwit Aunt Agatha, who sent a search party after us,' she faltered.

'It's okay Essie, it's not your fault,' said Tallitha.

'But it is, of course it is! Asenathe was never as strong as me. I should have saved her. I've looked for her for so many years,' she said sadly.

Tallitha took hold of Esmerelda's hand as she continued.

'It started to go wrong when we entered the deep caves. I was separated from Asenathe in Weeping Holes about ten days after we fled. We were tired and frightened and by this time we had certainly taken the wrong path. The caves were dark and slippery underfoot. One minute Asenathe was there and the next … I heard noises and saw something, but I can't remember anything about it. Then she vanished. She must have got lost in the labyrinth of tunnels and was taken. I searched for days, and became lost myself,' said Esmerelda looking distraught, 'I eventually got out with the help of some friendly Cave-Shroves.'

'Shroves? But surely they can't be trusted. Marlin and Florré have been acting so strangely lately,' said Tallitha.

'The Cave-Shroves are different from their distant cousins in Winderling Spires. They were good to me and without their help I would have perished.'

'What about the Shapeless Map?'

'The map is not like ordinary maps. The places are not in any order. I put down what I remembered from my travels through the caves, but you can't rely on the Shapeless Map. There's a certain sequence that you must follow to find your way through the caves, but we didn't know that at the time, so we became hopelessly lost.' Esmerelda stopped and poured herself a drink. 'There are unwritten rules in the underworld,' she said at last, 'rules that we don't understand.'

'But who makes the rules?' asked Tallitha.

Esmerelda's face darkened. 'They're made by Frintal Morrow, the ghastly Thane of Breedoor and Hellstone Tors. His henchmen and women are the Morrow Swarm who, along with Frintal, are the descendants of Edwyn Morrow. It's the Morrow Swarm who control which routes are accessible, and the Swarm allow the Murk Mowl and the Groats to charge tithes to use the tunnels.'

'The Murk Mowl and Groats, but what are they like?' asked Tallitha apprehensively.

'The vilest creatures and the most heartless, but the Murk Mowl are the worst,' she murmured. 'The map is my creation. I put it together after the first journey and have added to it since. There must be other ways through the caves, routes known to the underground creatures, although I never discovered these. Each time I've travelled a different path, all of which have turned out to be dead ends. Unfortunately my knowledge only extends part of the way under the mountains.'

'But how do you know Asenathe survived, and didn't perish?'

'I sensed it from the beginning, and when I returned the Cave-Shroves told me she was in Hellstone Tors, a captive of the Swarm and the Thane.' Esmerelda stopped abruptly. 'What's that noise?' she shouted, jumping to her feet.

Suddenly Tyaas fell through the curtain and Benedict landed on top of him with the Shrove hanging on to both of them.

'Get off me!' shouted Tyaas as he kicked Florré.

'Goodness, what are you two doing here?' asked Tallitha.

'We knew you hadn't made it to the sisters' apartment,' said Benedict pushing the Shrove to one side.

Florré stood snivelling by the curtain, waiting for Esmerelda to call for reinforcements, but she had other plans. She dismissed the Shrove, sending him with a message to the sisters that she would be teaching Tallitha that morning. Florré stumped off bad-temperedly, muttering to himself about the fickleness of the Morrow women.

Once he was certain Florré was out of earshot, Benedict

continued. 'We overheard the sisters reporting your absence to Great Aunt Agatha, so we decided to find you. Somehow we guessed you'd be with Essie so we pieced together the way. Not bad detective work, eh?'

Tallitha recounted all that Esmerelda had told her. Esmerelda watched as her excited young cousins lapped up the details of her adventures. They were so inexperienced, with no under-standing of what lay ahead of them. At that moment Esmerelda was certain she must return with them.

'Essie cannot accept that we're going to Hellstone Tors,' explained Tallitha.

'Well you're wrong, Tallitha. I've changed my mind about your intentions. I've decided to come with you. I know the mistakes I made and can guide you.'

'You can't be serious. Aren't you a bit, well, past it?' exclaimed Tyaas in amazement.

Esmerelda gave him a quizzical look and snorted. 'I'm not that old, Tyaas. I can guess what Cissie has said about me, but don't listen to everything she says. She's a good woman but she's never made the journey. Remember that map is all my work. I can also speak Ennish and some Shroveling.'

'Wow, how did you learn? Ennish is such a difficult language,' said Benedict, impressed.

'While I was living with the Cave-Shroves. I can smooth the way with them, otherwise they will thwart you at every turn. Cave-Shroves are fickle and mistrustful, but once they take to you then you're their friend forever. But they don't take kindly to strangers invading their territory.'

'You stayed with the Shroves? But for how long?' asked Benedict.

'That's another story, my friend. It was many months on one occasion. Some other time, perhaps when we are on our travels, I will tell you. We'll have plenty of time, particularly at night when the skies darken and we are huddled together against the northern winds. But some tales should not be repeated.'

Esmerelda looked distracted. 'For now we should separate. The sisters will never countenance our plans. That's why I sent Florré away. The less he knows the better. The Shroves are a strange lot and their allegiances are unfathomable. We'll meet to plan our journey and then we'll depart for the Tors.'

With that, Esmerelda swept through a door at the back of the room.

*

Later in the tree house they mulled over all they had heard.

'Can we trust her? We thought she was weird and to be honest, I still think she is,' exclaimed Tyaas.

'But she can hypnotise people. Anyway what choice do we have? If we don't let her come, she'll follow us anyway,' said Tallitha.

She helped Tyaas pack for their journey.

'She can speak Ennish too and she knows about the caves. After today I feel differently about her, don't you Tallitha?' asked Benedict.

'I think so. Cissie will need some persuading though. Come on, let's finish packing. No one ever comes up here, not even the Shroves, but we mustn't attract attention. I'll make my way to the schoolroom and you follow in about ten minutes.'

They rolled up their warm clothes and tucked matches and flasks inside. Tyaas packed penknives, ropes and a compass. Then he pushed the key to the tunnel deep into his bag and Tallitha packed the Shapeless Map. Then, one by one, they climbed down from the tree house and made their way back to the Spires.

Their adventure was about to begin.

Thirteen

The next few days went by in a flurry of clandestine activity. Cissie came round to their plan once she accepted they would be safer travelling together. She made parcels of dried food from the kitchen stores and sneaked these to Tallitha whenever the opportunity arose. Esmerelda had her own tried and tested remedies. She packed liquorice cordial for its revival properties, wild Barrenwort salve for healing wounds, and bitter moonflower for shock and soothing fevers. During her travels Esmerelda had studied the medicinal use of fungi and she prepared shavings of Amethyst Deceiver, Stinkhorn and Dryad's Saddle. She also packed the Death Caps and the Green Spotted Lepiota fungi which were deadly poisonous.

At dusk, on the day before their departure, Esmerelda called everyone together. She had instructed them to smuggle their backpacks to her apartment and over the preceding days, one by one, they had done so. Licks and Lap were fawning over their mistress, rubbing up against her legs and generally demanding attention when the others arrived.

'There, my pretty ones. Cissie will look after you whilst I'm away.'

She stroked their abundant fur as she inspected Tallitha and the boys to make sure they were wearing suitable clothing. Once the three were settled and Esmerelda had poured an elixir of the liquorice cordial, she revealed her plan.

'I expect you're wondering why I asked you to bring your bags up to my apartment?' she said mysteriously. 'Well, let me show you. I have a secret way of getting to the basement. Come, follow me.'

Esmerelda led them through her sitting room and into a corridor. There before them was a recess containing a large wooden cupboard.

'Open the doors, Tyaas, and take a look inside.'

It was a fairly unremarkable cupboard and it was empty.

'What use is this?' asked Tyaas, sounding bewildered. She was definitely batty, he thought to himself.

Esmerelda pressed a concealed button and then, from far below, they could hear a low rumbling noise. A smile appeared on Benedict's face.

'It's a dumb waiter!' he announced.

Slowly the realisation that they would be travelling in the dumb waiter began to sink in.

'I'm not going down in that thing!' exclaimed Benedict shrinking away from the whirring cupboard.

'It's quite safe. I've used it many times and I'm heavier than you. It means we can travel to the basement undetected. It comes out in the kitchens near to the escape tunnel. We'll use it tomorrow night when the servants are asleep.'

When the cupboard stopped making its noise, Benedict peered inside. He looked horrified.

'But it's so small and dark,' he wailed pathetically.

Esmerelda looked the boy up and down. He was a ninny.

'Come to my rooms tomorrow at midnight, but make sure everyone in the house is asleep. I'll be waiting for you. We must have a good day's start before they discover we've gone.'

*

The next night, when all was still, they set off for Esmerelda's apartment. It was pitch-black and the ancient house had an eerie conspiratorial silence after nightfall. The stair treads creaked and the floorboards groaned until somewhere on the fourth floor they lost their way.

'Look out!' whispered Tallitha hoarsely.

Coming down the corridor they saw the flicker of candlelight and the unmistakable long pointed shadow of Grintley ambling along in the darkness. Quickly they backed into one of the apartments and dived under a four-poster bed. But the old Shrove had heard a noise.

'What's that then?' he mumbled, hopping about and scurrying down the corridor.

Grintley followed them into the room just seconds after they had hidden themselves. He sniffed the air and peered into the gloomy interior. They held their breath and waited as he shuffled towards the huge bed. Then all at once there was a scurry as Licks and Lap jumped out of nowhere and made for the door.

'Damn critters,' he swore, kicking the cats and hobbling down the corridor after them.

Esmerelda's butterscotch cats had saved them!

'Come on, he's gone,' mumbled Tyaas, poking his nose round the door.

Eventually they located the enclosed staircase that led straight up to Esmerelda's apartment.

Their elder cousin was dressed for the part. She wore riding breeches and a dark moleskin jacket and her hair was tied in a long ponytail. She handed each of them a selection of brown-coloured leaves to chew.

'This is mugwort. Its special properties are used for maintaining energy. Keep it safe and chew at least three leaves each morning. Hurry, Cissie will be waiting at the bottom.'

Tyaas raised his eyes and winked at his sister. Esmerelda was a strange one for a Morrow woman. It was the servants who used these old-fashioned remedies. He chewed the bitter leaves and pulled a disgusted face.

Tyaas went first, his eyes gleaming with excitement. It was a tight fit and he had to tuck his knees up under his chin. As the doors closed he shouted, 'Make it go faster!'

'It isn't a fairground ride. Now, sit tight,' instructed Esmerelda and pressed the button.

The whirring started and Tyaas waited for the huge rush, but he was disappointed. It was much too slow for his liking. The bags went rumbling down next. Then it was Benedict's turn. He hesitated and looked quite peaky. As the dumb waiter came back up the shaft, whatever nerve he had, failed. He felt unsteady and looked at Tallitha for reassurance. Why was it that his cousins could happily do these adventurous things, without a moment's hesitation, and he was so fearful?

'Come on Benedict, don't be chicken,' teased Tallitha, gently pushing him forward.

Benedict eased backwards into the cupboard feeling helpless in the dark.

'Pull your legs up,' instructed Tallitha as she pushed him further inside.

Benedict tucked in his wobbly legs, wrapping his arms tightly round his knees and closed his eyes tight shut.

'Oh no,' he wailed as the cupboard trundled down the shaft.

It was ghastly in the total darkness of the wooden cupboard. The whirring noise of the dumb waiter inched down its rickety shaft, making Benedict's heart race. He could feel every rumble and thump as he imagined the flimsy box plummeting below and smashing into a hundred pieces. Down and down he went. He braced himself for disaster but with a final shudder he reached the basement. He was sweating, but he was safe.

At the bottom they followed Cissie through the shadowy

kitchen, past the sculleries where the smell of freshly laundered washing filled their nostrils, down the steps into the lower basement and along a stone-flagged passageway to a door at the end. It was much colder in the deep cellars and Tallitha's insides were awash with foreboding. She could hear the drains flowing beneath them and the sound of water drip-dripping in the gloom.

'The entrance to the tunnel is just behind those tanks,' said Esmerelda, pushing open the door to the boiler room.

The heavy metal door was encrusted with lichens and Tallitha's heart sank.

'What's it like in there?' asked Benedict shivering.

'It's pitch-black and icy cold,' said Esmerelda buttoning up her jacket.

Tyaas located the key and pushed it firmly into the lock. At first it would not budge. Esmerelda and Cissie lent their combined weight against the door and eventually the key turned and clicked. The metal door creaked open uncertainly on its hinges, letting wafts of freezing air into the boiler room. Inside the dark tunnel the old stone walls were grimy, soaked and blackened over the years from oozing, trickling water. The stench of stale air hit Tallitha in the face. It was going to be grim in this dark, wet place.

'You'll have to be brave, it's the only way to get out of the Spires without being seen,' urged Esmerelda watching their apprehensive faces in the candlelight.

They wrapped themselves up against the cold. As Tallitha turned to say farewell to Cissie, her nurse began fussing, giving them last minute advice and extra provisions.

'Take this, Tyaas,' she said handing him a bag of fruit. 'Tallitha, have you packed your warmest clothes?'

'We'll be fine. Please don't fret,' said Tallitha putting her arm around her nurse.

But it was all too much and Cissie began to dab her eyes. 'I'm frettin' about what's ahead of you. Look after them Esmerelda,' she pleaded, pushing a piece of paper into her hand. 'These are the directions to my brother's farm, should you need them. There'll be a welcome for you, aye, and a good hot meal. This will vouch for you.'

Cissie blew her nose and forced back more tears.

'Off you go. You mustn't get caught down here,' said Esmerelda urgently.

They gave Cissie one last hug and stepped into the dark tunnel. As the door clanged shut behind them, the hollow sound reverberated down the empty tunnel. Then they found themselves in total darkness and the kind of bone-coldness that took their breath away.

Esmerelda hurriedly lit the lantern and indicated for the others to follow her. As the candle spluttered and flicked its meagre light down the tunnel, an abundance of fat brown rats squeaked and scurried away, trying to escape through the gaps at the bottom of the wall. Tallitha screamed and jumped onto Benedict's back. Tyaas laughed and kicked one of the rats as far as he could.

'Take that!' he shouted with pleasure as a fat brown rat spun and landed splat in the muddy water, with its legs in the air.

'Be quiet, can't you?' Esmerelda shot them a desperate look

and pointed nervously above her, 'we don't know who's up there, listening.'

They stared at the uneven roof, which was dripping brown water. The tunnel walls were built of grey-green stones, splattered with the slimy marks of trickling moisture that had seeped out over the years. Green moss hung in web-like strands from the ceiling, trailing and catching in their hair. Underfoot was wet and slippery, and the atmosphere was dank and putrid.

'It smells awful,' said Tyaas holding his nose. 'Eurgh, what is this place?'

Esmerelda did not reply and hurried them onward. Big spiders and fat beetles scurried away at the noise of the four intruders.

'Not much further. Keep together. We'll be at the end soon. There are steps up to the next level,' said Esmerelda as she stepped through the dirty trickling water underfoot.

The tunnel narrowed and they turned sideways to squeeze through the shrinking space. Then round a slight bend and Esmerelda began climbing upwards.

'Where does it lead to?' asked Benedict, his eyes staring in the candlelight.

'You'll see soon enough,' said Esmerelda mysteriously.

At the top of the steps was a stone arch with lettering carved around the lintel.

'Lift the lantern so I can see,' whispered Tallitha, beginning to read out the warning.

'*Take care and be still so as not to awake the sleepers, all ye who enter here.*'

'Creepy –– what does that mean?' she said, as she passed underneath.

They stood huddled together in a large vaulted chamber. The walls had ledges along them and long wooden boxes sitting on each ledge.

'Is this what I think it is?' asked Tallitha grabbing hold of Benedict.

'I know where we are,' said Tyaas incredulously, 'it's the inside of the family mausoleum!'

The crypt was built in the shape of a pentagon and each one of the stone ledges held a coffin. In the centre was a plinth that held three stone tombs positioned one on top of the other.

'Why have you brought us here? To practice the black arts, I bet!' said Tyaas sarcastically.

Esmerelda smirked at his childish fear of the dead. 'Not today, Tyaas. It's the only way out of the grounds without being seen. If I'd told you where we were headed you'd have complained all the way.'

'It's creepy and cold,' said Tallitha, as she began to read the coffin inscriptions.

'Take a look around,' said Esmerelda. 'Happily there are four of us today so that will keep the spirits settled. These are our long dead Morrow ancestors. Some of these tombs are over three hundred years old,' she said, stroking an inscription with her fingertips.

'What do you mean, "keep the spirits settled"?' asked Tallitha nervously.

The sharp chilliness of the crypt began to seep through her outer garments down to her skin. She shivered uncontrollably.

'It's an old superstition from hereabouts. They say that an odd number of people at a burial or visiting the dead is considered ill-timed and unlucky, as it may awaken the spirits,' explained Esmerelda.

'That's superstitious nonsense,' said Tyaas looking apprehensively over his shoulder.

'Maybe,' said Esmerelda with a wry smile, 'but how do you know that for sure?'

Tyaas shifted from foot to foot. Damned Esmerelda, she made him feel so uncomfortable.

Benedict was transfixed by the house of death. So this is what it looked like inside. He had seen the isolated mausoleum from the distance of the Spires. It was as ghoulish inside as he had imagined, but also strangely fascinating. He began searching the nooks and crannies behind the coffins. Hidden at the back he discovered the funeral posies of the long dead. He picked up one of the wreaths and, as he did so, it disintegrated into a hundred brittle pieces in his hands. He jumped back, startled.

'Benedict! Stop acting weirdly,' exclaimed Tallitha.

But Benedict carried on snooping.

'Look at these inscriptions,' said Tallitha, absorbed by the names of the dear departed, 'I wonder who they were and how they died?'

The brass plaques had the names of the inhabitants of each coffin. Tallitha rubbed them clean with the sleeve of her jacket.

*'Here lies Septimia Morrow and Siskin Morrow, her husband,
laid here*

They died together, forever in our thoughts.'

'Eurgh, died together, what does that mean?' she whispered to
the others. 'Listen to this one:

'Peace Be With You, Arabella Dorothea
Dearest daughter of Bathia and Arthur Edwyn Morrow.'

'Come on let's get out of here. This place gives me the creeps,'
said Tyaas, 'You don't think they can hear us, do you?' he said,
gripping his lantern in the ghoulish tomb.

'The dead commune with us all the time,' said Esmerelda darkly
and too mysteriously for Tyaas's liking.

That shut him up. Tyaas looked at her wide eyed. 'W-W-What
do you mean?' he asked warily.

'We can't always see the ghosts in a physical sense, but they're
around us everywhere, watching us,' she said with a sinister air.

She looked steadily into the darkest corner of the crypt and
seemed to smile at something. Tyaas shivered and gave his sister a
desperate look.

'Let's get out of here,' he cried. 'I've had enough of the dead.'

'Help me open the door then. As I remember, it's heavy,' said
Esmerelda, pulling at the brass handle.

'How do you know it isn't locked?' asked Tallitha, heaving
on the door.

'Then we would be in a pickle,' said Tyaas trying to lighten the mood.

'This mausoleum is the tomb of Septimia Morrow. She was a strange woman from the family stories I've heard. She was the seventh daughter of a seventh daughter and so on. It's said she had very special powers indeed. Also she had an abiding horror of being buried alive and stipulated certain conditions for her own internment.'

Tyaas's mouth dropped open. What was she going to say next? His family was too eccentric and spooky for words.

'Unfortunately, some people were buried alive in days gone by. We know that because sometimes, when the coffins were opened, you could see that the person had tried to scratch their way out. So Septimia's coffin was never sealed and the crypt door was left unlocked so that if she woke, she could set herself free. She didn't want to be buried for eternity in this cold place.'

'Was she b-b-buried alive?' stuttered Tyaas looking horrified.

'No, but the possibility of escape was always there,' said Esmerelda gazing fondly at her long dead ancestors.

The uncanny atmosphere of the crypt had unsettled Tyaas and he was desperate to leave. He went over to the iron door and began pulling it open, but it was stuck fast.

'I think it's locked. I can't budge it!' he shouted, desperately

'Eurgh … eurgh … it's stuck. Probably hasn't been opened since the last time I was here,' said Esmerelda.

'Come on, Benedict, lend a hand,' said Tallitha sharply.

But Benedict was engrossed with the mausoleum. He liked its dead-stillness.

'Benedict, stop that and help us!' shouted Tyaas.

Benedict's head appeared over the top of the tombs as he fumbled in his bag.

'This is no time to start making notes on long dead relatives,' said Tallitha jokingly, watching him scribbling.

Benedict put his notepad away and went over to help his cousins. With his additional weight the door eventually began to scrape open.

'Pull harder … eurgh, it's moving. One final big heave should do it!'

The heavy door groaned open to reveal the howling night and the dark irregular shapes of the headstones against the moonlight. They clambered outside, pushing through the layers of tangled creepers snagging at their clothes.

'Where are we?' asked Tallitha, pulling leaves out of her hair.

Esmerelda looked towards the big house to get her bearings.

'We're some way from Winderling Spires. There's a gap in the boundary wall by that clump of trees. Once we're through, we'll head towards Shivering Water, it should take us until morning and by then we'll have a good head start.'

Tallitha and Tyaas stumbled through the dense undergrowth, tripping and falling over the gravestones in the dark.

'Ouch, that hurt!' cried Tyaas, rubbing his shin.

'Shine the lantern over here,' demanded Tallitha, who was caught in a bramble patch.

The graveyard was a muddle of broken headstones and burial plots which had sunk further into the ground, upending their grizzly contents back on to the earth from whence they came. It made Tyaas shudder as he fell to the ground and touched the side of a coffin.

'Let's get out of here,' he yelled.

'We need to make for higher ground, over there by the cemetery wall,' shouted Esmerelda but her shrill words were whipped away by the blustery squall.

She pointed towards the fallen headstones and they scrambled to the top and congregated around the lantern. The wind moaned through the trees as they looked back towards the light coming from the Spires. Overhead the moonlight struck the twisted branches and threw cruel shadows on the ground.

'Come on, let's go!' said Benedict unnerved by the deathly scene.

The wind shook the trees and made their ears sting with the cold. Owls hooted and the strange night noises feasted on the nervous travellers. Esmerelda took Benedict's hand and made off in the direction of the wall. Never before had they been so far out in the grounds after dark. Then a fox started calling to its mate in the distance. The distinct high-pitched piercing barks made Benedict freeze.

'What's that awful noise?' he squealed.

'It's only a fox, not a wolfhound,' explained Esmerelda. 'Come on, it won't hurt you,' she said, dragging Benedict through the darkness, willing him to pick up pace.

'You mean there are wolves out here?' wailed Tallitha, looking wildly around her.

'There are wild dogs in the forests to the north, but not here. Come on, we're nearly at the opening.'

Once through the gap, the ground became even underfoot and they found themselves on an old sheep-herders' pathway.

'This is the way to Shivering Water, now let's press on quickly.'

They had a few precious hours before the house awoke, their absence was discovered, and Agatha sent out a search party. On and on they tramped across fields and streams, over the dense scrubland of Burnt Heath. The rugged terrain and the heavy skies created a terrifying nightscape all around them, where the burgeoning shadows began to look like brooding monsters. The sight of the windswept heath unnerved Esmerelda and she looked surreptitiously over her shoulder towards the cemetery. Earlier, she thought she had heard someone behind them but she didn't want to alarm the others. Besides, Tallitha and the boys had been making too much noise for her to be certain.

*

But Esmerelda had heard a noise. The Shroves had been spying on them for several days. From the moment Florré returned with the gossip from Esmerelda's séance room, Marlin had been on to them. That nasty Morrow woman had tried to keep them out, had kept the interesting secret from them. On the night of their departure, Marlin watched Cissie disappear through the back kitchen, then he scampered off and the Shroves plotted in their lair. They decided to wait until the morning to break the news to the Grand Morrow. That would give the Shroves more time for their plan to take shape. So Marlin and Florré watched as Tallitha and the others escaped from the Spires. Their sensitive ears were made for eavesdropping and the long, echoing tunnel made it so easy to hear the noisy children, every step of the way.

Fourteen

After many hours tramping over rough ground, Tallitha was exhausted, fed-up and cold. Her feet were sore and her ears were aching, battered by the blustery winds and relentless rain. The cool miserly rain fell like spray, soaking their clothes and seeping down to their skin. Tallitha longed for her soft warm bed. She was already missing Cissie and her home comforts, and had started dreaming of buttered muffins and creamy hot chocolate. The empty wilderness stretched out before them, and the waterlogged ground clung in sodden clumps to their boots. Suddenly the weather deteriorated and the driving rain and drifting mist began to blur their sense of direction. They were slowly veering off course, further into the bogs to the west of Wycham Elva.

They stumbled on through the night, their voices calling out but being swept away by the fierce winds. Without warning, just as the sun was beginning to edge the darkness to one side, Tyaas

screamed. He had been dreaming about the adventures that lay ahead and had lost concentration, wandering hopelessly away from the others.

'Ahhhhh, help me!' he shrieked into the grey morning light.

Tyaas was sinking into the reeking mess and black sucking mud of the swamplands to the west of Shivering Water.

'Quick, he's going under,' shouted Tallitha. 'Come on Benedict!'

But Esmerelda grabbed hold of Tallitha's jacket, pulling her swiftly back.

'Don't move. Benedict, find the rope!' yelled Esmerelda.

Benedict clumsily threw the rope across the swamp but it fell short. Esmerelda dragged it back and flung it out again and this time Tyaas managed to grab hold just in time. He was up to his waist in mud that squelched and oozed as he struggled to free himself.

'Get me out, it's pulling me down!' he screamed.

'Keep still. The swamp will suck you under if you move!' shouted Esmerelda.

The three stood their ground and slowly began to pull him free of the sludgy gurgling mess, until he lay in a muddy heap at their feet. He stood up, immediately slipped, fell down again and slithered on the ground.

'Oh, you pong something awful,' said Tallitha screwing up her face at the sight of her mud-blackened brother.

Tyaas gasped and choked, trying to rub the thick stinking mud from his face.

'Ahh, it's disgusting!' he cried. 'One minute I was standing there and the next it dragged me under!'

He was shaking from the freezing mud and the shock of finding himself in the grip of the Gulping Mess.

'You must get those clothes off,' said Esmerelda looking for somewhere to shelter.

As the sun sneaked over the horizon they saw the misty expanse of the waterlogged swamp that almost had them in its clutches.

'Many travellers have been lost in there,' said Esmerelda, watching the popping vapours of the lonely mire.

'But where are we?' asked Tallitha.

'We've strayed too far west. Shivering Water is in that direction,' explained Esmerelda pointing towards the east.

Suddenly something caught her eye.

'What is it?' asked Tallitha nervously.

'Over there, can you see them by the shore of the lake?' whispered Esmerelda.

Something was moving along the water's edge. Then, out of nowhere, came a series of blood-curdling cries.

'Make for the rocks, quickly!' shouted Esmerelda dragging Tallitha behind her.

'Who are they?' asked Tallitha anxiously.

'It's the Murk Mowl,' said Esmerelda, visibly shrinking as she mentioned the name. 'Something must have forced them to the surface but they won't stay up for long.' Esmerelda peered round the rocks but the water's edge was empty. 'I think they've gone.'

'But what are they?' asked Tyaas.

'They're vile, evil creatures that live beneath the Out-of-the-Way Mountains in a foul place called Old Yawning Edges.'

Esmerelda reassured herself that the Mowl had left the shores of the lake.

'We can't go via Shivering Water now, it's much too dangerous.'

Esmerelda passed round the bitter moonflower and they sipped the luscious drink before ravenously tucking into bread and cheese. Esmerelda settled between the rocks and the others followed suit, wrapping their blankets around them against the cold. As they drifted off to sleep, Tallitha whispered, 'But what'll we do now?'

'Sleep now. We'll take a different route. Cissie's brother has a farm at High Bedders End, some miles from here. We'll have to skirt the swamp but hopefully we can avoid the Murk Mowl.'

With that, Esmerelda closed her eyes and snuggled into Tallitha's back. The boys were already asleep, their steady rhythmic breathing gently rocking the others into a heavy slumber. But Tallitha's sleep was overrun with wild chaotic dreams about the Murk Mowl chasing her through the deep caves, screeching and clashing their swords against the rock. She heard Cissie cry out, alone and frightened in Winderling Spires. Then, in her dream, the ghostly vision of the girl appeared in the tower.

The walk to the farm was pleasant compared to the endless trudge of the night before. The pastures hummed with insects and the tall grasses wafted aimlessly in the breeze. They passed through Sweet-Side Pasture, over Badger's Dyke and the sweeping hills of Dolly Moor Fell. The deep brown colours of the bracken, the vibrant purple heathers and sky colours of cornflower – blue and bright cerulean – reminded Tallitha of the embroidery sampler she had failed to complete.

Once on top, they could see the snowy peaks of the Out-Of-The-Way Mountains and, down below, the farm at High Bedders End. One final push and they would make it by twilight. Down, down they went, scraping their boots on the rough edges in Holly Pot Ghyll. The descent was steep, fast and exhilarating. Tyaas ran the last stretch, galloping down and flopping at the bottom. He shielded his eyes from the sun and gazed languidly at the others tripping down the side of the steep pasture.

'How far is it now?' he asked rolling over onto his stomach and chewing a cowslip.

'Not far at all. Let's keep going. We might arrive at Farmer Wakenshaw's in time for supper,' said Esmerelda.

'Food? Oh great, I'm starving,' said Tyaas and jumped to his feet.

Laughing and joking, they tramped through the dale, making their way to the farm at the other side of Summerset Beck. Tyaas was as free as a lark, throwing stones into the stream and planning in his mind's eye how he would build an enormous dam of branches and rocks. Eventually, tired and footsore, as the glowing embers of the sinking sun smouldered on the horizon, they entered the muddy farmyard. Two large dogs started barking and running towards them, but there was no danger. The dogs wagged their tails and jumped up to be petted.

'Sticker, Barney! Come here boys!' Farmer Wakenshaw called to his dogs, surveying the bedraggled visitors.

'Good day, Mr Wakenshaw. My name is Esmerelda Patch and this is Tallitha and Tyaas Mouldson, and ...'

'Aye, lass I know who you are, you're just as our Cissie described you. Dressed in all the wrong clothes though, there's no mistake. But you're most welcome here,' said the cheery farmer.

'But how did you know we were coming?' asked Tallitha inquisitively.

'We didn't know it was goin' to be you, but we knew someone would call. The old cock was a-crowing by the back door this morning and that's always a sign. The cock foretells the arrival of unexpected visitors,' explained Bettie, who was married to the farmer.

She stood at the kitchen door with her arms folded, red-faced from cooking, a woman not to be messed with, but cheery nonetheless. She looked askance at the four of them.

'Don't you know that old saying? There's much truth in country sayings and anyway, here you are to prove it. Did our Cissie tell you nowt?' asked Bettie, clicking her tongue in dismay at the peculiar ways of posh folk. 'Come inside and have some supper, you must be famished.'

Farmer Wakenshaw whistled and the dogs trotted obediently behind him, nestling down by the warm hearth. Josh Wakenshaw was a man with a happy disposition. He had ruddy cheeks, bushy eyebrows and abundant whiskers. He smiled so often that there were deep grooves in his weather-beaten face. His wife, Bettie, and daughters, Spooner and Lince, were sweet-natured too; happy with life. They welcomed the travellers into their parlour and gave them a supper of pheasant, partridge and a host of vegetables, followed by apple pudding and creamy yellow custard. Benedict could not recall a better meal or more cheerful hosts. Tyaas stretched out by the fire, yawned and rubbed his fat belly.

After supper, Esmerelda turned to her hosts. 'You haven't asked us where we're headed.' She looked gravely at the assembled company. 'Unless your family is threatened, I must ask you to keep our visit here a secret.'

Josh Wakenshaw looked at his wife and nodded. 'It's alright lass, we understand, don't we Bettie? You're welcome here. We've two small rooms above the barn. They're cosy and warm. Your secret's safe with us.'

'Course it is deary. Bless you,' said Bettie, stroking one of the snoozing dogs.

Esmerelda relaxed and they set about clearing the dishes. Later, Josh sat by the fire and lit his pipe while his daughter, Lince, began playing her flute and her sister, Spooner, sang old

Ennish ballads from the Northern Wolds. As night fell and the farm noises quietened, they sat and told stories of their different worlds, content in each others' company. Bettie came back from locking the hen coops and nudged her husband. Josh knocked his pipe on the hearth, nodded to Bettie, and cleared his throat.

'Well now, my dears, I 'spect you'll be headin' up through Ragging Brows Forest.'

'It's the only way to the caves that I know of,' said Esmerelda.

'Aye, you're right there lass.'

He hesitated and looked at Bettie who raised her eyebrows for him to get on with it.

'Bettie and me, we think you should be warned about some odd goings-on in the forest. It's 'appen what some folks say, round 'ere, any road.'

Josh Wakenshaw refilled his pipe, struck a match and drew on the tobacco until the room was full of bluish smoke. Tyaas moved from slouching next to Sticker and began to listen more intently, and Tallitha stopped talking with the sisters and sat on the sofa next to Benedict.

'You must get through the forest in daylight. Don't be abroad in Ragging Brows after dusk. It's a rum place, there's no mistake.'

Bettie patted the dogs and continued where he left off. 'The story goes that some folks went into the forest, a while back. They must have got lost and were still there at dusk.' She glanced at the wide-eyed faces glued to her every word. 'Now lass you look frit' to death,' she said to Tallitha.

Tallitha swallowed hard and looked swiftly at her brother.

'Nay lass, we don't want to frighten you, but you need to be warned, just to be on the safe side.'

'Aye, that's right,' said Josh, 'just so you're on the look-out, so to speak, for anything suspicious that comes your way.'

'But what happened?' asked Benedict nervously.

'They went in to Ragging Brows meaning to look for mushrooms, 'tis famous for its mushrooms, ain't it Josh?'

The farmer nodded and leaned back in his comfy chair, deep in thought.

'They must 'ave lost track of time and wandered in too far. It got darker sooner than they expected. In certain places that old forest is black as night.'

Bettie stopped and her husband took over the tale.

'Well they never came out again and were never found. So the story goes,' he said finally.

'But that's awful!' exclaimed Tyaas.

'Well it may just be a spooky story that people tell each other at night,' said Josh trying to lighten the mood.

'But what if it isn't? What are we to do?' asked Tallitha.

'There's no way round the forest,' said Josh, 'but best keep clear of the ravines, that's where the wild mushrooms grow, the Honey Fungus and the Destroying Angel.'

'We don't have a choice. We'll have to get through the forest by mid-afternoon,' said Esmerelda biting her lip.

Josh and Bettie forced a cheery smile, but their guests were not reassured and remained preoccupied. The dogs snoozed and Josh nodded off by the fire, letting his pipe clatter onto the stone hearth. Benedict was already falling asleep on the sofa when Esmerelda shook him, said goodnight to the Wakenshaws and they made their way over to the barn. As the boys snuggled down in their straw beds, Esmerelda took hold of Tallitha's hand and led her to the adjoining room.

'We must find the way through the caves. Will you contact Asenathe tonight? She knows you're connected to her. She's trying to help us reach her.'

Tallitha nodded. 'The last shadow-flight was easier, so I'm ready.'

As Tallitha began breathing deeply, Esmerelda started whispering the repetitive haunting words and releasing the sickly odour from her amulet. Then she dangled the shimmering pendant before Tallitha's eyes. The dazzling lights and Esmerelda's penetrating gaze soon brought Tallitha to a trance-like state. All at once she could feel the familiar drifting sensation: as though part of her was sliding away from her body, being sucked out and melting into a separate sphere. Her mind seemed to stretch, pop and snap, then *whoosh!* – she had entered the murky trance-like state where she began spinning upwards through the bright tunnel.

Tallitha found herself flying over the mountains where the spectre of the dark castle loomed like an enormous creature against the night sky. Tallitha swirled round the highest towers until she located the girl, dressed in black and sitting at a writing desk. The vision turned and beckoned to Tallitha to enter. As she approached, the girl smiled and pointed at the writing in front of her. At first Tallitha hesitated, then she moved towards the desk and stared at the strange words before her. The writing was in old Ennish script. Furtively, the girl reached out and touched Tallitha's hand. Suddenly everything blurred and the vision vanished. Tallitha found herself sliding fast down inside the bumpy tunnel and *whoosh!* – she was back in the hay barn with a sharp jolt. She gasped and opened her eyes, blinking in the candlelight.

'Can you can see her too?' asked Tallitha, coming round.

'I can feel her aura through you but I can't see her, not the way you can.'

Tallitha had a pinkish glow around her. 'She showed me some writing in Ennish. I'll be able to write down the words, although I don't understand their meaning.'

Esmerelda handed her pen and paper and Tallitha began to write the words automatically.

'*Canlayer trena ta serna fe la der et merle*
Certhe merlen setba na canya fe te la ye.'

'How peculiar,' said Esmerelda, 'it means:

The Tors are twinned, below and above,
Underground, go backwards through the Tors.'

Tallitha pulled a face. 'But that doesn't make any sense.'
'It's about the sequence underground. I don't understand

the significance but it's a real breakthrough. We'll work out the meaning in time,' said Esmerelda happily. 'Asenathe is a receptor. She's drawing you closer.'

'But why does this happen to me?' asked Tallitha, a little afraid.

'You're clairvoyant; you can see things that aren't in front of you. These powers have been handed down the female line of the Morrow family for generations,' explained Esmerelda.

'But why now?' asked Tallitha perplexed.

'You're leaving childhood behind you.'

Tallitha gasped. 'Can the three sisters see things too?'

'They've never revealed their powers to me, but then we've never been close.'

'What about you, Essie?'

'My powers are different. I can put people in a trance.'

As the moonlight shone down on Esmerelda's face she became pensive.

'I realised I had these powers when I was young. They're both a gift and a burden. You must be careful how you use them.'

'But what if I don't want this gift? Or what if I can't control it?' asked Tallitha apprehensively.

'It isn't a choice. You'll learn how to put yourself in a trance without my help. In time you'll work out the trigger, it may be a sound or a smell. Then you can control it,' explained Esmerelda.

'What if I can't bring myself back?'

Esmerelda smiled. 'It will take practice and skill.'

'How did you know I had the gift?' asked Tallitha tentatively.

'Cissie let something slip. She said you were able to read her mind, particularly when she was trying to keep something from you. Then when I hypnotised you, I saw the colour vibration surrounding you. She also told me you were fascinated by colours and from your sewing I could see you found it difficult to concentrate, to keep the colours separate. They become jumbled before your eyes, don't they, Tallitha?'

'Yes Essie, they always have.'

Esmerelda kissed a bewildered Tallitha goodnight and snuggled down into the straw bed. Tallitha stared at the moon, bright and high in the night sky. It was all beginning to fall into place. That's why she couldn't keep her stitches neat for Great Aunt Agatha and why she was mesmerised by Sybilla's fabrics. The colours entranced and confused her. Now she knew she was gifted in a very special way.

Fifteen

Marlin sat hunched in his Shrove hole, rubbing his whiskery chin and setting his duplicitous mind to work on what would serve the Shroves best. The Grand Morrow was an old woman who was past her prime, and he despised the sisters from the Crewel Tower with their high and mighty ways. There was a host of opportunities and no mistake. Marlin decided to hold a Shrove conclave, a special meeting with the other Shroves, Grintley and Florré. Within the hour they met together at the back of the fruit store. They were overexcited and their wet, slimy mouths could taste the delicious tang of disaster in the air. Their beady eyes were fixed on one another as they picked over each morsel of intrigue and plotted how to fix Cissie. The Grand Morrow would have to be informed about the children's departure, but not quite yet. Whilst sipping their berry juice, they hatched a devilish plan.

Early next morning Marlin slunk into one of the Shrove

holes near the kitchens and waited for Cissie to start her morning chores. Sure enough he heard her bustling about and chatting to Mrs Armitage about the daily menu. They discussed who was having what for breakfast, and when the fish and meat order would arrive for the evening meal. Marlin muttered away to himself, weighing up the pros and cons. Cissie was remarkably calm for someone who had been so underhand with the Grand Morrow. But he would spike her yet and make her pay. She would be sorry when he got hold of her. He sneaked off to find Florré and they hid themselves in Tallitha's bedroom to lay in wait for the nurse. At some point she would have to come into Tallitha's room and feign surprise at the young ones being missing. They would spoil her little game. No one could outmanoeuvre a Shrove, and certainly not Cissie.

As Marlin and Florré lurked behind the bedroom door, salivating at the thought of ambushing the servant and causing her pain, Cissie came wandering in with a pile of laundry. Marlin sprang out in front of her and Florré banged the door shut and locked it. They stood malevolently, staring at her in a most peculiar way, their venomous hatred leeching out of their eyes.

'Well I never, what are you two doing in Miss Tallitha's bedroom? You two have a nerve, I'll say.'

But the Shroves were not interested in being scolded by Cissie. They grabbed her by the neck and pulled her struggling onto the bedroom floor. Marlin put his cold hand over her mouth and held her arm tightly behind her back, weaselling right into her face, sniffing and breathing his foul breath all over her. His closeness made her feel sick with the stench of his vile, odorous body. She pulled away and shielded her face.

'Let me go this instant, you're hurting me,' cried Cissie.

But Marlin pushed her arm further up her back and she yelped out in pain. Florré made a growling noise at the back of his throat and towered over her, baring his twisted yellow fangs as if to bite her neck. At that moment Cissie realised she was in grave danger and kept very still. The ill humour between the Shroves and the servants had always been there, bubbling away beneath the surface with snide comments and acid looks, but this was different. She had never been so terrified in all her life. She whimpered and turned her face to the wall, screwing up her eyes to get rid of the terrifying spectacle of the Shroves leering over her body. Then Marlin spoke.

'Tell 'em now where they'd be gone to, tell 'em. I'll nip 'er harder and I'll bite ya deep,' he threatened.

He licked his wet lips and twisted her arm further up her back. Cissie thought it would break. She felt sick with pain.

'Please … you're hurting me. I don't know what you mean,' cried Cissie.

Marlin gripped her harder and the spit dribbled down his chin and landed on her face as he revealed a ghastly set of brown teeth. He curled his lip and bared his fangs, rearing up like a ferocious wild animal waiting to strike its prey. Tallitha had been right about Florré that day in the Crewel Tower, the Shroves were evil. Why hadn't she listened to her? She thought Tallitha was being fanciful and imagining things. Now the Shroves were out of control with bloodlust and meant to hurt her. Spit was flying in Cissie's face as they lifted her, pushing her violently against the wall. The Shroves were stronger and more agile than Cissie, and their combined force took her breath away as she groaned and slumped down the wall.

'Oww, get away from me. Please, leave me alone,' moaned Cissie struggling for air, but Marlin would not release his grip.

He hissed and his eyes sunk back into his skull as he reared up, loomed over her crumpled body and bit her hard on the side of her face. She could feel his disgusting fangs puncture her skin as the blood trickled down her cheeks and she cried out in pain. Florré watched the violent struggle, hopping up and down and salivating at the sight of Cissie's blood oozing from the jagged wound on her cheek. She cried out.

'Tell 'em now,' he growled again.

Cissie could stand the pain no longer.

'Ohhh … they've gone to find Miss Asenathe.'

'Where 'ave they gone to, woman? Tell 'em now,' demanded Florré.

'I don't know.'

Marlin bit her again and she wailed uncontrollably.

'Agggh leave me alone, please. They've gone to Breedoor, to Hellstone Tors.'

Cissie fell to the floor sobbing as she mopped the blood from her lacerated face. Marlin and Florré moved in closer and towered above her as if to finish her off. A victorious smile lit up

Marlin's evil eyes and Cissie knew in that moment that he meant to kill her. She gasped and hid her face against the wall waiting for the pain to begin. But the Shrove hesitated.

'I'll get ye, one day, woman,' he said murderously with his devilish face right next to hers.

He motioned to Florré and they slithered out of the bedroom, banging the door behind them.

Cissie lay on the floor like a wounded animal, shaking and whimpering. She was in shock. What was she to do? All the plans had gone so horribly wrong. If she told Lady Agatha now about the children's disappearance she would see the Shrove's mark and would ask too many questions.

But Cissie was already too late. As soon as Marlin had wiped the fresh blood from his lips, he went to the Grand Morrow and broke the news, relishing every second of his story and his mistresses' despair. Upstairs in Tallitha's bedroom Cissie heard the dreadful cries of the Grand Morrow wailing from below. Marlin had got to her first.

Oh no, thought Cissie, I'm done for.

'Enough!' the Grand Morrow yelled. 'Bring her to me at once!'

As Cissie opened the door of the morning room Agatha Morrow's body shook with rage. Cissie froze at the sight of her mistress's distress.

'Is this true?' she shouted, shaking her fist at the servant.

'Yes your ladyship. I'm sorry I couldn't stop them,' pleaded the abject Cissie.

Agatha stood up, gripping the arms of her chair.

'That's a blatant lie. Marlin has told me you were in on their ill-conceived plan from the beginning and that you even stole food for them!'

Cissie threw a hateful glance at the Shrove and held a handkerchief to her face.

'How could you be so foolish? What made you assist Esmerelda, after what happened the last time? What about the children, the poor children? You have endangered the lives of the ones you most care about!' Agatha paced the floor glaring at Cissie and crying out in distress. 'She is my only surviving heir and now she is lost forever!'

Marlin licked his feverish lips and grimaced, relishing every moment of Cissie's disgrace and the Grand Morrow's sorrow.

'They'll never come home. Oh Cissie, what have you done?'

Agatha paced the room, wringing her hands, crying out as the enormity of her loss began to sink in. Cissie stood with her head down.

'Or worse, they'll be captured by the Morrow Swarm and murdered. My Asenathe is gone forever. Why couldn't Essie believe this and stop torturing us with her foolishness. Her original stupidity was the cause of me losing my only child and heir!' cried Agatha. She fell into inconsolable bouts of weeping, a wretched heap on the sofa.

'Oh please, my lady, I'm sure they'll be safe. Esmerelda will look after them and Benedict is a sensible boy,' pleaded Cissie. She ran to her mistress's side but was hastily rebuffed.

Agatha sat up and called for her smelling salts.

'Benedict you say, who exactly is he? Do we know him? I have never met him. Oh Lord, a stranger in my house and I know nothing about him!' cried Agatha and flounced back onto the sofa.

'No, no my lady, not a stranger as you suggest, he's a relative, a cousin. The Lady Snowdroppe introduced him to you, I'm sure she must have. He's a sweet boy, studious and more careful than Tallitha and her brother. He will be a good influence.'

'Never heard of him. Are you imagining things, Cissie? Snowdroppe, you say? I will speak to her directly. Marlin, I dare say you're there listening to all this,' shouted Agatha.

Marlin scurried to his mistress's side, pushing Cissie out of the way.

'Go directly and summon Lady Snowdroppe. I must talk to her about the children.'

Marlin slunk off rubbing his hands with glee. He had to disguise his delight at the way everything was turning out. Agatha sat on her sofa sniffing and haranguing Cissie.

'Why did you listen to Esmerelda this time when I know you've resisted her wild schemes in the past?'

'It wasn't Miss Esmerelda who started it, but Miss Tallitha and Master Tyaas. They found out about Lady Asenathe, and Esmerelda discovered their plans. She promised to keep them safe on the journey. There was no use trying to stop them. At first I lied to Tallitha about knowing Lady Asenathe, I really did, but she was determined to go and got it out of me. I'm so sorry my lady.'

'Silence, you could have told me, but decided not to. I could have stopped them!' shouted Agatha, enraged by Cissie's duplicity.

'I hoped they would find Lady Asenathe this time. I was trying to do some good!' pleaded Cissie.

'Good! Are you mad? They will never find her. She's gone forever. If I have come to terms with that as her mother, why can't everyone else? You have served my family for years, and I trusted you. Get out of my sight and leave this house immediately.'

Agatha broke down sobbing and Cissie fled from the room. She had done a bad thing without meaning to. She had betrayed the Grand Morrow when she had meant to help find her missing daughter. She was confused and ashamed of herself. She had helped Tallitha against her better judgement and now this had happened. The Grand Morrow had banished her from Winderling Spires.

Cissie set off for Wycham village and her sister's cottage. She needed time to think and to be as far away from the Shroves as possible. They were pure evil and she knew they were out to get her.

*

While Agatha consoled herself, alternately weeping, drinking sweet tea and eating an abundance of strawberry fondants, the news of the children's departure eventually reached the inhabitants of the Crewel Tower. Edwina and Sybilla, all of a twitter with the mayhem and excitement, came down from their apartment and joined in the gossip and general upset that pervaded the house. Their day was spoiled again, of course, but they consoled themselves by sitting in the grand sitting room and nibbling lemon tarts and fresh blackberry pies. After considering the situation, they decided they had good reason to be distraught and demanded attention from the servants, calling on them to do this and that. After all, Sybilla's daughter and Edwina's grandchildren were now missing. Sybilla was particularly exercised at their recklessness. The thought of those children going out in the middle of the night made her feel quite faint.

According to the two sisters, the commotion had definitely aged Agatha. She looked peaky and her skin had become sallow with all the constant fretting and weeping. Sybilla and Edwina took it in turns to sit with their sister, alternately and insidiously reminding her of the dangers out in the wilds of Wycham Elva and beyond to Breedoor. Each new bout of wailing made Agatha look even more haggard and older, much older. The sisters quietly relished these diminutions in Agatha's demeanour and ate monstrous amounts of sweet tarts, wearing the pastry cook out with their insatiable demands for more sugared cakes. But what were sisters for, if not to give comfort when comfort was needed?

Eventually Snowdroppe arrived, late as usual. She flounced into the library as though nothing had happened and she expected the world to dance attendance on her needs. She was dressed in apple-green velvet with sparkling emeralds at her throat and dangling from her ears. She swept towards Agatha and kissed the air ever so lightly by the side of each sunken cheek.

'Well dear Aunt, this is a to-do, is it not?' said Snowdroppe admiring herself in the sitting room mirror as she glided past.

The Grand Morrow glared at Snowdroppe, her dislike pasted all over her distraught face.

'Did you know anything about these dreadful plans?' demanded Agatha.

Snowdroppe bristled as she sat opposite the Grand Morrow. How dare Agatha speak to her in that off-hand tone, accusing her in that superior manner? She took her time answering, ordering tea from Marlin and demanding lemon rather than milk. She sipped it slowly.

'Why, Aunt, what do you mean? They're my children after all and of course I'm concerned. But heaven knows they're always up to some prank or other. Tallitha especially, she is so headstrong.'

Agatha cut her short, shocked at Snowdroppe's total lack of motherly concern.

'Your children are missing. They may be injured or taken prisoner by the border tribes and all you can do is to complain about Tallitha.'

Snowdroppe sighed, raised her eyes and looked unperturbed.

'I shouldn't worry if I were you, Aunt Agatha. Essie will take care of them, won't she? Try not to fuss so much, you'll wear yourself out,' said Snowdroppe pouting and rising from her seat. 'Well, if that's all I have an arrangement with Maximillian.'

But Agatha was not letting her off that lightly.

'No it isn't. Who is this Benedict? What was he doing in my house?' she demanded, staring hard at her nephew's vain, superficial wife.

Snowdroppe was momentarily caught off guard. She faltered, forced a simpering smile and sat back down again.

'He's … why he's a distant cousin. You remember meeting him, dearest Aunt, of course you do. He came for tea.'

Snowdroppe gave Agatha a patronising smile, the sort one would give to an old woman who was losing track of things.

'I'm old but I'm not stupid. I've never met this boy. Whose cousin is he?'

Snowdroppe was cornered. Agatha could be a tiresome old witch.

'Why Aunt, I thought he was your cousin of course. He's been having lessons with …'

'What do you mean a cousin of mine? Having lessons? I don't like strangers in my house!'

Agatha was aghast at Snowdroppe's off-hand manner and in her house too!

'You had better hope he is more sensible than your wayward children and will take care of them. I suppose they must have struck up a friendship. Be more careful in the future, Snowdroppe. This is my house, not yours! I want to know what goes on in it. If you must introduce anyone else into my circle you will tell me first. Do you understand?' said Agatha forcefully.

She gripped the chair and stared at the simpering female before her. What on earth did Maximillian see in her? Well he was soused as a herring most of the time, so he probably couldn't see very much at all. Her family, her dear family was disintegrating before her very eyes.

Snowdroppe regarded Agatha coolly. One day, she would teach her a lesson. Agatha Morrow would rue this day, she would make certain of that! Snowdroppe raised her eyebrows disparagingly and stood up. Revenge is a dish best eaten cold.

'That will be all. I will keep you posted should there be any developments,' Agatha threw the words at the self-regarding creature that stood before her.

'Most kind,' said Snowdroppe sarcastically and left Agatha to stew.

Later, when Snowdroppe was certain she was unobserved, she conferred with the Shroves on the latest rumours. Marlin and the others were enthralled by her. The balance of power was shifting in Winderling Spires. Soon they would be dancing to her tune.

But the strange old house was quiet without Tallitha and Tyaas. Agatha demanded the family rally round and that everything should return to normal. She ordered Marlin and Florré to be despatched to follow the children and they duly departed, but returned within a few hours having been unable to pick up a good enough trail. Shroves were renowned for their keen sense of smell so their inability to find the scent was frowned upon by the Grand Morrow. But Marlin knew where the children were headed. He was quite content for them to continue on their journey and he smiled inwardly at the deception played out in the grand house. There were more interesting plans afoot. So the Shroves spent their days engaged in their favourite pastime, snooping on the Morrow women, pretending to offer consolation, but secretly enjoying the women's distress and watching their every move.

Sixteen

Waking up to the sounds of the farmyard, the clattering of the breakfast dishes and the women chattering to each other, made Tallitha yearn for Winderling Spires and dear Cissie. Tallitha turned over and buried her head under the blankets. She missed the strange old house and her nurse's affection. She had taken so much of her old life for granted.

Tyaas bounded onto Tallitha's straw bed holding a struggling lamb that was ba-ba-ba-ing for its mother.

'Ah she's sweet,' said Tallitha, 'let me hold her.'

Tallitha petted the lamb as it frolicked about on the straw, trying to get back to its mother, with Tyaas catching it, falling over and laughing.

'Isn't this great?' he said.

But Tallitha didn't reply. She looked distracted.

'What's up?'

She stroked the lamb then clutched it to her chest.

'I miss home.' Her voice trailed off into a whisper. 'What if we've made a mistake and we never see Winderling Spires or Cissie again?' she said plaintively.

Tyaas did not understand his sister. First she wanted to be free of Winderling Spires and all her responsibilities to search for Asenathe, and now she wanted to be at home again.

'Buck up Tallitha,' he said, 'you wanted an adventure, and now we're really having one.'

'I know,' she said pathetically. 'I don't know what's wrong with me. I'm scared,'

Tyaas was amazed. 'But what are you scared of?'

'The future,' said Tallitha quietly, 'and of Ragging Brows Forest.'

*

Saying goodbye to the Wakenshaws was hard. The farmer and his family had been delightful company and the warm beds and good food had been such a blessing. As the dogs barked and they waved to their friends, they looked back at the idyllic farmyard and the safety of Josh and Bettie's cosy homestead.

'Goodbye and take care,' shouted Lince and Spooner from the doorway.

'Remember, keep out of the forest at night and you'll be fine, my dears,' said Bettie with an attempt at a broad smile.

'Come and see us on your way back,' shouted the girls.

The four travellers made their way up the steep side of the dale towards Ragging Brows Forest. It was a hard climb and with every step Tallitha thought about the dangers that lay ahead of them. The Wakenshaws' story had unnerved her. Spending a night in the dark forest was to be avoided at all costs.

'How much further?' asked Tyaas, stopping to take a breather.

Esmerelda shaded her eyes from the bright sunlight. It was another beautiful day but all she could see ahead was the steep incline, way into the distance.

'It's a fair way yet,' she said, 'let's take a rest.'

So they shared Bettie's stotty cakes filled with cheese and homemade pickle. Later they made their way over an old mineshaft which was littered with slate and shale. Benedict was excited about every new plant and insect he discovered. The flowers were abundant, poking out in clumps over the hillside and Benedict would not be hurried.

'Look here's a beautiful specimen, a dog violet, wait, what about this meadow-sweet?'

He kept stopping to examine the butterflies and crane flies, and to make notes on each insect that came in his path.

'Come on, Benedict,' insisted Tyaas. 'We aren't going to get very far if you keep this up.'

But Benedict ignored Tyaas's pleas, sauntering along at a snail's pace and within a few minutes he was at it again.

On the hillside Tallitha could see the outline of the forest which stretched way off into the distance. Thousands of tall pine trees stood row upon row like sentinels up into the sky, guarding the edge of the ragged forest. Behind the outer rim of trees the heavy darkness percolated between the branches making Tallitha feel deeply uneasy.

'It looks worse than I feared,' said Tallitha quietly, peering nervously ahead into the gloomy depths of the dismal pine trees.

They picked their way through the undergrowth, hoping to make good headway, but within an hour they realised they had gone in a complete circle.

'I don't understand it,' said Tyaas scratching his head, 'we've been here before.'

'We must have gone the wrong way when we crossed the stream back there. Or was it over there?' said Esmerelda looking puzzled.

All the trees and pathways looked the same and it was becoming abundantly clear how easy it would be to become completely lost. The memory of the Wakenshaws' story began to play over in Tallitha's mind. Tyaas took the compass from his pocket and sighed.

'I thought I'd worked out how to use this compass. We're heading north, aren't we, Tallitha?

But Tallitha was unsure. She began to feel panicky as the light slowly faded. Over-hanging branches and dense foliage blocked their way and as they walked deeper into the forest, Esmerelda began to look nervously about her.

'Is it getting darker?' she asked.

Tyaas shrugged his shoulders and checked the compass

again. After their near-disaster in the Gulping Mess he kept it in his pocket at all times.

'Tyaas are you sure you know how to use that?' asked Benedict. 'Here let me have a go.'

'No, leave off. I can do it,' shouted Tyaas.

He pushed Benedict away and hugged the compass to himself shielding it with his hand.

'We should be skirting the eastern edge of the forest. Let's keep going in this direction,' said Tyaas sounding more confident than he actually felt.

Tyaas went first, using his knife to hack down the stubborn, tangled bracken, while Tallitha and the others scrambled through the undergrowth behind him. Slowly the light ebbed away as the gloomy patches of the forest became darker still. Suddenly Tallitha grabbed hold of her brother.

'Wait a minute. Listen, all of you.'

They stood perfectly still.

'I can't hear anything,' whispered Benedict.

'I know,' said Tallitha, turning quickly to look over her shoulder, 'it's much too quiet.'

A heavy, deathly silence bore down on them. Dusk was settling and it was getting murkier with every step. Tallitha stared into the gloomy twilight and it seemed to her as if something was watching their faltering steps, luring them ever further into the heart of the dark forest.

*

A Skink was hiding close by. They could not see her, but she could see them. Ruker had been stalking the travellers for some time and had watched them lose their way several times. She was an artful forester, skilled in all the woodland ways, able to survive in the harshest conditions. She operated by stealth and surprise, always ready to pounce or to escape through one of the tunnels in the forest floor. The four friends had been drawing attention to themselves, noisily tramping through the undergrowth and calling out to each other without a care. Ruker felt nervous to be out in the forest as evening was drawing in. She looked quickly this way and that, peering into the shadows, watching for any sign that the wild dogs were on the move. The Black Hounds would soon be out, foraging for their night feed. Ruker knew she had to intervene or these strangers would meet a sorry end. She crept out in front of them, sprang up quickly from the undergrowth and coughed.

'Ahhhh, who are you?' gasped Tallitha hiding behind her brother.

Tyaas laughed, 'It's okay, she's a Skink. Aren't you, my friend?'

The Skink grinned. She was lithe and graceful, built for climbing the tallest trees. Her long dark hair was pulled into a braided plait but it was her eyes that attracted them. They were almond shaped, brown and beautifully slanted, peering out beneath a heavy fringe. She blinked slowly and tightly held her sabre in its leather tabard.

'You scared me,' said Tallitha realising that the Skink meant them no harm.

'I'm Ruker, come with me. You aren't safe out here,' she said authoritatively. 'I can smell the wind, it is changing,' she said mysteriously, raising her head and sniffing at the air.

'Why should we follow you?' asked Esmerelda suspiciously.

'It's up to you, but the Black Hounds will be out soon, and you don't want to meet them,' she said nervously. 'The wind will deliver your scents straight to them. They're extremely nasty and will devour you as soon as look at you. So are you coming or not?'

Ruker's voice sounded like the noise of the wind through the forest, gruff and raw and in full command of the situation. The four travellers knew they had no choice so they quickly followed the Skink as she high-tailed it through the undergrowth.

*

Tallitha raced after her, the wild dogs uppermost in her mind. She didn't fancy being their supper that night. One minute they were running along the forest floor and the next, Ruker was pushing them, one by one, down a dark brown hole in the earth. The leafy entrance was camouflaged with knotted branches and layers of wet sodden leaves. One by one they tumbled down a narrow shaft and landed in a heap at the bottom.

'Ouch, where am I?' shouted Benedict falling on top of Tallitha.

'Owwww – it's pitch-black down here!' cried Esmerelda trying to stand up and banging her head.

'Watch it. You can't stand up,' said Ruker. 'You have to crouch down, like this.'

She bent down on all fours to avoid the tangle of overhanging branches and pushed Benedict into the same position.

'But where are we?' asked Tallitha.

'We're in a Skink burrow. We have hidden routes under the forest to avoid ending up as fodder for the wild dogs,' she grinned and nodded upwards.

The others followed her gaze, knowing they had better make the best of it. The Skink lit a number of small waxed sticks and handed one to each of the travellers. In front of them was a long dark twisting burrow. The underground path curled under the boughs of thousands of interwoven tree roots which had been twisted together overhead and formed into a low arch.

'Come, follow me.'

The Skink moved at a tremendous pace, darting and diving over tree roots, throwing back instructions to the others.

'Leap over here. Mind that branch. Keep to the left, watch the roof here, it sags.'

Ruker barked orders the whole length of the tunnel, intermittently looking over her shoulder to make sure that no one had fallen behind. Tyaas was in awe. Who would have thought the Skinks were so clever? The burrow was an amazing feat of engineering, and this was one fine Skink. After a few minutes Ruker stopped, held up her hand and signalled for them to halt.

'This is the end of the tunnel. We have some climbing ahead of us. I suppose you know how to do that?' she asked sarcastically.

From the look of them she wasn't sure. They certainly weren't dressed properly. Their boots were too new and she could see their hands were unused to manual work. They would be sore and chapped by the end of this climb. Tyaas and Tallitha nodded,

Esmerelda said she could just about manage it, and Benedict went pale.

'I'm afraid. I'm not good with heights,' he stammered looking warily up the cavernous shaft above him. Ruker roped them up just in case of any mishaps.

'I'll go first, followed by you,' Ruker said pointing at Esmerelda. 'Then you, girl, then the scared one, then the boy. Clear about that? Then let's go, quickly now.'

Ruker began to climb up the inside of the hollowed tree using the foot- and handholds.

'Watch out for any falling debris,' she shouted as twigs and leaf litter fell on top of their heads.

It was an arduous climb and they had to make several stops for Benedict who wobbled and froze.

'Stop looking down. Just keep going, you won't fall, and if you do, you'll land on me,' said Tyaas spitting out pieces of bark that were showering down on top of him.

'This is my worst nightmare,' howled Benedict pathetically. 'I'm trying my best.'

'Come on, don't stop!' said Tyaas pushing Benedict from behind.

At the top, Ruker opened a trapdoor and they stepped out on to a solid wooden platform. The view before them was spectacular, way over to the grey mountains shrouded by cloud in the distance. They had just climbed up the inside of a huge redwood and were high above the tops of the trees.

'Welcome to Hanging Tree Islands,' said Ruker with a flourish and a bow as she proudly showed off her world.

'Wow!' said Tyaas, 'it's incredible, and so high!'

Tallitha and Tyaas skipped over one of the rope bridges overhanging the dark forest below. All around were the twinkling lights of the Skink village built at the top of the tree canopy way above the edges of the Ragging Brows Ravine, hundreds of feet below. The treetops were interlinked with rope bridges, rope swings and ladders which connected all the tree-dwellings. Benedict stepped onto the rope bridge, swayed and tightly closed his eyes.

'Be calm, my friend,' said Ruker, 'you're safe up here.'

Benedict stared at the deep chasm of the ravine and began to shake. Esmerelda fumbled in her bag and pulled out slivers of her special mushrooms.

'Here, eat these – they'll steady your nerves.'

Benedict chewed pieces of the Dryad's Saddle and Ruker placed a blindfold over his eyes. It worked, and despite protests they were soon at Ruker's front door.

The Skink's dwelling was one of many scattered amongst the high branches of the redwood trees. Each residence was a smooth, round construction made of interwoven straw and mud with pointed roofs. They were all individually paint-washed in muddy colours, sludgy green, washed out ochre and walnut brown. Inside the hut there were a number of small burrow-like sleeping chambers leading off from a central room. This was where all the cooking and eating took place. Ruker was immensely proud of her cosy home and she ushered her visitors inside. She lit the lamp and settled her guests around the glowing stove.

'Now tell me, what possessed you to go into Ragging Brows Forest at dusk?'

Ruker prepared food while Tallitha told her about their adventures and where they were headed.

'You have a hard road ahead of you. Who'll show you the way through the Out-Of-The-Way Mountains?' she asked, handing them supper.

'We don't know yet,' said Tallitha sheepishly, seeing herself and the others through Ruker's trained eyes.

'It's a maze of treacherous shafts and tunnels. Even those who make the caves their home only know certain parts of them.'

Ruker studied the travellers. They were about to enter an underground world that was laced with danger. They were completely unprepared for the trials ahead of them. Esmerelda bristled.

'I've been some of the way before and we've been given a clue to the way through the caves. We just have to work it out.'

Benedict looked at Tyaas for confirmation but he shrugged his shoulders.

'Have we? When was that?' asked Benedict, perking up.

'Last night, Tallitha contacted Asenathe when you were asleep. She saw a riddle written down. It said:

The Tors are twinned, below and above,
Underground, go backwards through the TORS.'

'Mmm,' said Ruker scratching her head, 'but what does that

mean? Twinned with what? How can you go backwards? It's difficult enough going forwards in those deep caves.'

'I'll have a go at solving it,' suggested Benedict.

That evening he pored over the words and kept asking them questions. Did they think it meant this? What about that? But it was no good, nothing seemed to fit.

After supper Ruker suggested a stroll around Hanging Trees, and everyone but Benedict agreed.

'I'll stay here and decipher the puzzle. Besides I may get stuck on a rope bridge and spoil your fun,' he said, sounding slightly put out.

So Benedict snuggled down into the cushions on Ruker's floor. When they left him he was sitting happily with pen and paper scribbling away trying all sorts of combinations to solve the riddle.

It was windy and the rope bridges creaked and groaned across the village. Tyaas leapt across each bridge without fear. He was extremely nimble, almost outdoing Ruker with his ability to race across the rungs without touching the sides.

'Come on, this is great fun. Woooooooooh!' he shouted as he sped across.

'Wait for me!' screamed Tallitha with delight.

They were happy and free, safe amongst the tall trees.

'What are they doing?' asked Tyaas, pointing at the Skinks who were flying through the air from tree to tree on long rope swings. 'That looks amazing – can I have a go?'

'Not tonight. It's too dark for inexperienced tree skimmers.

But you can try tomorrow,' said Ruker.

'You bet,' said Tyaas 'it looks incredible!'

The lights from the Skink dwellings lit up the evening sky like twinkling stars, and Tallitha thought it was the most magical place she had ever seen. On their way home Ruker suggested popping into The Wild Oak for a draught of beer. The ale house was run by a Skink called Neeps who was an old travelling companion of Ruker's. It was bright and noisy inside the tavern and the cheerful Skink behind the bar gave them a winning smile.

'Good evening, ladies and gents. What will you have? Tonight we have a number of guest ales, bottled though, we can't get draught up here,' said Neeps chuckling.

Tyaas had never drunk ale before and chose half a pint of Taddy Brown Pot. Tallitha had a pint of Shepherd's Tipple and Esmerelda had a Black Chocolate Malt Ale. Ruker and Neeps had their favourite drink of Old Badger Stout, with bags of Pig's Trotter Crisps all round. They sat round the rustic bar chatting and watching the comings and goings of the ale house. Skinks were an adventurous lot, Tallitha could see that. Both male and female Skinks came into the bar carrying sacks over their shoulders, and began to show one another the contents.

'What's in those bags?' asked Tyaas.

'The day's catch, probably rabbits and squirrels for supper,' explained Neeps.

He was shorter than Ruker but more heavily built, with fair hair pulled into a stubby ponytail at the back of his head. He had brown and ochre-coloured beads around his neck and two silver earrings in his left ear. Tyaas thought he looked like a real pirate, a swashbuckler of the high trees! He was cool.

'So what you doing in these parts?' asked Neeps winking at Ruker.

The Skinks leant on the bar, supping their stout and studying the travellers.

'They're headed for Breedoor,' explained Ruker.

'Are they now?' said Neeps quizzically.

But Neeps knew they would never make it through alone. Either the Black Hounds would see them off in Ragging Brows Forest or the Murk Morrow would destroy them in the caves.

'That means you'll be going underground. Been down there before have you?' asked Neeps, twiddling with his earrings.

Esmerelda coloured. Neeps's humorous expression said it all. He thought they were ill-prepared for such a journey.

'I've been down there, many times in fact,' Esmerelda blurted out.

'But you 'aint actually ever made it to the other side, have you?' asked Neeps.

His brown eyes twinkled as he teased the wary travellers. Esmerelda shook her head and supped her ale.

'Seems to me, you need a guide,' he said. 'Someone who knows these parts, and may have half a chance of getting you in and out of the caves in one piece.'

'Do you know anyone who would be willing to help us?' asked Tallitha innocently.

Ruker grinned at Neeps and continued. 'Well, Neeps and I

are old travelling companions. I'm not saying we've been all the way through the Out-Of-The-Way Mountains, because we ain't, but we know our Shroves from the Murk Mowl,' she laughed.

'Aye and we know the dangers underground. Been pot-holing manys a time in Weeping Holes and Startling Caves,' said Neeps slapping Ruker on the back and chinking their glasses in memory of long gone escapades.

'Ain't that a fact? Those were the days, got the scars to prove it!' shouted Ruker and downed the rest of her ale in one glugging mouthful.

She lifted her trouser leg to reveal an old purple-coloured wound. Neeps laughed and lifted his hair to reveal his ear with the top half missing. Tyaas marvelled at the two of them.

'So, will you help us?' asked Tyaas, beguiled by the Skinks.

He was elated at the thought of travelling alongside these dare devils.

'I think we might just do that,' said Neeps, 'I'm due some leave, and we take it in turns behind the bar, so the others can manage things whilst I'm away.'

'How splendid' said Esmerelda perking up at last. 'That definitely calls for another round of drinks, bartender.'

'Here's to us' said Tallitha and Tyaas in unison, smiling and chinking their glasses

'Bottoms up!' shouted Neeps.

When they got back to Ruker's dwelling Benedict was snoring, fast asleep on the cushions, so they covered him up and sat down to a nightcap.

'So tell me about the Black Hounds,' said Tallitha, supping her hot drink.

'Ah, those critters,' said Ruker, her face becoming serious, 'they're vicious dogs who roam the forest at night. That's the reason we live up here,' she said patting the walls of her home. 'They're savage and will kill you in an instant. They hunt in packs too, very nasty. Some people were killed a while back looking for mushrooms. Here one minute and gone the next. We heard their screams from way down there. Dragged into their lairs they were and, well, you can guess the rest.'

Tyaas shuddered. So the awful story was true.

'But how will we get past them? Won't they smell us?'

Ruker grinned and started to undo her long plait ready for bed.

'Skinks have ways and means, don't you worry. All will be revealed in the morning,' she said mysteriously and bid them goodnight.

They scrambled into their warm pods and snuggled down. Almost before her head touched the pillow, Tallitha fell asleep but in the night something disturbed her. A dreadful wolfish howling could be heard from down in Ragging Brows Forest.

'What's that?' she said terrified, sitting bolt upright in bed.

'Shut up, Sis,' shouted Tyaas, 'it's just the dogs howling.'

Tallitha pulled the blankets over her head to keep the dreadful noise at bay. What would they do if they came across those hounds? They had killed the travellers when they were searching for mushrooms. But at some point Tallitha did fall asleep. Images of rushing headlong through the trees filled her dreams, with the Black Hounds snapping at her heels.

Seventeen

The next morning wonderful sizzling sounds came from the kitchen and the smell of smoked bacon and scrambled eggs wafted through the morning air and greeted the hungry travellers still drowsy from their over-indulgence of the night before. They happily tucked into the hearty breakfast while they discussed plans for the day ahead.

'Any success with the riddle?' asked Esmerelda handing round the mugwort leaves.

Tyaas pretended to chew but when Esmerelda wasn't looking, he spat them out of the window.

'Riddle?' asked Benedict distractedly, 'Oh that … sorry, nothing made sense to me.'

'Perhaps there's an easy answer, it might be staring us in the face,' said Tyaas sticking out his tongue at his cousin.

'Okay brain-box, what do you suggest?' snapped Benedict,

but Tyaas shrugged. It wasn't his thing, riddles and puzzles. He was stumped.

'Maybe it'll make sense once we're in the caves,' said Ruker trying to keep the peace between the boys.

'I suggest we start for the mountains tomorrow. It's a long hike to Startling Caves. First we need to show you tree-skimming,' said Ruker laughing. 'It's like flying. You'll love it,' she said looking at Tyaas's excited face.

'Ooooh wait a minute,' said Benedict alarmed, 'that sounds dangerous.'

'Shut up Benedict and stop being a baby. Of course we want to try,' said Tyaas scowling at his cousin.

'No we don't!' snapped Benedict, his face turning sour.

'Well, those of you who want to try tree skimming, come with me. There's another way down, using the redwoods, it just takes much longer. Why don't you give it a go, Benedict, and come with us?'

'Okay, I'll watch, but I'm not promising anything,' said a moody Benedict.

Ruker led them to the tree school in Hanging Trees where all the little Skinks learnt how to tree-skim. A collection of rope swings were tethered to the trees and the young Skinks just hopped on and off as the fancy took them. All the ropes had bulging knots in the bottom so the Skinks could fly through the trees, sitting comfortably on the knot, or the dare-devils amongst them could fly through the air standing up.

'Here Tyaas, take hold of this rope and lunge out as far as you can. There's a skill to it, just watch me and you'll get the hang of it.'

Ruker jumped onto the knot, deftly skimming the trees all around her. It looked fantastic and Tyaas was soon flying through the air behind her.

'Aaaaaaaaaaaaaaaahhh,' he yelled at the top of his voice. 'Come on Sis, it's incredible.'

Within seconds they were flying above Ragging Brows forest, skimming the trees in all directions. But Benedict would not budge, and scowled at them from the platform.

'Come on Benedict it's easy,' said Tallitha as she returned to their jumping-off point.

'I'm staying put,' said Benedict folding his arms.

Later, as they made their way back for supper, Tallitha walked next to the Skink. Images of the wild dogs had plagued her for most of the day. She put her arm through Ruker's.

'Where will we sleep tomorrow night?' asked Tallitha, peering below her.

'Don't worry, there's another Skink settlement at the northern edge of the forest. We'll be there before nightfall,' said Ruker putting her arm round Tallitha's shoulders.

But Tallitha was far from reassured. She twisted her hair in and out of her fingers and stared down into the gloomy forest. A dense mass of fir trees and endless woody darkness greeted her gaze as the impenetrable forest seemed to go on and on forever. She shivered and moved closer to the Skink. What if those hounds were down there, the pack circling on the forest floor, just waiting for them to come back down?

*

Morning came and Neeps arrived bright and early.

'Just before we go,' he said, 'you'll need this.'

He took a bottle from his pocket and began dabbing their clothes with a thick green smelly liquid.

'Ugh, what is that smell? It's vile!' said Tallitha, holding her nose.

'Essence of forest I'm afraid,' explained Ruker. 'It's to put the Black Hounds off our scent.'

'Excellent,' said Tyaas. 'Dab away my friend.'

He laughed, twirled around, lifting up his arms so the Skink could dab the disgusting aroma under his armpits and all over his clothes.

'Eugh, Tyaas you are quite revolting' said Tallitha as they fell about laughing at Tyaas's antics.

'Come on, Tallitha, this includes you!' said Neeps rubbing the green gunge on Tallitha's clothes.

Later, with their bags packed snugly on their backs, they left Ruker's home. The Skink fastened the door behind her and they started off on their journey. Despite Benedict's protests they persuaded him to cross the swaying bridges, but he refused to attempt the rope swings.

'If you won't try the tree-skimming it will take much longer,' explained Neeps, exasperated with the foolish boy.

'I'm not doing it. You can't make me,' said Benedict.

His stubbornness meant they had to go the long way round, over the maze of inter-connecting rope bridges. On their journey they met many Skinks, so Ruker and Neeps passed the time of day with their neighbours. To do otherwise for a Skink would be considered the height of bad manners. By early afternoon they had not made much headway at all.

'Come on, Benedict, do hurry up, this is taking forever,' snapped Tyaas.

'I'm doing my best. Ahhhh! But it's so wobbly,' shouted Benedict grabbing hold of Tyaas.

'Hold the ropes and stop looking down,' said Ruker as she steadied Benedict, 'There's the redwood tree, not much further now. Do hurry up, Benedict.'

*

Down and down they climbed, intermittently stopping to coax Benedict out of his fears. Once at the bottom they came to a twisting burrow and crept along the earth floor until they reached the leafy camouflaged shaft at the end.

'Come on, nearly there,' said Ruker pulling herself out of the hole, quickly followed by Neeps.

He extended his hand to Tallitha but as she scrambled through the foliage, a familiar tingle started to churn in the pit of her stomach. She glanced warily at the fading light and swallowed hard. Dusk was falling and the birds were silent. How could this have happened? Damn Benedict!

'It's too dark. Let's go back in the burrow,' pleaded Esmerelda, grabbing hold of Tyaas.

They stood together, huddled against the spectre of the dark wood, desperate to escape the deepening shadows that were gathering in ghostly shapes all around them. Tallitha narrowed her eyes and peered way ahead into the twilight. All she could see was the criss-cross of branches fading into the darkening distance.

'This is your fault, Benedict', said Tallitha sharply. 'If you hadn't been such a scaredy-cat we would have been out of this forest by now.'

'Stop having a go at me,' he whined.

'Shhhh, stop it, both of you', said Tyaas apprehensively, staring into the greyish light.

He pulled up his jacket collar to protect his throat, blinking nervously in the twilight.

Tallitha turned to speak to the Skinks. 'Ruker,' she said softly, 'where are we?'

But Ruker and Neeps were far ahead, ripping through the thickets, gesticulating to the others to follow them. Esmerelda's heart missed a beat, and fear began to eat away inside her. With each slipping second it was becoming more difficult to see the misty path before them. The dark forest grabbed at their resolve and swallowed their flagging spirits. Tyaas called out to the Skinks, but they had vanished amongst the thickly tangled undergrowth.

'What shall we do?' asked Tallitha, looking warily behind her.

She was afraid that something unspeakable was lurking, licking its jaws and sharpening its claws, ready to pounce.

'We have to get out of this dreadful place,' said Benedict looking wildly about him.

The owls hooted overhead, mocking the hapless intruders, seeming to herald their impending doom. Suddenly Tallitha could bear it no longer and she grabbed hold of Tyaas's hand. She raced down the path, keeping her head down, trying not to think about what may be stalking them just beyond the branches.

'Just run, Tyaas, and keep going, no matter what happens!' Her thin voice crackled with fear.

'Quick, follow them,' cried Esmerelda to Benedict.

They fled in raggedy bundles, their clothes flying wildly behind them into the seeping mists of the forest night. Brambles snagged at their hair and tore at their faces as the moon shone down, making strange pointed shadows all about them. Tallitha's uneven breathing caught in the back of her throat as she stumbled headlong over the forest floor.

'Just keep running. We must get ...'

But Tallitha was prevented from finishing what she was about to say. Out of nowhere Ruker lunged at them, roughly pushing them under the bushes. Then Neeps jumped out, dragging Esmerelda and Benedict in with the others and diving in on top of them.

'Ouch! Hey, what's happening?' shouted Tyaas as he struggled to get out from under Neeps, but the Skink held him fast and slapped his hand over the boy's mouth.

He took the bottle from his pocket and began dousing the area around their bodies.

'This should keep them at bay,' he said as he worked furiously, dribbling the green liquid on the ground by the edge of the thicket.

'What do you mean?' asked Tallitha, her voice shaking.

Her frightened eyes shone in the greying light, riveted on the Skink's every move.

'Be quiet,' said Neeps harshly under his breath.

In the earthy darkness of the tightly packed thicket Tallitha could sense that the Skinks were on their guard as their strained bodies protected them against the encroaching danger. Something had scared them. Ruker held one hand over Tallitha's mouth and the other was poised on the hilt of her sword. Neeps put his finger to his lips to signal absolute silence. Tallitha's heart was pounding as she stared at their drawn faces, scratched and dirty from dashing headlong through the brambles as the approaching menace saturated the dark wood all around them.

Suddenly, out of the night came a rustling sound, in the distance at first, then moving swiftly towards them through the undergrowth. Tallitha looked at Ruker for reassurance, desperate that the sounds should not foretell what she feared the most. But Ruker's eyes were filled with terror. The sound was the unmistakable pad-pad-padding of the wild dogs' paws treading on the fallen leaves. It was the nightly rampage of the Black Hounds; the hideous pack was scavenging for fresh prey. Pinpricking fear immobilised Tallitha as she waited for the moment when the dogs would strike. Their low belly-growls filled the night as they snarled at each other, ferreting away in the leaf litter, their paws scratching violently at the dirt, eagerly sniffing for the scent of their next meal.

The sound of the pack came closer as the smell of rancid meat and damp fur filled the air, making Tallitha want to retch. Ruker held her tightly and pulled a scarf around her mouth to suppress her screams. Then the dark blur of the Black Hounds pounded past their hiding place, baying and snarling at the unholy prospect of a feeding frenzy. Suddenly, one of the hounds broke free from the pack and stopped next to their thicket, sniffing the night air and absorbing all the forest smells that surrounded him. The large scruffy hound had been distracted by something. Maybe it had smelt them out!

As Tallitha peered through the branches, shards of moonlight fell on the beast's head and exaggerated the hooded blood-red eyes, as the enormous fangs and the drooling, dripping jaws pointed upwards towards the moon. She could hear the wild dog's dreadful panting, and smell its foul murderous breath. The monster sniffed again, dripping saliva on the forest floor, its fat tongue lolling by the side of its huge brown teeth. Then the hound turned towards the thicket and projected its enormous gaping jaws in their direction. Tallitha stiffened and closed her eyes, waiting for the dog to strike and the pack to seek them out.

Suddenly the wolfish hound sprang into the air and with an appalling deep-throated howl began chasing after the pack. There was a cacophony of terrifying baying and blood-curdling howls as the dogs took chase after some poor creature whose life was extinguished within seconds. The dark forest was filled with the sounds of death, cries of pain, the manic tearing of flesh and a final whimper into bleak nothingness.

*

The friends remained frozen, huddled together against the horrific night. Time passed slowly, punctured by the sound of their shallow breathing and Tallitha's intermittent weeping in the eerie silence. At last, when they were certain the dogs had finished off their prey and had left their part of the forest, the Skinks crawled from under the bushes. Tallitha's bleary face was scratched and smeared with mud and tears. Tyaas starred vacantly into the distance, shocked by what he had witnessed. It was Esmerelda who took charge and roused the bedraggled friends. She passed round the liquorice cordial and they nibbled pieces of Dryad's Saddle as they ran helter-skelter through the deep dark pockets of the forest night.

Later, as the moon shone down and the big buster moths fluttered idly past them, the Skinks pushed them down another muddy hole and they found themselves in the safety of a Skink burrow.

But Tallitha could not stop shaking, nor could she forget the sight of the Black Hound as it stopped by their thicket and licked its terrifying jaws. They had all been a sniff away from death. In the warmth and safety of the Skink village it took Tallitha many hours to fall asleep. Horrific images of the hound's salivating jaws crowded before her eyes whenever she tried to close them.

Eighteen

When Tyaas woke the next morning the full horror of the previous night came flooding back and he hid beneath the covers. Esmerelda busied herself with practical tasks but she too was shaken by the terrible risk they had taken. Ruker's cousin, Kitty, had given them shelter and the Skinks were talking on the balcony of Kitty's home when Tallitha joined them for breakfast.

'Neeps and Tyaas have gone to get provisions. It'll be another day's hike before we get to Startling Caves. How about staying here for the night and starting out tomorrow?' asked Ruker.

Tallitha was relieved to stay away from the terrifying forest for another day.

'I'd like that, if it's okay with Kitty?'

'Sure, I love having my cousin to stay. It's no problem at all.'

Tallitha rested on Kitty's balcony. In the morning light she could see the edge of Ragging Brows forest and, far ahead, the

clouds, like damp cotton wool clinging to the tops of the grey mountains. She closed her eyes and breathed deeply. The thought of ever coming across those hell-hounds again filled her with abject terror.

In the evening they ate a hearty meal of meat patties and blueberry pie, but as the hours ticked by and night approached, the apprehension about descending once more into the forest invaded Tallitha's thoughts. That night she dreamt again of the wild dogs and she cried out fitfully, waking the others.

Eventually morning came and the travellers departed, leaving the safety of the Skink village the way they had entered it. Soon they were through to the edge of the forest, and Tallitha breathed a sigh of relief as she scrambled over the last of the brambles. She hastily looked over her shoulder and caught Esmerelda doing the same.

'I hope the caves will be better than this dreadful forest,' she said as they exchanged glances.

But Esmerelda's face betrayed no emotion. She turned away and said nothing.

The Skinks maintained their gruelling pace and by the turn of the afternoon they had crossed Smear-Seat Knells and were walking alongside Deepdale Beck. As evening drew close, Tallitha became anxious as thoughts of the hell-hounds returned with the ebbing light. The Skinks could smell her fear.

'Where are we staying tonight?' she asked the Skinks hesitantly.

Ruker and Neeps had already planned the location of their camp site.

'By the Ruby Waterfall about a mile from here. We'll be sheltered from the elements. Let's make haste,' said Neeps urgently.

'The wild dogs can't get us, can they?' she asked.

Neeps shook his head. 'We'll be safe, for now,' he said guardedly.

As the sun was setting, they reached the edge of Wycham Elva by way of the steep-sided Hellsnip Pass. Way over the next ridge was the mysterious land of Breedoor.

'This is the border crossing,' said Neeps. 'From here we enter Breedoor and rugged mountain terrain. There's no turning back once we go underground,' he said sounding unusually serious for the happy-go-lucky Skink.

As they scrambled across the stony incline at the foot of the Out-Of-The-Way Mountain, huge rock faces and boulders barred their way. Their ascent became steeper, and as Tallitha looked upwards she saw the immense scale of the grey mountains towering above her.

'We're here,' said Ruker, pointing to a sheltered recess near the entrance to the caves.

Tallitha's heart sank. The dark underground world was down there, lying in wait for them to enter its domain.

*

The camp site was on a ledge overhanging the entrance to Startling Caves. Ruker, ever resourceful, had been collecting wood and she started to make a fire and pull together the makings of a meal. Sweet tea was a treat after their day's march, and they quickly ate their boiled eggs and flat hunks of bread. Tallitha was getting used to feeling extremely hungry after a hard day's trek and then savouring every mouthful of the simple outdoor fare. She was grateful for every bite, and thought back to the extravagant meals she had taken for granted at Winderling Spires … and all the waste.

Ruker explained her plan whilst the others congregated around the crackling camp fire, sipping the last of the hot tea.

'Tomorrow we'll enter Startling Caves. The entrance is fairly even underfoot although on a steep descent. When we arrive in the Weeping Cavern there are a number of routes under the mountains. We know Esmerelda became lost in Weeping Holes, so we'll avoid that path. Do you agree, Esmerelda?'

Esmerelda raised her head and nodded at Ruker.

'Only a small section of the cave system has ever been explored by non-cave dwellers and this knowledge, although scant, has been handed down amongst the folk who live around here. The cave system is many miles deep, twisting back on itself, confusing the best potholers and cavers. Legend has it that the deepest part is at Old Yawning Edges which is thousands of fathom deep. But I warn you, the caves are fraught with danger and are inhabited by those who will not welcome our presence.'

As Ruker continued her description of the caves, the enormity of what they were about to embark on began to take shape in Tallitha's imagination, and her thoughts turned to the creatures that inhabited the underground world. She remembered Esmerelda's reaction to the Mowl by Shivering Water. She had been absolutely terrified. Tyaas, on the other hand, was excited by the prospect of their descent into the cold dark world.

'Wow!' said Tyaas, 'will we see stalagmites and stalactites?'

'You will see all the amazing "tites",' said Ruker laughing.

'The deepest vertical shaft is over a thousand fathoms, and the largest cavern is big enough to hold all of Winderling Spires.'

Ruker suddenly stopped and blushed, realising her mistake.

'You know Winderling Spires?' Esmerelda inquired looking quizzically at the Skink.

'We worked there, like many Skinks, when we were young. I realised who you were when I first saw you. I'm sorry, I should have said something.'

'But why didn't you?' asked Tallitha feeling hurt.

Ruker poked the embers of the fire. 'You might not have wanted to know me; someone who had worked in your gardens. I suppose I felt a bit out of your league.'

Benedict snorted insensitively and Tyaas flashed him a savage look, then punched him into silence. Tallitha's breath caught in the back of her throat and tears came into her eyes. Esmerelda immediately went over and took Ruker's hand.

'My friend, it is us who are not worthy of you. You have been kinder to us than we deserve. You've sheltered us, fed us and saved our lives more than once. We are honoured to be your equals.'

Ruker lifted her eyes from under her heavy fringe and smiled. 'I hoped you'd understand,' she said. 'I have wanted to tell you but I felt ashamed.'

'Never feel that,' cried Tallitha. 'The people who live at the Spires will never be your equal, they are greedy and selfish,' she said hotly.

'She's right,' said Tyaas. 'No one cares about anyone else in that house, except Cissie of course.'

When they began to talk once more, a different stronger relationship prevailed amongst them. In the wilderness, where danger was present at all times, the friends relied on each other for their very existence. Tallitha finally understood that out there in the desolate wild places, the riches of Winderling Spires counted for nothing.

After supper, Ruker and Neeps perked up and began to recount tales of their adventures.

'There was one time when we came upon those sleeping snakes,' said Ruker. 'Do you remember?'

'They didn't 'arf give us a fright. When I nearly …,' said Neeps, continuing with the story, and adding one or two embellishments of his own.

Tyaas was gripped by their tales and his face shone with excitement and anticipation. These were real adventurers, not like his make-believe boyish games. He couldn't get enough and kept urging them to tell him more stories. Esmerelda was unusually quiet. She sat poking the embers of the fire, lost in thought.

'What's up?' asked Tallitha.

'It's being here,' she whispered and glanced at the mouth of the underground world waiting to gobble them up.

'You promised to tell us what happened down there, remember, when we were in your séance room?'

'I know what I said, but now we're really here,' she said, her voice faltering.

They all fell silent, distracted by thoughts of what awaited them in the sunken world.

'Come on Essie,' said Tyaas, buoyed up with the Skinks' heroic tales. 'It can't be that bad, can it?'

The look on Esmerelda's face was enough to turn milk sour. 'Yes Tyaas, it can. Down there,' she said gravely staring in the direction of the caves, 'there are things you couldn't imagine.' She trailed off, swallowing hard.

Her eyes took on a desperate look and she put her head in her hands.

'You have to tell us,' insisted Tallitha.

The Skinks stoked the fire and settled down. They loved a good tale and they knew from the look on Esmerelda's face that this story would take some telling.

'I should have told you earlier. But in truth, I've been avoiding this moment. I desperately wanted to try again to find my cousin Asenathe and I thought if I told you everything, about the real dangers down there, you might change your mind.' She bit her lip and took hold of Tallitha's hand.

They huddled round the fire and Esmerelda began.

'Remember, I told you I'd been absent for many months and that the Cave-Shroves looked after me.' Esmerelda's face looked haunted as she began to recount her darkest memories. 'In the hours after I became separated from Asenathe I was distraught and out of my mind. I'd lost any sense of direction and wandered deep into the heart of the underground chambers. Round and round I went, dazed and quite mad with grief. I later found out that, somehow in my agitated state, I had entered a strange subterranean maze and any hope of making my way out unharmed was negligible. This place was the sunken world of Asphodel, the powerful Queen of the Dark Reaches.'

'Asphodel!' shouted Ruker in astonishment, 'we've heard of her evil ways.'

The Skinks exchanged glances as Esmerelda continued.

'The deep maze, a labyrinth of complex tunnel systems, protects Asphodel's upper kingdom from unwanted entry from below. The caves are patrolled by the Groats, Asphodel's hideous creatures of the lower world. I learned later that Asphodel lives above ground, although the exact location is unknown. About the second day of my wandering I was captured by a Groat patrol and taken to one of their holding stations to await my fate. Days went by and I learned from the other prisoners about the dark world beneath the Out-Of-The-Way Mountains. The underground kingdom is ruled by two powerful tribes that constantly vie for power. Sometimes they work together when it suits their purposes, and at other times they fight, capturing and occupying parts of the other's territories. The Groats, I have already mentioned, the other tribe is the Murk Mowl.

Tallitha jumped at the mention of their name. 'You mean those dreadful creatures we saw by Shivering Water?'

Esmerelda nodded. 'Now you can understand why the sight of them terrified me.'

'Hang on, I'm confused,' said Tyaas. 'I thought you said that Lord Frintal made the rules down there,' he said pointing below him.

'Yes he does. Well, they all do. They have an unholy alliance that keeps the tripartite in place; Lord Frintal and the Morrow Swarm, Asphodel and the Groats, and the Murk Mowl.'

'What's a tripartite?' asked Tyaas.

'It's a power-sharing arrangement, sometimes good, but on this occasion extremely wicked, where three different groups share the power and the spoils within their orbit. If one group does a bad thing they turn a blind eye, knowing they are all as evil as each other. They play games, lying and cheating all the time,' said Esmerelda.

'After a few weeks languishing in this hellish prison, I was taken to Asphodel so she could decide what to do with me. The caves were a grim sight, filled with the lost souls who did the Queen's bidding. Asphodel never materialised and one of her Groat Captains saw me instead. I asked about Asenathe and the Captain laughed in my face. He told me that Asenathe was gone forever and I would never see her again. I was to be sold to the Murk Mowl, and he invited one of their Chieftains to inspect me and offer a price. He was a horrific creature, much worse than the Groats, with stinking breath and translucent skin as though the colour had leaked out. I knew the fate that awaited me would be worse than death.'

Esmerelda hands began to shake.

'Poor Essie, why didn't you tell someone?' asked Tallitha.

Esmerelda shook her head and handed round the liquorice cordial. Everyone took the reviving drink apart from Benedict who was staring below him. He was transfixed by the cave entrance.

'Later I was taken to a dark underbelly of a prison. Unbeknown to me the politics of the underworld was working in my favour as the Groats fell out with the Murk Mowl over unpaid border tithes, and Asphodel forgot about me in the many battles and skirmishes that followed. The prison was an unruly place. Order broke down and one day when the guards were distracted, I escaped.'

'You escaped! Wow, that's amazing,' exclaimed Tyaas excitedly.

'This isn't some make-believe tale. I did it because I had no choice; it wasn't some act of heroism. Don't be fooled, Tyaas, about what it's really like down there. Make no mistake, it's truly horrific,' she put her hand on the boy's arm. 'It was escape into the unknown, or certain death at the hands of the Mowl.'

Tyaas coughed nervously and Tallitha returned Esmerelda's steady gaze. Her terrified eyes shone in the firelight and Esmerelda continued.

'Some time later, the Cave-Shroves found me wandering. I was out of my mind. I lived with them for many months and when I regained my strength they helped me back to Wycham Elva. They became my true friends. I learned Ennish and

Shroveling during this time.' Esmerelda fell silent.

'That's some tale,' said Ruker. 'I've heard about the strange tribes from the underworld, but in Breedoor you never can tell myth from reality.'

'Ain't that a fact,' said Neeps. 'There are many stories of adventurers getting lost down there,' he added, nodding towards the caves.

'That's why I'm scared now we're here,' she whispered. 'Having to go back into that unrelenting darkness fills me with terror,' said Esmerelda, turning her weary face towards the black mouth of the cave.

'Well, there's no turning back now,' said Ruker, 'let's get some sleep. We've a hard journey ahead of us. Things will look better in the morning.'

The travellers tucked themselves down for the night, each one absorbed by their own particular fear that Esmerelda's story had awakened. Again Tallitha could not sleep. She was distracted by a series of whooshing sounds as the nightly bat flight filled the air. The dark blue sky was covered with hundreds of bats, their winged silhouettes blotting out the moonlight. Benedict crawled from under his blanket and huddled next to Tallitha to watch the nocturnal spectacle.

'Do you think they're vampire bats?' asked Tallitha nervously.

'Maybe they're the Hairy-Legged Vampire Bats, waaaahhh,' teased Benedict, making a ghostly wail.

'Stop it, you're not funny. Go away!' she shouted giving her cousin a thump.

'They might get tangled in your hair,' teased Benedict.

Tallitha tucked her head under the blanket and gave Benedict a final kick. She wasn't worried about the bats, but the thought that somewhere, deep in the caves, lurked the creatures of Esmerelda's tale, the Groats, the Murk Mowl and the Cave-Shroves. The thought of descending into the dark place filled her with foreboding, and the sweet sanctuary of sleep evaded her as she tossed and turned and tried to block out the distant howling of the wild dogs on their nightly rampage in Ragging Brows Forest.

Nineteen

Esmerelda's story made Ruker all the more determined to organise the ramshackle party, so after breakfast she gathered everyone together. As she outlined the dangers that lay ahead, the boys started to snigger.

'This is a serious business you two, so stop laughing and pay attention. The other night in the forest was a close shave. We must be more careful.'

'Sorry,' muttered Tyaas, smirking behind his hand.

'Every climbing or pot-holing expedition has a leader. That's me, folks, and what I say goes. Neeps and I know the dangers ahead so he'll be my deputy. I don't want any argument when I give instructions. I'll use this yellow chalk on the cave walls so we can follow each other and retrace our steps if necessary.'

Benedict was not paying attention. He was an unlikely adventurer with no stomach for the thrill of exploration. Ruker could not make him out at all.

'Are we avoiding Weeping Holes?' asked Esmerelda. 'It's on the map, but I've become lost there before.'

Ruker nodded. 'We'll follow your old route to the Weeping Cavern, by way of the Shapeless Map but no further. So I need you up here next to me. Benedict, you'll come next, with Tallitha and Tyaas following, and Neeps bringing up the rear. Okay?'

'Aye, aye Captain' said Tyaas sarcastically.

'Stop it Tyaas. This isn't a game!' snapped Ruker. 'Now let's rope up and remember to put on an extra layer of clothing because it will be cold.'

'There'll be all kinds of insects and animals down there. Remember it's their habitat, not ours, so we need to show respect,' said Neeps. 'Cave entrances can be home to bears and wildcats. If you see anything untoward, follow my lead and give them a wide berth. Come on, let's go.'

They stepped behind the wall of water and into the dank, dripping cave. The ground was slippery, and the air was filled with a fine wet spray that hit their faces. Tallitha stared round in the gloom and shivered. The cold dark cave was even more inhospitable than she had imagined.

'Use your lanterns, it will be pitch-black from now on,' said Neeps urgently.

Immediately the narrow pathway sheared to one side as they descended deeper and deeper into the coal-black darkness. Fat scaly beetles and leggy insects scurried away and black rats nosed out of their holes to see who had disturbed their slumbers. The cave opened out into a sheer drop and the travellers were forced to crawl around a narrow ledge. Below, they saw a group of wildcats catching fish at the edge of a deep pool. The cats eyed them suspiciously, hissing intermittently, but were more interested in catching their breakfast than stalking their visitors.

Down and down they trudged, ever deeper into the dripping, cold darkness. The light from their lanterns randomly danced along the cavern walls revealing patterns in the rocks the colour of wet seals. As Tallitha rounded a corner she noticed some chalky scrawled writing and tugged on Ruker's arm.

'They're warnings, messages from one explorer to another,' she explained.

'Can they help us with the riddle?' asked Tyaas.

'Not that I can see,' said Esmerelda translating the script on the walls. 'They're about the Mowl,' she said guardedly.

'What do they say?' asked Tallitha.

'They explain where the Mowl have struck,' explained Esmerelda.

'Struck?'

'Where they've killed. It's best not to know. Now come on.'

Suddenly the path became narrower and the ceiling dropped downwards. Dripping, soaking darkness surrounded them and in the slimy wetness underfoot, Esmerelda slipped.

'Ahhhh, my ankle,' she winced as she fell to the floor, dragging Tallitha down with her.

The noise of her piercing scream reverberated through the maze of tunnels, bouncing off the cave walls, echoing into nothingness. Esmerelda hurriedly applied the Barrenwort salve to her ankle.

'I'll be fine. Sorry I cried out. You okay?' she asked Tallitha.

The girl's face was etched with fear. Being down in the steely-dark world was terrifying. Tallitha helped Esmerelda bandage her ankle and they followed the others in silence.

All at once the Skinks stopped as the path abruptly forked into two uninviting black holes, one much bigger than the other. Ruker and Neeps lifted their lanterns and began surveying both entrances.

'Which way?' asked Tallitha, hoping it was the larger of the two holes.

'Down here to the right,' said Esmerelda, peering at the map.

Tallitha recoiled. The thought of squeezing into the cramped space made her heart pound.

'Sorry Tallitha,' said Ruker, 'but the other tunnel will take us back to the surface.'

'But it's so dark,' she whispered, peering into the blackness.

'Crouch down on to your hands and knees. Blow out your lanterns.'

'What?' exclaimed Tallitha, 'but it's horrible in there.'

'You won't be able to manage a lantern in the narrow gaps,' explained Neeps, 'we'll be next to each other.'

'But …,' said Tallitha.

'No "buts" Tallitha,' instructed Ruker forcefully and led the way into the seeping hole.

*

'Where are we?' asked Tyaas as he crawled into the dark wet tunnel behind Neeps.

He could hear the Skink's heavy breathing in the slate-cold tomb.

'Lava tubes formed through volcanic activity, millions of years ago,' Neeps coughed as grit entered his mouth.

They crawled through the tunnel, pushing their backpacks in front of them as the gap narrowed alarmingly. The tubes were rough and their hands became lacerated from the jagged rocks on the tunnel floor. Ruker called back instructions to them.

'Okay, there's a twist ahead of you. Lie flat and be warned, it's very tight.'

Tight! How could it get any tighter? Tallitha wondered. The sheer weight of the rock formation bore down and she felt the full force of nature all around her. As the space became ever more compact, she began to feel panicky as the rock face pressed down and scraped her scalp. She imagined being trapped in the cold stone ground that would forever be her grave. Benedict was the first to complain. Tallitha heard his rapid, frightened breathing coming up behind her in the darkness.

'It's just like a coffin. I can't breathe. It's so awful. What if we get stuck?' he cried out.

'Just stay calm. I don't like it either. It'll soon be over,' said Tallitha trying to keep her nerve steady.

'Let's go back. I can't bear it,' pleaded Benedict.

'Stop it!' said Tallitha pushing on his head with her feet, 'you have to keep going.'

'You're nearly through. Keep moving and you'll come out into a cave,' whispered Ruker hoarsely into the darkness, willing the terrified Benedict to calm down.

So Benedict closed his eyes and inched forward, whimpering all the while. At last the lava tube came to an end and they climbed out into the great expanse of the Weeping Cavern, their clothes sodden and their faces smeared in dirt. They hurriedly lit their lanterns and stared at the enormous space before them. It was filled with hundreds of stalagmites and stalactites and Tyaas could not believe his eyes.

'It's fantastic!' he said rubbing grit from the palms of his hands.

'Come, follow me,' said Ruker, 'but be careful underfoot, it's wet.'

They edged round the huge cavern, a small band of wary bedraggled explorers, dwarfed by the enormity of the grand cathedral-like space, tiptoeing onto the flat stones as rivulets of water ran this way and that under their feet. Tyaas lifted his lantern to scan the crevices of the ancient roof more clearly. He was fascinated by the sheer scale of the cavern, with its fingers of multicoloured gnarled rock sticking up like tentacles all around him. The rippling arched roof gleamed in the lantern light as copper, silver and golden seams of colour glowed overhead, while the ever-dripping droplets of water plopped into dark pools in the cavern floor, echoing into the sunken distance.

Something intermittently bright caught Tyaas's eye, just for a second. There it was again, blue and shimmering, like sunlight through flimsy butterfly wings. Tyaas motioned to the others and pointed upwards. The dappling azure lights danced overhead, following them as they walked through the cave.

'They're like tiny stars. What are they?' asked Tyaas scanning the roofline.

'I'm not sure,' said Esmerelda cautiously, grabbing Tallitha's hand, 'but I don't like it.'

'Over here,' said Ruker, making for a gap in the rocks.

They followed the Skinks behind a fissure in the rock and waited. Neeps fumbled in the backpacks. 'We may as well eat,' he said sharing the dried fruits and biscuits.

But Esmerelda was not hungry. She stared distractedly around her.

'What is it?' asked Tallitha nervously.

'I've seen those blue lights before. I'm going back to see if they jog my memory.'

But before she could leave, Ruker pulled her back.

'You aren't going anywhere alone. If for some reason we're delayed, make camp here,' she instructed the others.

'Can't I come?' pleaded Tyaas.

'No, definitely not,' said Ruker firmly.

Ruker ignored Tyaas's continued pleas, took a lantern and left the shelter with Esmerelda at her side. Once out of earshot, Esmerelda confided in Ruker.

'Those lights are harbingers of something, I saw them when I was here with Asenathe, but I can't remember what happened,' she said, sounding perplexed.

They walked round the perimeter of the cave searching the roof crevices with the lantern, but the lights had vanished. The central cavern had a number of smaller enclaves and recesses. Esmerelda's curiosity got the better of her.

'What's in here?'

Without waiting for Ruker's reply, Esmerelda slipped through the opening.

'No Esmerelda. Don't go in there!' exclaimed Ruker bounding after her.

But it was too late. When Ruker followed Esmerelda she was standing with her hand over her mouth, her desperate eyes reflecting the ghastly sight in front of her. She pointed to a corner of the cave where two rotting corpses were bound together in death, locked in irons, their hollowed eye sockets betraying the time they had lain there, side by side, in their grizzly grave. The smell of putrid flesh and decay filled the space.

'What is this dreadful place?' asked Esmerelda, horrified at the sight before her.

'I tried to stop you. It's a Murk turrow. They keep their prey in here and feast on their bodies,' explained Ruker. 'It's a gruesome pantry for the Murk Mowl and a warning to intruders.'

Esmerelda's body trembled with shock. The loathing she felt for the Murk Mowl came bubbling up as she stumbled outside the turrow and was violently sick.

'We can't tell the others,' she cried, wiping her hand across her mouth, 'it's so vile.'

On their return through the cavern Ruker filled the flasks

and Esmerelda slapped water in her face to get rid of the smell of death. As she stood by the side of the pool, she tugged at Ruker's shirt and pointed up at the purple-blue lights moving in and out of the rock fissures high above them.

'There they are again,' whispered Esmerelda, apprehensively.

'Come on, let's get back to the others,' shouted Ruker, quickly grabbing Esmerelda's hand.

They jumped over the rivulets of water with the blue lights moving in and out of the high fissures above them. But now they were certain that the lights were chasing them.

'Quickly, they're gaining on us,' shouted Esmerelda desperately, as she leapt from stone to stone.

Suddenly, in a series of erratic movements, the blue lights took on grotesque bodily forms as they sprang from behind the rock face, leaping out and revealing their hideous grey torsos. Bounding downwards in swift zigzag movements the creatures scaled the rock face, landing in the encampment below and emitting a series of horrific high-pitched battle cries.

'Run everyone, Tallitha! Tyaas! They're coming!' screamed Esmerelda, but it was too late.

As Ruker raced into the encampment she saw a horde of grizzly grey creatures pinning down her friends. The fat Groats turned and hissed, spitting at Ruker and flashing their shocking blue eyes.

'Don't look into their eyes, keep your heads down!' shouted Esmerelda recalling their true potency.

The azure lights were the eyes of the captors who had

mesmerised Esmerelda and kidnapped Asenathe. Her cousin had not just vanished in the caves, the Groats had stolen her away and had bewitched Esmerelda, leaving her for dead.

Ruker immediately averted her eyes and punched one of the Groats hard in the back. He screeched and lurched sideways, freeing Neeps who pounced on another Groat and buried a knife deep in his bulbous leg.

'Take that!' he shouted as he pushed the knife deep into the flesh and pulled it out dripping with blood and gore from the Groat's thigh.

'Arrrrrrrrrrrrrrrrrrrr,' the creature wailed, spitting obscenities at the Skink.

There was a desperate sound of howling and moaning as the Groat clutched his bloody leg and fled, scaling the wall with his sucker-feet, dripping ooze and blood as he limped up the cave wall moaning and screeching. Ruker pulled her sword, lunged for another Groat and sliced his arm in one deft movement, blood bursting in fast spurts from the deep wound.

'Got ya!' she shouted, spinning round and landing a series of blows on the back of a Groat's head.

The cave was a mess of flying bloody bodies, flashing swords and a cacophony of terrifying screaming and shouting. Tallitha leapt on a Groat who had Tyaas by the throat, but the creature flung her roughly to the ground, kicking her against a rock. She fell dazed to the floor as the Groat put his sword against her throat. Quick as a flash, Esmerelda and the Skinks fell on the Groat and dragged him away from Tallitha whilst trying to wrench Tyaas from his grasp. The Groat held the boy fast, hissed at the encroaching Skinks and delivered

Esmerelda a glancing blow on the side of the head. The throng of Groats regrouped, assembled in a corner of the camp then took flight, carrying Tyaas, limp and bleeding, up the cave wall. Tallitha watched helplessly as her brother disappeared before her eyes.

'They've got Tyaas!' shouted Tallitha incredulously. 'Help him Ruker, Neeps help him!'

Ruker grabbed her sword and began to scale the cavern wall but the sheer rock was impossible for the Skink to climb. By the time she had reached the first footholds, Tyaas's body was being dragged up the rock face high above her. Then the boy vanished behind a collection of stalagmites.

'No, please no!' shouted Tallitha, 'Tyaas, Tyaas – let him go, I beg you!'

The Groat, who had secreted Tyaas away, turned and leered at Tallitha, hanging by his long springy arms, sneering devilishly in her face, before slithering quickly away.

'Where's he gone? What will they do to him?' wailed Tallitha. 'Will they kill him?'

'Not while we have this one, they won't!' said Ruker.

She pushed her foot firmly on the neck of an oily Groat who writhed on the cavern floor, foaming at the mouth and uttering Groat curses.

'Shut up and keep still or you'll feel this steel in your back!' yelled Ruker.

'Benedict, bind his arms and wrap his suckers tight so he can't escape.'

'Ohhh, he smells awful!' said Neeps holding his nose.

'Aye, he looks pitiful now his friends have gone,' said Ruker, 'but he still has the power to transfix us with those eyes. Blindfold him!'

Esmerelda moaned in pain, and Tallitha began searching for the Barrenwort salve and the bitter moonflower.

'Essie, drink this, can you move?'

Esmerelda pulled herself up, giving the Groat a severe kick with her foot.

'Come on, Benedict. Tie him to that rock. Tallitha, you too,' insisted Neeps.

Tallitha leapt to her feet and began binding the Groat's arms behind his back.

'Where have they taken him?' she shouted at the Groat.

His dark oily skin glistened with sweat in the lantern light. The skin hung in folds around the Groat's face and his mouth was a gruesome envelope of skin flaps and bubbling spit. His ears sat like grey cauliflowers on each side of his bald head. As he panted, he revealed his razor-sharp teeth in two rows on the top and bottom of his mouth. The Groat was injured but refused to speak.

'Tell me!' she cried kicking him.

'They won't harm Tyaas as long as we have this creature,' said Benedict helping Tallitha bind the Groat's arms.

Ruker raised her sword. 'We've asked you once! Where have they taken him?'

With her sword pressed up against the Groat's throat, Ruker was poised to strike. But still the Groat refused to speak.

'Shall we kill him now? Finish him off?' suggested Neeps with his knife pushed under the Groat's ribcage. Ruker was enraged, but shook her head.

'First he must tell us where they've taken Tyaas!' she shouted, drawing blood.

The Groat moaned as the blood trickled down between the fleshy folds of his neck.

'Hold off Ruker!' said Esmerelda finally coming to. 'If he won't talk of his own free will, I'll make him.'

She took a phial and began to make a potion of Stinkhorn and Amethyst Deceiver to loosen the Groat's tongue. She added water, crushed the fungi and shook the mixture furiously. The Groat pulled away, clamping his mouth tightly shut.

'Neeps, force open his jaw,' demanded Esmerelda. 'Ruker, hold him!'

The Skinks held down the Groat, forcing his mouth open with the point of a knife while Esmerelda poured the green foaming liquid into the gaping hole. The Groat choked and gagged as the liquid ran down his throat. Then his eyes lolled back in his head as the potion began to take effect.

'Come on, he's ready now,' said Neeps, pulling the creature to a sitting position and revealing his gruesome body, covered in raised sores and battle scars which had healed badly over the years.

'Tell us where they've taken our friend!' Esmerelda demanded, shaking him.

'I'll take his blindfold off. He can't do us any harm in this state,' said Neeps.

The Groat stirred but refused to speak. His bulging hooded eyes barely flickered and bloody saliva ran from his fat grey lips. Esmerelda held his chin and slapped his face.

'Where have they taken him? Answer me!' she shouted.

But the Groat refused to speak. Ruker slapped him again. 'Answer her, now!'

Ruker pushed the knife into the Groat's belly. He groaned and blood began oozing from his wound.

'Speak, or I'll kill you!' shouted Neeps. 'I'll slice your throat from your chin, down to your belly!' he shouted, sticking the blade into the Groat's neck.

'Arrgggh, wait,' he muttered, 'to the … Sour Pit Chimneys,' the Groat spat out the words like bubbling venom.

'Why have they taken him there?' shouted Esmerelda into the Groat's face.

'It's where w-we take prisoners,' he spluttered, coughing up more blood.

'Where will they keep him?'

The Groat flopped forward and Ruker slapped him again. He moaned and moved his heavy head to one side.

'In the prison caves. On the n-northern r-r-rim,' he said slurring.

Esmerelda slapped the Groat to bring him to consciousness. 'Keep awake, do you hear me? How do we find him?'

The Groat let out a deep, unsettling chuckle. 'Errr, he'll be n-near the top, you'll have to climb down.'

'Is he lying?' asked Esmerelda looking round at the others.

'Will they harm him?' asked Tallitha anxiously.

'Maybe,' taunted the Groat. 'Depends …,' he smirked in his drugged stupor and his head slumped to his chest.

Tallitha made a whimpering noise and clutched Esmerelda's hand.

'Shush, Tallitha,' said Esmerelda, 'it'll be okay.'

Esmerelda stood in front of the Groat and lifted his head. This was her opportunity and she was not about to waste it.

'Now listen to me! Wake up!' she demanded, 'you're going to tell me what these words mean.'

The Groat smelled of stale meat and sweat and as Esmerelda moved closer to him, she took a deep breath. Then she uttered the words that Tallitha had seen written down in the trance.

'The Tors are twinned, below and above,
Underground, go backwards through the TORS.'

The Groat refused to answer. Esmerelda hit him on the side of his head. He winced and began to slur, his speech befuddled by the drug.

'It means … errr … the r-route under the m-m-mountains,' said the Groat moaning and coughing up blood.

He vomited on the floor.

'What's the meaning of the riddle?' demanded Esmerelda, disgusted at the vile creature.

The Groat's head fell forward, and Esmerelda punched him again. 'Tell me or we'll finish you off!'

'You have to go b-b-backwards,' said the Groat his eyelids flickering open, revealing his blue eyes now dulled with the drug.

'What do you mean, go backwards?'

The Groat chuckled drunkenly and blood trickled from his fat lips.

'Come on!' shouted Ruker pushing her sword into the Groat's belly.

The Groat moaned in pain and knocked the sword away.

'The l-l-letters,' the Groat winced, 'turn the letters backwards in the TORS.'

Esmerelda's face lit up as she grasped the meaning. 'You mean find the locations with the letters, but backwards, as in S-R-O-T?'

The Groat grimaced and nodded.

'Yesss, follow them in s-s-sequence,' said the Groat groggily.

'Which places?' shouted Esmerelda shaking him.

He slumped forward and she hit him again. He groaned, lifted his head and blood oozed from his neck. The friends crowded round to hear every utterance from the vile creature.

'First, to Sour Pit Chimneys,' said the Groat.

'Then where? Come on, tell us!' she shouted.

'Then to ... to Raven Stones.'

The Groat slumped forward. Esmerelda lifted his chin and shook him.

'Old Yawning Edges,' The Groat chuckled wickedly.

'Then what?' asked Esmerelda.

The Groat smiled a sickly, vicious smile that made his fat lips bulge to reveal his sharp carnivorous teeth.

'Then to the T-T-Throes of Woe,' he said chuckling malevolently, 'but you'll never make it that far.' He licked his lips and sneered.

'Tell me about the Throes of Woe. What dangers lurk there?' demanded Esmerelda becoming frustrated with the Groat's insinuations.

'You'll find out,' said the Groat curling his lip and snarling.

Ruker suddenly hit the Groat with the butt of her sword and he fell solidly in a heap on the floor.

'Hey, what did you do that for?' demanded Benedict.

'We don't want him overhearing our plans. Also I really don't like him,' said Ruker giving the Groat a kick with her foot. 'He won't wake up for a good while.'

'We'll take him with us. We can barter with his life if necessary,' said Esmerelda.

Neeps sat thoughtfully, wiping the blood from his sword. 'The Groats could have killed us, so why didn't they?' asked Neeps. 'There's something afoot and no mistake,' he said nervously.

Ruker nodded at her friend. 'They outnumbered us for sure. These caves hold many secrets, there's something here we don't understand,' said Ruker, warily.

'There's evil. I can feel it in my bones,' said Neeps. 'The evil is waiting and biding its time. It's old and vengeful, and it will harm us if it can. Something devilish is going on,' he said, his words trailing off.

'We've only been to the edge of Sour Pits before, but no further,' said Ruker, turning to Esmerelda.

'Aye, and that was bad enough,' interrupted Neeps. 'That means we'll have to go down the Shrunken Butts.'

'Then the map is no good from here on in,' she said sadly pushing it into her pack. 'No wonder I became lost so often.'

Neeps tied his ponytail into a stump at the back of his head, and looked nervously into the darkness. The way through the caves had been revealed to them but they still had one pressing problem. They had to find Tyaas and rescue him. Ruker knew the only way to the Sour Pit Chimneys was through a narrow pothole. She braced herself to forewarn the others about the next stage of their perilous journey.

'We'll need all our strength to deal with what's ahead of us. The way to Sour Pit Chimneys is down a narrow dark pothole, called Shrunken Butts. I'll go first, roped up, and make a series of bolt-points where I'll leave small tallow pots to guide you. Neeps will send down three bags, hiding the rest up here. I'll wait at the end of each section and manoeuvre the bags through. Then you'll follow, one by one and Neeps will come last with the Groat. Does anyone have any questions?'

No one spoke. The prospect of descending into the dark pothole was almost too much to bear. Ruker and Neeps prepared the ropes for the long pitch down, tying hitches and knots in several places. Tallitha watched as the Skinks busied themselves organising the equipment. She could tell they were nervous and afraid of what was yet to come. Tallitha twisted her hair in and out of her fingers, while a heavy feeling of dread gnawed away inside her.

Twenty

When Tyaas woke some hours later, his head throbbed and his body ached. He winced as he lifted his hands to his temple and felt something warm and sticky. He licked his fingers and tasted his own salty blood. In the gloomy half-light he crawled towards the edge of the cave and peered over the deep shaft. Down below he could hear the distant sounds of the Groats in the darkness. Then he remembered the eyes of the vile creatures, and how they had snatched him from his friends. Tentatively, he reached down and touched the smooth sides of the vertical shaft. There was no way up or down without a rope, and even then it would be near impossible. Tyaas saw a faint greyish light coming from the gaping entrance at the head of the shaft. He slumped on his back, scared and miserable. Now he was a prisoner of the Groats.

Later, when all was still, a Groat guard left food and a strange-tasting amber drink. Tyaas quickly ate the pot of sloppy

food, trying not to think about the lumpy ingredients floating at the bottom. Almost immediately he yawned and curled up on the cave floor. He dreamt of strange frightening creatures and attempting to escape but making no headway, his feet too heavy to move, like weighted stone.

*

The space in the lava tubes was generous compared to the narrow twists and turns of the Shrunken Butts. They lowered themselves into the pothole one by one, following the guide rope and the small yellow chalk marks glowing in the tallow lights. They grasped at the indentations in the rock wall whilst using the rope to guide them down the inky cavity. About halfway down, Benedict began to shake.

'The thought of what's below us is terrifying,' he moaned, 'I hate the dark,' he whimpered.

'Then stop thinking about it and don't look down. Just keep going,' said Tallitha inching further down the abysmal hole.

'I'm stuck,' he bleated. 'I can't move, something's caught!'

'What's going on?' Ruker whispered hoarsely from the tallow point.

She shone the lantern up the pothole and it alighted on Tallitha's desperate face peering down the shaft.

'It's Benedict,' she whispered. 'He says he's stuck.'

All they could hear was Benedict's whining in the darkness. Benedict was a complete drain. Tallitha felt the rope tighten around her waist as Esmerelda began her descent.

'Essie, can you help Benedict? He's got himself snagged somehow.'

They waited, clinging to the rock face as the boy continued whingeing, while Esmerelda unhooked his jacket. They heard her speak to him, encouraging him to move down the shaft. Then Tallitha felt the rope slacken and she began her descent to the next tallow point.

Slowly they eased their way down the shaft, snagging their clothes on the rocks and gasping as the rope tightened and pulled them up sharply. The pothole echoed to the sound of Ruker's voice as she guided them through the impossibly tight spaces.

'Okay, move left. That's it. Now further right and drop down to the next foothold. That's right,' she said, urging them round the tight bends.

Even with the blindfold, the Groat had no trouble with the pothole. His rubbery body was made to navigate the tight spaces as he elongated and stretched round the trickiest bends. He was tethered to Neeps and the Groat had to keep stopping so the Skink could catch up with him. Neeps was a skilled knife-thrower, a fact he had shared with the Groat before their descent. Eventually Tallitha and Benedict reached the bottom and eased their way out of the hellhole.

'That's the sound of Sour Pit Chimneys,' said Ruker, gesticulating towards the roaring water.

They crawled along a narrow ledge with the turbulent waterfalls flowing beneath them.

'It's vast. Please tell me we don't have to go down there!' pleaded Benedict.

'Yes, I'm afraid we do. Some of the shafts are beneath the water. We'll have to manoeuvre round those without falling down one,' explained Ruker.

'Tyaas is somewhere down there,' said Tallitha despondently. 'Maybe he's in one of the northern chimneys? What do you think, Neeps?'

Neeps tuned to the blindfolded Groat and prodded him. 'We're standing over the Sour Pits now. Is our friend in the last shaft?'

The Groat grunted.

'How can we trust him?' asked Esmerelda suspiciously. 'He could be lying to us.'

'We have no choice. If Tyaas isn't there he knows we'll kill him, don't you?' said Ruker, pushing the Groat with the point of her sword.

They had to find Tyaas before it was too late.

'I can see why they're called chimneys,' said Benedict. 'The rock formation is impressive.'

'Oh do shut up, Benedict, you've caused enough bother for one day,' snapped Tallitha. 'Tyaas is a prisoner somewhere down there. Stop wasting time on stupid geology.'

Whilst the others discussed how to tackle the next stage of the journey, Benedict's face burned with rage. Ruker roped them up and one by one they climbed down the steep rock face, apart from Benedict who needed the Skinks to steady him all the way down.

'Come on Benedict, nearly there,' said Neeps guiding the shaking boy from one crevasse to the next.

'Ahhhh, my feet are slipping,' he shouted.

'Be calm, we've got you,' insisted Ruker.

Within a short time they were all assembled on the top of the chimney shafts. Only then did the enormity of the sieve-like rock structure become apparent. Water rushed in fast flowing streams at their feet and roared down several of the larger shafts, as they made their way towards the northern chimneys above the water level.

'Be careful, it's slippery,' said Neeps, 'and avoid the streams, they're deeper than they look.'

They held on to one another, using the stepping stones over the streams and keeping well away from the steep slippery edges of the shafts.

'What's down there?' asked Tallitha, leaning over the edge of one of the dry chimney shafts. It was sheer, dark, and very deep.

'Groats,' said Ruker abruptly. 'They live down there and come up here to fish.'

'I don't want to see any more of those horrible creatures,' said Tallitha pulling a face.

But already it was too late. From the time Tyaas had been taken, the Groats had been tracking their intruders.

*

After wading through the shallow water above the raging

waterfalls, they reached the head of the northern chimney. The scale of the shaft was breathtaking, broad and wide across its cavernous mouth, and endless into the black bottomless silence. Calling out to Tyaas was out of the question.

'Let me abseil down!' said Tallitha excitedly. 'It isn't far to the first cave entrance. Look there,' she said pointing down the shaft.

'It's much too risky,' said Ruker.

'I'm the smallest and it does make sense,' insisted Tallitha.

'I'm not sure,' said Esmerelda, 'it's so dangerous. What if you fall?'

'Essie, I have to find my brother.'

Esmerelda didn't argue further. She knew what it was like to have lost someone.

'Come on, I'll be fine. I can do it.'

Ruker relented. There was no other way of reaching the boy.

'Okay, we'll winch you from this rock and hold you with our combined strength.'

Neeps held the Groat with the knife at his throat while Esmerelda and Ruker made the abseil point firm and secured Tallitha to the winching tackle.

'Wish me luck!'

Tallitha leant back over the vast drop below as the others counterbalanced her weight.

'Pull on the rope three times if you find him and four if you don't. We'll signal with two pulls when we've received the information. If there's danger and we want you to stay put we'll pull five times,' said Ruker. 'Ready. Okay?'

'Easy-peasy, piece of cake,' said Tallitha full of bravado.

'Be careful, please be careful,' said Esmerelda nervously.

The drop below was cavernous and certain death awaited Tallitha if she slipped or if she got stuck. She knew they had no rescue plan for that. As the travellers held their lanterns over the fathomless drop, with a bounce and a smile Tallitha stepped from the edge, fearless and determined to find her brother. The chimney wall was smooth, and relatively easy to abseil down as long as she didn't think about the drop below. Tallitha soon got into a repetitive rhythm – land, bounce and jump – land, bounce and jump – as the others held the rope and watched her disappear into the sooty blackness.

Tallitha's heart raced furiously as she bumped down the chimney wall.

'Eurgh! Eurgh! Don't look down, don't look down,' she said to herself as she abseiled further into the pit. Desperate grunting noises emanated from deep within her throat as she landed momentarily and then pushed off again over the abyss. Her arm muscles ached and her thighs trembled but she kept up the gruelling pace.

'Eurgh, eurgh – just a bit further,' she whispered to herself, 'then it'll be over.'

The further down she went, the darker it became, with only flashes of light from the lanterns above to guide her. The intermittent beams made jagged patterns down the chimney wall, momentarily revealing the cave entrances within her reach. Tallitha had to be as fast as lightning to absorb sufficient information as the beam of light struck the rock face to guide her on the descent. She had a split-second of light, then she had to spring further down the black shaft – land, bounce and jump …

At last a cave entrance came into view, and with a determined manoeuvre she landed nimbly inside the small round space. Her hands were sore from rope burns and her legs buckled underneath her as she slumped to the floor. Slowly her eyes became accustomed to the darkness and she peered nervously around the space. But it was empty. Tyaas was nowhere to be seen. Downhearted she walked to the edge and looked up at the others but it was pitch-black apart from the occasional beam of light flashing in the heavy darkness. She tugged on the rope four times. At the top of the shaft Ruker and Neeps looked despondently at each other and pulled twice more on the rope.

But Tallitha was not about to give up. She had noticed another cave just below her. She spat on her palms, rubbing her stinging hands together and steeled herself for another perilous decent. Once again she stepped out over the abyss and began abseiling down the chimney shaft.

'What's she doing?' asked Neeps as he felt a huge tug on the rope.

'I don't know,' said Ruker anxiously turning to Esmerelda, who threw her hands up in despair.

Far below, Tallitha repeated her rhythm of landing, bouncing and jumping. But once again the next cave was empty. She pulled on the rope four times. This time her heart sank.

'What's happening?' demanded Esmerelda, looking warily over the edge.

'She's pulled on the rope again. She hasn't found Tyaas,' explained Ruker, running her hand desperately through her hair.

Ruker grabbed the Groat. 'Okay you loathsome creature, what's going on?'

The Groat clamped his mouth tightly shut.

'Where's Tyaas? What have they done with him?'

Neeps pushed the edge of his knife into the Groat's neck, nicking the skin so that the blood slowly began to trickle down his throat.

'He's no use to us, let me finish him off!' said Neeps angrily with his knife poised to slice the Groat's neck.

But before Ruker could answer, there was a series of high-pitched screams and the fat Groat smirked. Esmerelda grabbed Ruker and pointed towards the cavern roof. Twinkling above them was an array of purple-blue lights. Ruker raced to the chimney shaft and pulled on the rope five times.

*

Far below in her cave, Tallitha felt the rope tug, one-two-three-four-five times! She closed her eyes, put her head in her hands and waited for the noise to begin.

There was a cacophony of blood-curdling screams as an army of Groats landed at the top of the chimney and surrounded the hapless explorers. Ruker and Neeps never had a chance to strike back as the bright blue eyes of the Groats mesmerised their captives and dragged them back to their lair.

Twenty-one

Tallitha heard the screaming and froze. The Groats must have captured the others. She sat in her cave waiting for the Groats to find her. They were sure to discover the rope. She could hear her friends being dragged away from the top of Sour Pits. Then all became deathly quiet. In their haste to capture the intruders and free their comrade, the Groats had somehow forgotten all about Tallitha. She waited and waited, listening for any sound, clutching the rope which hung down the shaft of the chimney, hoping for a signal. Anything at all, that would let her know her friends were still alive.

*

The prisoners were taken down a series of narrow passageways and left in a cave that looked out over the shaft of the chimney. There in the corner slept Tyaas, curled up and snoring deeply. Esmerelda shook him firmly.

'Tyaas, Tyaas, it's me, Essie. Wake up.'

But Tyaas moaned and turned over. Esmerelda smelled his breath and the cup that had held the amber liquid.

'He's been drugged,' she said flatly, 'it's a heady potion. We mustn't drink anything they bring us.'

The Skinks immediately began sizing up the problem, peering up and down the chimney shaft.

'They brought us in the back way then they barred the entrance. That Groat told us the only way in here was by scaling the chimney wall, which was a lie. Perhaps Tallitha's cave is in the same shaft,' said Neeps optimistically.

'Shine the lantern. Let's try and pinpoint where we are,' said Ruker.

Esmerelda shone the lantern up and down the walls of the immense shaft. Outside the span of the single beam of light, the chimney shaft was totally black. As the lantern moved along the rock face Benedict saw something move.

'There, over there! I can see the rope!'

'I can't see it,' said Esmerelda.

'Hanging by that greenish mark in the rock,' said Ruker pointing upwards.

Across the abyss the rope hung limply down. Then it moved like a snake, twisting down the rock face. Esmerelda shone the beam of light along the length of the rope until it alighted on a pair of feet. Sitting, with her legs over the edge, sat Tallitha, twisting the rope round her fingers. As the beam of light struck her she leapt up and began waving madly at her friends. Now that they had found her, what were they going to do? One thing was clear. Somehow they must climb up to her.

*

In time, Tyaas woke up.

'Ohhh my head,' he groaned. 'Am I glad to see you lot.'

Eventually the guards brought them food, which they immediately threw down the shaft. They noticed the Groats push back a rock at the rear of their cave.

'There'll be a Groat patrol outside, so there's no use trying to get out that way,' whispered Neeps.

'Seems to me we have no alternative, we must climb up to Tallitha. Then we can escape from there,' said Ruker.

'That's easier said than done,' said Esmerelda narrowing her eyes and peering into the darkness.

'What do you think?' asked Ruker scratching her head.

'It's impossible,' said Benedict.

'Nothing's impossible' said Neeps, 'we have to be positive.'

The Skinks went into a huddle. Tyaas watched them talking animatedly to one another and making complicated hand gestures, as though they were sizing up the width of the shaft. Eventually they turned round.

'We have a plan,' said Ruker triumphantly.

'Yes and it might even work!' said Neeps, and Ruker pushed him.

Benedict groaned, 'No, no, it won't work. We'll all be killed. I'm staying here.'

'Shush, Benedict, and listen for once,' said Tyaas.

His cousin was embarrassing.

'Remember the rope swings in Hanging Trees?' said Neeps.

Benedict groaned again.

'We have to get Tallitha to swing her rope over here. It just depends on the angle. It's tethered securely so ...'

'No way – you're all mad!' shouted Benedict.

'Shhhh! Shut up, will you? The Groats will hear us,' snapped Esmerelda.

'Now just watch,' insisted Ruker.

She flashed the lantern to attract Tallitha's attention. Then Ruker began to mime what she wanted Tallitha to do, to swing the rope over to their cave. Tallitha stood at the edge and swung the rope out over the chasm but there was insufficient weight to reach the other side.

'No. Show her, like this,' said Neeps excitedly. 'She needs to tie knots in the end, like at Hanging Trees. She has to make a rope swing.' He began tying knots in Esmerelda's scarf. 'Shine the light on me so she can see.'

Tallitha copied the Skink and this time she ran to the edge of her cave, thrusting the rope out over the abyss as far as she could. They watched in silence as the rope flew across the chimney void, picking up speed, but again it fell just short of their cave. Tallitha shook her head and raised her hands in the air. Then Ruker had another idea. She gesticulated wildly to Tallitha to try once more.

'Stand next to me and hold me steady. I'm going to reach out for the rope,' explained Ruker. 'Once we have it this side we can add more knots to give it weight.'

The Skink leaned out over the ledge as far as she dared. As the rope swung towards her she caught it firmly, almost slipped, and was pulled to safety by the others.

'Well done!' said Esmerelda grabbing hold of Ruker.

'What now?' asked Tyaas staring out over the blackness.

'Good question. How can we swing over there without dashing our brains out on the other side?' asked Neeps frustratedly.

Benedict sat on the edge of the cave. 'I have an idea,' he said cautiously, 'not that I'm necessarily going to try it. But you lot might be crazy enough.'

'Okay brainbox, what is it?' asked Tyaas.

'You could use clothes for padding, on the soles of your feet. Then when you sit on the knot, you can use your feet as brakes when you hit the wall on the other side.'

Ruker looked impressed. 'It might work. But will you be able to do it?'

Benedict went pale. 'I don't know. But I'm not going first,' he said looking sick.

It was agreed that Neeps would go first. He tied his shirt and jacket to his feet and Ruker held the rope firmly until her friend was sitting snugly on the big knot.

'I'll guide you to the edge to reduce the swing, then I'll let go. Make no noise at all, not a squeak,' she said sternly.

Neeps swung out over the abyss, gathering momentum as he moved soundlessly through the steely darkness, the air whistling past his face. With a thud he slammed into the rock face on the other side of the chimney and raised his thumb to indicate success. Lithe and brave, he advanced in quick crab-like movements, deftly scaling the rock face using the rope and crevices in the wall to pull himself up to Tallitha's cave. Then Neeps leaned out and swung the rope back to the others.

Next it was Esmerelda's turn. Apprehensively she sat on the big knot. Ruker let go and she flew out into the stomach-churning darkness. Esmerelda's climb to the cave was arduous. Her arms shook with the sheer effort of hauling herself up the rock face. The others watched terrified as she faltered, shining the lantern as she ascended in slow jerky movements. Eventually she made it.

'That was dreadful. I never thought I'd make it,' she cried, hauling her exhausted body over the ledge and falling into Tallitha's arms.

Again the rope went flying back across the pit. This time Ruker turned to Benedict.

'I can't leave you until last. If Esmerelda can do it, then you can. It's your fear you must conquer.'

Ruker handed him the rope.

'But I hate heights,' he wailed.

Benedict had been steeling himself. His face was ashen and his stomach was awash with fear. He wrapped his feet as Neeps had demonstrated and Ruker helped him on to the rope swing.

Benedict whimpered.

'Remember, no noise.'

Ruker let Benedict go and he swung out over the ghastly chasm.

Benedict kept his eyes tightly shut and stuck his feet out rigidly in front of him. In a matter of moments he felt the full force of the rock wall as it collided with the padding. His chaotic heartbeat was erupting out of his chest in terrifying bursts. He froze, unable to open his eyes. What was he doing in this dangerous place? It had been foolish to come along in the first place. He kept his eyes screwed tightly shut.

'Errr, o-o-oh no, oh help me,' he whined.

Tallitha whispered down to him. 'Come on Benedict, you can do it. Pull yourself up using the handholds, just like Neeps.'

The only emotion forging through Benedict's body was absolute churning terror. Shaking uncontrollably he reached out for the first crevice, trying to remember the basics of Tyaas's training at Winderling Spires. But each movement was torturous as he focussed on the drop below him – to certain death and OBLIVION! He couldn't stop the terrible shaking which made the rope wobble over the abyss. He peered helplessly at Tallitha with tears rolling down his cheeks.

'I can't do it,' he cried, 'I can't move!'

Benedict was stuck and so they were all stuck on both sides of the chimney, just waiting to be picked off by the Groats. Whatever nerve Benedict had mustered for the flight across had now vanished. Ruker raised her lantern and signalled to Neeps.

The Skink looked down the shaft at the helpless boy and braced himself. Unfortunately he knew what he must do next.

'Damn that awkward boy,' Ruker said under her breath, 'he's been nothing but trouble from the start.'

'We should have left him behind, like I said,' whispered Tyaas.

What if something should happen and they both fell to their deaths? Tyaas watched as Tallitha and Esmerelda held the rope and the brave Skink stepped off the edge of the world and into jaws of the dark chasm. The rope heaved as it stretched further down the shaft, pulling taut under Neeps's added weight. Benedict put his head down, screwed up his eyes and whimpered.

'Shut up, Benedict, please shut up,' said Tallitha, hugging herself nervously.

It was unbearable to watch. Tallitha could see the strain on the Skink's face as his neck muscles tightened and he manoeuvred his way down the rope. He descended the shaft crab-like, using both the wall and the rope, which he twisted round his leg. The rope strained under Neeps's weight and jarred Benedict who moaned pathetically as each movement rocked his body.

'If he doesn't shut up, the Groats will be upon us,' said Ruker staring desperately at Neeps, willing him to make it to the bottom of the rope.

But somehow the Skink's foot slipped and in the awful confusion that followed he let go of the rope. In an agonising split-second, the others watched in terrifying slow motion as Neeps lurched towards the rock face and miraculously clung on to the wall like a spider, his fingers digging into the small crevices and his feet managing to position themselves on the chimney wall, while Benedict swayed helplessly next to him.

'What will he do?' cried Tallitha 'He can't stay like that.'

They all knew that Neeps had one chance to save himself before his arms gave way and he plummeted to his death. Desperate pairs of eyes watched as Neeps swiftly turned in one daring movement, lunged for the rope and grabbed it, swinging out over the chasm with his legs flaying madly below him.

'Ahhhhhhhh,' shouted Benedict as the rope lengthened and jerked over the shaft.

Ruker put her head in her hands in horror. The Groats would hear them and unless Neeps could steady the rope and control Benedict's fears, they were done for.

But the Skink had nerves of steel and arms that were adept at climbing the tallest trees. He pulled himself up the rope with deft hand-over-hand movements until he was standing with both feet squarely on the knot.

'Give me your hand, Benedict,' Neeps instructed as he towered over the cowering boy. 'You're going on my back. Grip your legs round my middle. Hold on, but don't strangle me.'

The sweat dripped from the Skink's face as he yanked Benedict on to his back.

'Ahhh, I'm slipping,' yelled Benedict as he gripped on to the Skink.

'Shut up and hold tight or we'll both fall,' said Neeps desperately.

He began climbing the chimney wall using the rope and the

hand-holds as Esmerelda and Tallitha steadied the rope from above. His muscles bulged with sheer exertion and he made grunting noises at the back of his throat that seemed to propel him up the shaft. With a final groan the Skink hauled himself and the miserable Benedict up the last stretch of the rock, over the edge of the cave entrance and lay exhausted on the floor. Neeps pulled his trembling body to a sitting position and mopped his brow on his sleeve.

'T-Thanks,' stuttered Benedict and reddened.

'You almost killed us both,' said Neeps and stared in disbelief at the foolish boy.

Tyaas and Ruker followed in quick succession making the task look easy as they rapidly scaled the chimney. When Tyaas arrived in Tallitha's cave he hugged his sister, and she kissed him far too much for his liking.

Ruker roughly grabbed Benedict by his collar. 'You nearly killed Neeps with your stupidity. Let this be a warning to you,' hissed Ruker shaking with rage. 'The next time I'll leave you to rot, do you hear me?' she shouted into the boy's sullen face.

Benedict lifted his head as if to say something, but changed his mind.

'We need to find the way out,' said Ruker turning her back on Benedict, 'Tallitha, have you searched the cave?' she asked, trying to compose herself.

'There's a boulder covering the exit,' she said staring anew at Benedict. Perhaps she had been wrong about him after all.

They moved the boulder to reveal a small gap and Ruker

was the first to crawl through. One by one they followed her into a dismal tunnel and began creeping upwards along a dark low passageway that turned back on itself like a spiral. Up and up they went until eventually they came to a huge cavern to the north-west of Sour Pit Tunnels.

'Wow, look up there,' said Tyaas, shining his lantern on the cavern roof which writhed and twisted like a snake.

In the light the roof shone black and silky, covered with roosting, squirming bats jostling for position, their rodent-like faces peering down at the unwelcome visitors.

'There are thousands of bats,' exclaimed Tallitha.

'That must mean we're near the surface,' said Neeps.

'We must press on before the Groats notice we've escaped. Once at Raven Stones we're outside their territory, they won't follow us there,' said Ruker.

'Let's get out of here!' cried Esmerelda, peering up at the writhing black roof. 'They seem really agitated.'

As if the creatures had overheard Esmerelda, they began to swoop, darting towards the visitors. Esmerelda covered her head and began to scream.

'Stop shouting, you're scaring them,' said Benedict.

Suddenly the whole bat colony took flight and the cave became a mass of black-winged creatures flapping in their faces. Esmerelda froze as the bats swooped around her and she screamed and screamed. Ruker grabbed Esmerelda and dragged her from the midst of the whooshing creatures but it was too late, she had made too much noise.

Far below, near the prison entrance, a Groat warder stirred and looked up from licking his spongy grey suckers. He shouted irritably to his companion and they ambled over to the cave. It was empty. The Groat scratched his head and looked out over the void. Then the Groat picked up the battle horn and blew it loudly three times. Now every Groat within hearing distance would be stampeding up the tunnels or scaling the walls ready to do battle.

Ruker heard the horn from deep within the caves. Now they were being hunted. They must reach the Raven Stones before the Groats caught them. On and on they raced through the dripping darkness.

'We have to rest,' pleaded Tallitha, 'I'm so thirsty and my feet are aching.'

Esmerelda stumbled behind her, tired and weak with hunger.

'If we stop, they'll catch us,' said Ruker.

So they crawled, through dripping caves, slipping and sliding on the wet, slimy surfaces. Eventually, when sufficient distance had been put between them and the Groats, Ruker began to look for a place to rest.

'Here behind these rocks,' she said.

They fell to the floor with exhaustion and Benedict began foraging for the little food they had left. 'I have some biscuits, what about you?'

Esmerelda had potions but nothing else, Ruker had some soda bread, Tallitha some dried fruit and Tyaas had two stale buns. They put the food in the middle and looked at it despondently.

'What are we going to do? Our remaining bags have been

taken by the Groats. We have some water and this paltry amount of food. We're done for,' murmured Tallitha.

'It's my fault,' said Esmerelda, 'I'm sorry I panicked, but the bats …'

'Stop it all of you. It's no one's fault,' said Ruker trying to rally their spirits. 'We'll feel better once we've rested. Neeps and I will take it in turns to sleep, come on let's use our bodies for warmth.'

They nestled together behind the rocks, falling asleep within minutes. Neeps was on first watch. Perhaps it was the strain of the climb with Benedict but eventually his eyelids became heavy with sleep. He woke himself up with a start but within seconds his head sank to his chest again … perhaps he would just shut his eyes for twenty winks …

Twenty-Two

It was Benedict who stirred first. Staring down at him were two pairs of bright eyes. He screamed and grabbed Neeps who shot bolt upright.

'What the devil? I must have dozed off. Who are you?' demanded Neeps.

The Cave-Shroves pointed at Esmerelda and chuckled. They had smaller features than the Shroves at Winderling Spires, and were altogether much more cheerful.

'Ernelle and Pester, am I glad to see you!' cried Esmerelda shaking hands with the Cave-Shroves.

'These are my dear friends, the ones who took care of me. They won't bite. Will you, my pointy-eared friends?'

'We're here to help you,' said Ernelle gravely.

She turned to Pester and whispered something in Shroveling. Esmerelda could tell from their twitchiness that they were alert to approaching danger.

'You must follow us to Raven Stones and then to our village. The Groats are hunting you,' said Pester, her face twitching in the gloom.

'We've laid a false scent to put the Groats off our trail but it won't fool them for long,' said Ernelle. 'Come, hurry now.'

They followed the Cave-Shroves through a series of wet, sloping tunnels that went deeper into the belly of the mountain. Icy cold water dripped down, soaking their hair and the ground was slippery underfoot. The Cave-Shroves were cunning little creatures and their ability to see in the dark made the route seem easier. The path twisted and turned under the red veined walls and at regular intervals one of the Cave-Shroves scampered off down a side tunnel to leave a false trail for the Groats.

At last, there before them was the path up to the Raven Stones Ring.

'Come,' said Pester, 'we must pass through the ring of stones, then onward to our village.'

Tallitha pulled Tyaas to one side and pointed at the carvings at the foot of the stones.

'Look, it's those ravens again. They're the same carvings that were in Winderling Spires.'

Tyaas shrugged his shoulders, he couldn't remember. Tallitha ran her fingers over the outline of the raven carvings.

'Come, hurry now,' said Ernelle.

The Cave-Shroves disappeared behind a fissure in the rock. When Tallitha squeezed herself through, she saw Ernelle standing below a dark shaft, calling out in Shroveling.

'What's she doing?' asked Tallitha

'Shhh,' said Esmerelda, 'just watch. I'd forgotten about this, it's really something.'

Suddenly a large basket landed with a thump at Ernelle's feet and Pester climbed inside.

'Tyaas, you get in. There's room for two,' explained Esmerelda.

Once Pester and Tyaas were tucked inside, the basket began stuttering up the shaft, hauled by a team of Cave-Shroves peering down from above.

'This is one of our secret entrances,' whispered Ernelle, pushing Tallitha and Benedict in next.

The Cave-Shroves inhabited a secure world, protected from their enemies in the heart of the cave system. Once at the top Esmerelda was warmly welcomed by an elderly Cave-Shrove named Snouter who fussed over her long lost friend. Cave-Shroves were smaller than the Shroves at Winderling Spires, with sharper, more quizzical features and a kind disposition.

'Well, you've led us a merry dance. We've been tracking you for days but the Groats got to you first.'

Esmerelda turned to her host, 'Snouter, these are my friends. Snouter knows everything there is to know about these caves,' said Esmerelda, putting her arm round the grey-haired Cave-Shrove.

Snouter chuckled and led the way to the communal hall. The village was built into a series of caves, hollowed out from the side of the rock face with ladders leading up to each dwelling. The sight before them was a welcome one to the hungry travellers. The table was full of bread, cakes, pies and buns, fruit and nuts and a selection of skewered grilled rat and baked blindworm puddings. The Skinks devoured the steaming puddings and the tasty rat, but Tallitha and Tyaas shied away from eating the unusual fare.

'They aren't used to these delicacies so forgive them,' explained Esmerelda, a little embarrassed. 'But it's a long time since I tasted these puddings and they're a welcome treat.'

Esmerelda tucked in and ate three chunks of roasted meat and two hot puddings in quick succession. When the others had finished eating, Snouter wiped the meat juices from her lips and pushed her plate to one side.

'Now then, why have you returned after all this time? Is it to look for your cousin?' asked Snouter, passing round sweet delicacies.

'I'll never give up,' said Esmerelda dabbing her mouth.

The Cave-Shroves exchanged glances.

'The Dooerlins are vicious hunters, and you'll have to pass through their territory next,' said Snouter gravely.

'Dooerlins!' said Tallitha laughing. 'But surely they're make-believe?'

'They're far from make-believe,' exclaimed Pester. 'You prob'ly know them as the Murk Mowl.'

Tallitha gasped. So maybe it was true, what Cissie had told them, about children being secreted away in the middle of the night. Tallitha shuddered at the thought of the Murk Mowl roaming Wycham Elva at the dead of night, or even entering Winderling Spires itself.

'It's dangerous in their domain. There are few who make

it through alive,' said Snouter, playing with the crumbs on the table.

'What else have you discovered since I was last here?' asked Esmerelda. 'There is something, isn't there?'

'We've heard things, and if what we've heard is true, it might not be worth the perilous journey ahead.'

Esmerelda drank her ale and motioned for Snouter to continue.

'After Asenathe was taken by the Groats, she was handed over to the Swarm. She was a prized possession given her connection to the Grand Morrow, and at first the Thane intended to ransom her back to Wycham Elva, but he was persuaded into another course of action.'

Benedict pushed back his hair and excused himself. He looked decidedly odd.

'Mind if I have a lie down? I feel a bit queasy,' he said, quietly rubbing his stomach.

'There are sleeping spaces over there,' said Pester, indicating a mezzanine level at the side of the cave.

'What's up with him?' asked Tyaas, watching his cousin disappear up the ladder.

Ruker stared after Benedict. There was something decidedly odd about that boy, something she couldn't put her finger on.

'What happened next?' inquired Tallitha.

She was more interested in hearing about Asenathe than Benedict's indigestion.

'She married the Thane's son, Arden Morrow.'

Esmerelda gasped. 'What! But who persuaded the Thane to change his plan?'

'Queen Asphodel had a hand in it. She didn't want Asenathe to return to Wycham Elva,' said Snouter cautiously.

'Asphodel again,' said Tallitha under her breath.

'Surely Lord Frintel and Asphodel could have secured a huge ransom for Asenathe,' said Ruker.

'It's a strange turn of events. Asenathe left Winderling Spires to escape one arranged marriage and she ended up being forced into another one,' said Esmerelda sadly.

Ernelle and Pester became twitchy and looked to Snouter to take the lead.

'Well that's not what we heard. The marriage wasn't arranged,' said the elderly Cave-Shrove.

'What do you mean?' asked Esmerelda, perplexed.

'It was a love match. Arden and Asenathe persuaded Lord Frintal to let them marry. Asenathe is no longer a prisoner, as far as we know. She stayed in Hellstone Tors because she wanted to,' explained Snouter.

'As far as you know ... but how did you hear this?' exclaimed Esmerelda.

'Our spies overheard it from the Groats,' explained Pester.

'I don't believe it!' Esmerelda gripped the edge of the table. 'After all this time I must see her. If she's happy and wants to stay in the Tors, it must be of her own free will, not because she was forced into marrying this Arden. Am I right?' she said looking at the others.

'We can't give up now. We'll never know the truth and I don't trust something third-hand, no offence,' said Tallitha.

'Particularly coming from those sources,' said Ruker.

'Very well, but your journey will be extremely dangerous. The Murk Mowl have formed a pact with Asphodel so they will work with her to capture you. News will reach her of your escape from the Groats so her spies will be everywhere. It's the second time you've outwitted them, they won't like that,' said Snouter turning to Esmerelda. 'It was never intended that you should survive. The plan was to kill you when Asenathe was taken, but that failed and you escaped.'

A shadow flitted over Esmerelda's face as the implication of Snouter's words sank in.

'You mean Asenathe's kidnap was planned?'

'That's also what we heard,' said Snouter.

'B-But I thought we were just unlucky, when we got lost in the caves,' Esmerelda said quietly as her face turned ashen. 'But that means someone from Winderling Spires must have betrayed us, all those years ago.'

'Who would do a thing like that?' asked Tallitha anxiously. 'Think back Essie – who first told you about the marriage between Asenathe and Cornelius Pew?'

Esmerelda knew only too well who had told her. She averted her eyes from Tallitha.

'Essie – what is it?'

Esmerelda swallowed hard. 'I'm afraid it was your mother. It was Snowdroppe.'

The colour drained from Tallitha's face.

'Mother!' cried Tyaas, 'but why would she do that?'

'She said she was helping us at the time, but have you ever known Snowdroppe to help anyone but herself?'

Tyaas jumped up from the table and lashed out at Esmerelda. 'How dare you accuse our mother of such a thing? Tallitha, tell her it can't be true!'

Tallitha looked crestfallen. 'But Essie's right. Our mother doesn't care for anyone and Father is no better. I'm sorry, Tyaas, but maybe there's something to this story. Mother would only do this to gain something. But what?'

The assembled company waited for someone to say what was obvious to everyone except Tallitha and Tyaas. It was Esmerelda who finally spoke.

'She would achieve great power from this change in fortune.'

'What do you mean?' asked Tallitha, apprehensively.

'Through the children she would have, eventually. You're the heir Tallitha, now that Asenathe is gone. It's through you that Snowdroppe will rule Wycham Elva once Agatha is dead, and then Winderling Spires will be hers.'

Tallitha peered out from underneath her dark lashes. There were tears in her eyes. It must be true. Tallitha's mind was swimming with ghastly images of her mother betraying the Morrow family.

'But why did she do it? What's her connection with the Tors?' asked Tallitha.

Pester shrugged, 'We don't know, but Marlin, Grintley and Florré are all involved somehow.'

Tallitha bit her lip. Oh no, not them again – the Winderling Shroves were always involved somehow.

'The Shroves must have been reporting back to Snowdroppe all this time,' added Esmerelda.

'But how do you know the Shroves at Winderling Spires?' asked Tyaas.

'We have links going back for generations. Grintley and Florré were visitors here but we banished them from Raven Stones many years ago,' said Ernelle.

'Now Grintley works for Snowdroppe and Florré works for my mother and Aunt Edwina. The old sisters discuss the family all day long. The Shroves at Winderling Spires must have been eavesdropping for years. I feel sick with the thought of it,' said Esmerelda, her voice rising in despair.

'But why were they banished?' asked Tallitha.

'We discovered they were being paid for passing closely guarded Shrove secrets to Asphodel, so we expelled them from our community. At first they went to the Dark Reaches then we heard they had left the Out-Of-The-Way Mountains for good.'

'I can't bear to think of our mother doing this. Is she really this wicked?' asked Tyaas, his voice cracking with emotion.

Tallitha went over to Esmerelda and nestled into her side as the horror of what she had been told began to sink in.

*

The next morning the Skinks were busy planning the route

to Old Yawning Edges.

'I'm afraid we can't enter Murk Mowl territory with you. It would put our village in danger,' said Pester.

Esmerelda nodded, 'I understand. Which way shall we go?'

'Pass through the Raven Stones Ring, then round the top of Old Yawning Edges avoiding the Murk Mowl. There's a small winding tunnel at the back of Raven Stones,' explained Snouter. 'It's hidden behind a boulder. You'll see it once you're in the second cave along from the ring.'

'Not another tunnel!' said Benedict, 'I'm getting tired of this.'

'Stop it!' shouted Tallitha who was still brooding about their mother's betrayal.

Benedict pulled a face and took himself back to bed to sulk.

It was Esmerelda who broke the silence. 'Maybe Snowdroppe didn't act alone. She was young and had just married your father. Perhaps the Shroves …,' suggested Esmerelda trying to soften the blow.

Tears fell down Tallitha's cheeks.

'It was Mother, and it doesn't matter, she still betrayed you,' she said, her voice faltering. 'There's always been something distant about her. She doesn't love us.'

Tallitha bit her lip and wiped her eyes.

'Come and sit next to me,' Essic offered.

But Tallitha shook her head. It was too much to bear. Their mother didn't love anyone, including her own children.

Twenty-Three

Early the next morning the travellers began their journey. Ruker located the winding tunnel that would lead them over the top of Old Yawning Edges.

'I'll go first and you follow me,' said Ruker.

The entrance hole was small, dark and wet. Benedict took one look inside the narrow tunnel and shook his head.

'I'm not going in there,' he said flatly.

The others stared at him.

'We've no idea where it leads. I'm staying put,' he said stubbornly.

'Do come on Benedict, stop being tiresome,' said Tyaas, sharply.

'There isn't a choice. We can't go back, this is the only way,' insisted Neeps.

'I've had enough. You can't make me,' said Benedict finally.

Tallitha rolled her eyes in frustration. 'Come on, Bumps,' she said cheekily.

'Shut up, just shut up!' shouted Benedict thunderously.

He was behaving worse than usual. Ruker knew she could not persuade him.

'Once we're through I'll come back for you. Then you'll know we're safe,' she said trying to placate him.

Benedict pouted and sat down to wait.

The others struggled through the winding tunnel, crawling on their hands and knees, eventually making it to the other side, wet, exhausted and bitterly cold. Almost immediately the air smelt fresh. Way below them, the pitted rim of Old Yawning Edges leered up at them with its gaping, terrifying mouth. Down through the cavernous gap they could see hundreds of Murk Mowl, the size of worker ants, going backwards and forwards about their odious business.

'I'll go back for Benedict,' said Ruker.

She quickly departed leaving the others to peer anxiously down into the jaws of the deep pit that waited hungrily before them.

*

As Ruker made her way back through the tunnel, she was seething at Benedict. Not only had he endangered the life of her dear friend, but he had become more difficult of late. The icy drippiness of the tunnel saturated her clothes for the second time that day. Eventually, she pulled herself out of the tunnel and poked her head round the side of the boulder. But there was no sign of Benedict. She called his name to make sure he hadn't fallen or injured himself, but he was nowhere to be seen. Blast that selfish boy, she said to herself. But Ruker had a strange feeling. She had half-expected something like this from Benedict, some disappearing act, something to attract everyone's attention. But where was he? Surely he wouldn't wander off alone. She made a final search of the cave then decided to head back to the others. Exhausted, Ruker pulled her soaking body to the end of the tunnel and hauled herself out.

'Where's Benedict? Is he behind you making a fuss?' asked Tallitha peering into the dark hole.

Ruker shook her head. 'When I got to the other side he'd vanished.'

'What do you mean? He can't have done. Did you look for him?' asked Tallitha.

'Of course I looked everywhere within reach. He's a damned nuisance.'

'But where is he?' asked Tyaas, sounding alarmed.

'Benedict isn't the sort to go wandering off alone,' said Ruker, 'maybe he's been taken.'

'Taken? What shall we do?' exclaimed Tallitha anxiously.

Ruker and Esmerelda exchanged glances. They knew if Benedict had disappeared, that was it. They would have to leave without him.

'You look exhausted, Ruker. Take a rest and have some of the liquorice cordial. I suggest that Neeps and Tyaas go back to make absolutely certain he isn't there. Then by the time they return we'll have had time to decide what to do,' suggested Esmerelda.

The pair set off and retraced Ruker's steps, but they were also unsuccessful. Neeps poked his head out of the tunnel.

'No. He's definitely vanished.'

Someone had to make a decision.

'We must press on without him,' said Ruker finally.

Tallitha gasped and Esmerelda took her hand.

'If he's been taken, and we go looking for him, chances are the same will happen to us. I agree with Ruker. He wouldn't have gone off by himself. He's too scared down here in the dark. There's nothing for it but to continue.'

'What, leave him here all by himself? But that's awful. Would you do that to us?' asked Tallitha.

'I told him what would happen the last time he disobeyed me. We can't split up and go searching for him, not down here,' said Ruker angrily.

'But Ruker, Essie ...' pleaded Tallitha.

'As the leader of this expedition I have the final word. Our safety cannot be jeopardised for one person. We must go forward. I'm sorry but there it is.'

Ruker flung her pack over her shoulder and began to rope up.

'But it's so dark and lonely down here. What if he ...?' but her voice trailed away.

Tallitha broke into a sob. Tyaas tried his best to comfort his sister but she shrugged him off. Benedict could die all alone down here in the darkness and they were responsible. They were leaving him.

'Tallitha, I wish there was another way. He shouldn't have stayed on the other side.'

'You shouldn't have let him,' wailed Tallitha but she knew Ruker had no choice.

Maybe it was her fault for letting him come along in the first place.

Tallitha tried pleading with the Skinks, but they were adamant. Benedict was lost in the cold, dark hell.

'Okay, pay attention,' said Ruker, 'the next part of the journey is hazardous. There's an over-hanging ledge, crumbling away in places so I'm going to rope up. I'll use the carabiners to anchor us into the rock face, then should anyone stumble we can catch them. Like this …' Ruker demonstrated the safety mechanism of the ropes and began screwing the carabiners into position.

It was a slow hard climb to the over-hanging ledge. Tallitha's legs were shaking from the sheer effort of hauling herself up over such a long distance. Her arm muscles throbbed and her fingers stung from grasping the jagged edges of the rock. Finally she felt her fingers creep over the edge and Ruker pulled her to safety.

'Don't look down whatever you do,' she whispered, hauling Tallitha's body onto a narrow pathway.

Tallitha pressed her body flat against the rock wall. Through the cracks in the ledge she could see into the Murk Mowl's kingdom. Tallitha screwed up her eyes and concentrated on moving along the thin strip of rock that was the only buffer between her and the cavernous drop below. They crawled along at a glacial pace. The bulging rock face forced them to hang on to the rope and lean out over the fathomless pit below in order to manoeuvre the twists and turns in the cave wall.

Esmerelda could not resist peering down. Below, the Murk Mowl moved up and down the rock face, foraging for their young in the stone funnels. Their yellow pod-like feeding nurseries dangled from the cavern wall, bouncing up and down whenever a Mowl entered or left. The pods resembled rubber sacks containing bundles of writhing kittens, the mewling sounds from the Murk litters echoing up the cavern walls. Esmerelda's thoughts turned to the Murk Mowl's prey, both dead and alive, sordidly stored in the grizzly Murk turrows scattered throughout the caves. She gasped and averted her eyes.

Tyaas whispered in a strained voice, 'Ruker says we have to wait here. There's some sort of problem.'

Ahead of them, Esmerelda could hear the Skinks speaking in hushed tones.

'Come on, but be prepared for something shocking,' said Tyaas over his shoulder.

As Esmerelda rounded the bulge in the cave wall, the reason for Ruker's warning confronted them. There before them was a long tunnel filled with Murk turrows.

'We either go through this tunnel or we find another way,' said Tallitha, horrified.

'We don't have a choice,' said Esmerelda raising her head.

'This must be the Throes of Woe.'

Above the tunnel was a pattern carved in the rock.

'B-but it's the same pattern that was embroidered on the sampler I found,' whispered Tallitha.

'Maybe that Groat was trying to trick us,' said Neeps. 'This tunnel could lead us into even more danger.'

Inside, the hideous chambers went downward into the darkness.

'Let's find out where it leads. Tyaas, will you come with me? Neeps can stay with the others. It will be sickening down there, I should warn you,' said Ruker.

'I'll come,' answered Tyaas without hesitation.

'We won't be long,' said Ruker and with that they stepped into the turrow.

By the lamplight, Tyaas witnessed the despicable work of the Murk Mowl. Each chamber held a creature, or parts of them – long dead and preserved in yellow glistening gel. Ruker held a handkerchief to her face to keep out the stench of rotting flesh. In front of each turrow there was a small trench, filled with the bodies of rotting vermin and beetles. Tyaas mouthed to Ruker, '*What's that?*'

'It's full of poison, to stop the rats and insects eating the Murk fodder.'

Tyaas's terrified eyes shone in the flickering light. What if the Mowl should discover them? They would end up like these dead souls. The sordid place reminded Tyaas of the mausoleum at

Winderling Spires. It was the smell of the dead and the lingering presence of the spirits, their ghostliness in death pervading each crevice of the dank chamber.

At the end of the tunnel Ruker covered the flickering candle and gingerly poked her head round the corner. She indicated for Tyaas to stay out of sight. As the ledge wound round the rock face, there was a group of Mowl sitting on their haunches tearing at hunks of raw flesh, guarding the way out. Their heads bobbed up and down at the feed, ravaging their food like voracious animals, pieces of raw meat and blood dripping down their faces and splattering their grizzly hands. Tyaas heard the crunch of bone and the wrench of flesh, and pressed himself flat against the stone wall of the turrow, his breath coming in rapid bursts. In a heartbeat Ruker grabbed Tyaas and moved like lightning, ripping back past the turrows.

'What's wrong?' asked Esmerelda as they emerged shaking from the tunnel.

'Mowl,' was all that Ruker said as she hurried along the narrow ledge. They inched forward on their hands and knees trying desperately not to displace a stone or disturb any cave creature that would alert the Murk Mowl. They might have succeeded had Tallitha not suddenly swayed and dropped her backpack. She let out a whimper and they held their breath as they watched the pack falling in slow motion, bouncing off the cavern walls. They prayed it would lodge itself somewhere between them and the Murk Mowl, but it didn't. As it landed with a heavy thud, there was a second or two of agonising silence. Then it started. The deadly Murkish screams came rushing up the cavern, piercing the air. The battle cry of the Murk Mowl filled Old Yawning Edges as the Mowl spotted the intruders and took flight to catch them.

'Quick, get off the ledge! Move, Tallitha!' shouted Ruker.

But Tallitha had lost her nerve. She was stuck between Neeps and Tyaas.

'Tallitha, move forward, please!' urged Tyaas.

She remained shaking on the ledge. 'I can't. I'm too scared to move. I'll fall!' she cried helplessly.

'Come on Sis, let me help you,' begged Tyaas desperately.

But Tallitha bent her head, shaking with fear as the Murk Mowl scaled the cavern wall and pounced on her. The others didn't take too much finding either. They were no match for the Mowl. Violently, the Murk Mowl dragged the prisoners to their foul lair, sniffing all their sweet-smelling body scents, assessing their tastiness and licking their fat lips.

*

Later, when the prison was quiet, Esmerelda pulled herself up to the grille and called to the others. She knew Neeps was somewhere near her. She had heard him cry out as he was thrown on to the cell floor after a period of interrogation. At some point Tallitha replied, whispering into the darkness.

'Essie, I'm here with Tyaas. They've taken Ruker to be interrogated. I hate to think what they are doing to her.'

But Esmerelda knew what the interrogation would entail. She had endured these tortures herself so she sat in her black hole waiting for the terror to be visited upon them. Some time later, Ruker returned and although Tallitha called out to her there was no response.

The days passed slowly and the routine in the prison was monotonous. They were woken early each day and taken one by one to a washing room. The water was freezing and the guards poked fun at them as they shivered under the icy blasts. Breakfast consisted of water and biscuits, followed by a basic meal before the lanterns were doused at night. The only safe time to communicate was at dead of night when the guards were dozing. Ruker and Neeps had been cruelly treated, and suffered greatly from their wounds. It was many days before they spoke to their friends. Tallitha was in the next cell to Ruker and very slowly she was able to piece together what had happened to the Skinks.

'I told them very little,' whispered Ruker through the grille. 'Only that we were looking for Asenathe and they laughed in my face.'

'What about our helpful friends?' asked Tallitha, concerned about the Cave-Shrove's safety.

'Nothing. I said nothing,' she said finally.

But in their dark lonely cells, the grizzly horror of the Murk turrows filled their waking thoughts and haunted their dreams, night after endless night.

Twenty-Four

After a week of unrelenting grime and cold, one morning after a measly breakfast the prisoners were dragged along a series of gloomy tunnels. Ruker and Neeps were the worse for their experiences. Neeps had a red oozing gash across his forehead, and Ruker had deep bruises on her face and neck. The others looked dishevelled after days in the damp dark cells. Esmerelda had circles under her eyes, plagued by the thought of ending her days as Murk meat. Tallitha looked thin, her hair had lost its abundant shine and her eyes had a fearful glint in the lamplight.

'Do you think they're going to kill us?' she whispered.

Her cousin didn't know what fate awaited them. She reached out and squeezed Tallitha's frozen fingers in the darkness. Suddenly the Murk Mowl barked orders at them and they stopped at a solid rock face. The Murk guard pushed the Skinks up on a ledge and untied their hands.

'Climb,' ordered the guard pointing to a series of rope ladders suspended from the cave wall.

The Skinks raced up into the darkness.

'What's up there?' asked Tyaas hesitantly.

Esmerelda faltered, fearing the worst but began climbing nonetheless. They had little choice with the Murk Mowl right behind them. It was a tough climb. They were weak from days spent in the damp cells. Tallitha's breathing became more laboured the higher she climbed. She was exhausted, but the ladders reached way up into the black shaft above them. Suddenly Esmerelda gasped and pointed up the shaft. There, up above, was a bright crack of daylight. Then the brightness hurt her eyes. At last they were coming out into the sunlight.

Tallitha heaved her tired body out of the shaft and fell onto a grassy mound into the cool breeze at the very top of the Out-Of-The-Way Mountains. Esmerelda stretched her arms and breathed deeply as the clean fresh air filled her lungs and the sunlight fell upon her dirty swollen face.

'Move, now!' ordered the Murk Captain, jabbing the hilt of his sword into her side. 'Follow me.'

They had escaped from the knife-cold darkness. Tallitha gathered Tyaas to her side and peered out underneath her fringe at the Mowl's appearance in the glaring sunlight. Their blood-drained flesh hung in deep folds and their rheumy fish-eyes protruded out of hooded pouches in their thick, rubbery faces. Their ears were full of metal piercings which had been trained into bizarre shapes and only added to their ugliness. Tallitha hoped the Mowl would not hurt them. She breathed in the sweet smell of the grasses and felt their feathery touch as she moved ahead through the summer meadow. She gazed heavenward at the freedom of the sea birds coasting on the wind currents, and felt the invigorating biting wind on her sunken cheeks.

The Murk Captain led them down a steep path, littered with rock falls, to a wooded ravine and a stream which chuckled away at their feet.

'Sit there, no talking,' ordered the guards.

From the opposite side of the ravine, Ruker spied a party of Groats moving heavily down the hillside. There was a hurried exchange, then the prisoners were handed over to the Groats and the Mowl disappeared down a hole in the mountain, back from whence they had come.

The Groats rounded on their prisoners and taunted them mercilessly for daring to escape, nicking their skin with their swords and swearing oaths to kill them. As the day edged towards dusk, the Groats led them further down the ravine and into a glade. There before them was a large tent, the colour of the forest with royal insignia painted on the awnings.

'Get inside,' ordered the Groats, pushing them viciously with the butt of their swords.

Tallitha and the others huddled together, their eyes fixed on the Groats who guarded all the exits. Inside, the tent was laid out like a sumptuous palace with velvet cushions and silken drapes surrounding a large central platform.

'What is this dreadful place?' asked Neeps, staring at the feathered specimens that adorned the tent.

Placed around the room were a number of birds, noisily squawking and flapping their wings at the visitors. Three shiny ravens preened their glossy feathers in a large domed cage, occasionally pecking at each other in annoyance whilst two vultures sat stone-like on either side of the podium, chained to their wooden plinths. Occasionally their eyelids moved, revealing their hard black eyes that observed their visitors with malice.

It was not long before a tall, thin woman entered the main tent. Her hooked nose resembled the beaks of the threatening birds who caw-cawed reverently at her entrance. As she walked across the podium, wild ocelots roamed about her sandalled feet, spitting ferociously at the noisy birds.

'Quiet, my pets,' she drawled.

The woman was dressed in a black dress that trailed behind her on the floor. Her waist-length hair was the colour of charcoal streaked with strands of white. She positioned herself on an ornate chair and idly surveyed the prisoners. Four Groats stood to attention at her side.

'Who is she?' mouthed Tyaas into Tallitha's ear but his sister shook her head.

Tyaas was mesmerised by the way the woman held herself. There was something worryingly familiar about her.

'All stand for Asphodel, Queen of the Dark Reaches,' shouted one of the Groats and stamped his staff on the floor.

'Oh no,' whispered Esmerelda under her breath, 'I feared as much.'

The prisoners stood for the haughty Queen. She was stick-thin with a fierce glint in her ebony eyes. Asphodel clicked her fingers and one of the Groats returned with a plate of food which the Queen toyed with in front of her hungry visitors. She tossed morsels to the ocelots that scurried backwards and forwards at her feet, gobbling the food, hissing and spitting at each other. Asphodel nibbled bird-like portions, desiring all who surveyed her to notice the thinness of her angular body. Tallitha's heart began to race. What was it about this woman that unsettled her so?

'She's a sorceress,' whispered Tyaas in Tallitha's ear.

'Silence!' shouted a Groat, poking his staff into Tyaas's ribs.

Asphodel whispered to one of the Groats, who hauled Tallitha before the Queen.

'Come here Tallitha and let me see you, close up!' demanded the Queen who circled Tallitha, touching her hair and peering right into her face.

The Queen was much older than Tallitha had first thought, with crows-feet wrinkles etched at the corner of her eyes, and deep furrowed lines by her mouth and nose. Her long hair was fastened with black pearl clasps at intervals in the long tresses. She stretched out her spindly hand and raised the chin of the unkempt girl before her.

'Tell me child, what were you doing snooping about in the Dark Reaches?'

Tallitha gazed past the Queen and refused to answer. Asphodel flashed her granite eyes and clicked her brittle fingers, making a snapping noise next to Tallitha's ear.

'Have it your own way, stupid girl. Bring that boy Tyaas to me now!'

A vehement Tyaas was roughly placed next to his sister. The

marble-hearted Queen pursed her mouth into an evil smile and reached down into a velvet pouch, which was fastened to her belt. She opened the draw-string, plunging her talons inside and lifted out a wriggling purple reptile. Asphodel stared into the reptile's hooded eyes and held it tightly by the neck. It writhed under her pinching grip, lashing its viperish tongue in the Queen's face. Asphodel flung her head back, and mad peals of laughter filled the tent. Then she viciously nipped the creature to annoy it even more. At the sight of the reptile, Ruker and Neeps strained to get out of their fastenings but were savagely lashed by the Groat guards. Then Asphodel held the creature above the boy's head.

'This is a Helly Dragon, isn't she a pretty one?' said Asphodel. 'She's deadly poisonous and will bite your brother when I drop her down his neck. So, Tallitha, I will ask you once more. What were you doing in my kingdom?'

Asphodel spat out the words in Tallitha's face. The Queen loomed above her and Tallitha reared back, squirming out of Asphodel's reach, trying to avoid her perfume which had the pungent aroma of rotting fruit.

'Don't hurt him! We came looking for my cousin Asenathe,' she spluttered nervously.

'Still fascinated with her?' she laughed wickedly.

She held the Helly Dragon over Tyaas's shirt and made as if to drop the creature down his back.

'Leave him alone. It was my idea to look for Asenathe,' shouted Esmerelda, moving towards the podium.

The Groats pulled on the ropes to restrain Esmerelda who jarred against their strength. Asphodel started at the sound of Esmerelda's voice and her face twisted into a malevolent sneer.

'Bring her closer, that I may see her better,' she ordered and stamped her feet.

She recognised her instantly.

'Ahhh, you're a fool to come back here. You should have been destroyed many years ago. But we'll do it now,' she said and bared her sharp white teeth. 'Take her outside and execute her immediately.'

Tallitha gasped and Asphodel laughed, roughly pushing her to one side. Almost at once there was a scuffling noise at the rear of the tent and someone fell, tripping over the awnings.

'P-Please, please don't hurt her, Mother,' the small voice pleaded.

In the moments that followed, every one of the friends became completely still, their mouths falling open in utter disbelief. It was a voice they recognised but found difficult to reconcile with the strange place they found themselves in. Everything happened in a dream as the figure of Benedict slowly emerged from the back of the tent. Tallitha stared wide-eyed at him in horror.

'Benedict, this can't be true!'

Had she heard him correctly? He had said the word, 'Mother', to that vile woman. Asphodel was Benedict's mother! But it made no sense. He was their cousin and his parents … but she had never met them, had she?

'But, hang on a minute,' said Tyaas in a state of confusion. 'I don't understand. What happened, Benedict? Where did you go? Are you drugged or something?'

Benedict shifted uncomfortably from one leg to the other.

'You traitor,' shouted Ruker. 'You nearly had us killed in the pits!'

She strained with all her might to free herself from the Groats. At that moment she wanted to strangle Benedict with her bare hands.

'But we trusted you. You've betrayed us!' shouted Tallitha, 'and I was so worried about you,' she cried. 'I even blamed myself.'

Benedict's cheeks reddened and he pushed his floppy hair out of his eyes. 'I didn't mean to … I meant to help you when you dropped the sampler. I suppose I was showing off to impress you.'

It was then that Tallitha saw clearly how weak Benedict was. She remembered her initial feelings towards him, that he was a strange, awkward boy. Now she knew why. She should have trusted her initial instincts. Now it was much too late. She felt sick with dread.

'Benedict, come to Mother,' Asphodel said and clicked her fingers.

Benedict shuffled towards the Queen and sat at her feet, trying to avoid the gaze of the shocked faces all around him as Asphodel stroked his head like a pet.

'There, why don't I tell your little friends all about it?' she said venomously, relishing their betrayal.

Benedict looked beseechingly up at his mother and began playing with the hem of her dress.

'B-But don't hurt Essie, p-please Mother,' pleaded Benedict.

He flinched slightly and turned away from Asphodel's savage face. He knew his mother was capable of unspeakable cruelty.

'But why shouldn't I?' she said, petulantly turning her red-raging eyes on Esmerelda.

'Please, p-please Mother,' begged Benedict, averting his eyes from her stony face and raising his hand to protect himself. Benedict cowered before his mother. Tallitha could see that Asphodel was a heartless fiend. She was uncertain in that moment whether the Queen would strike him or give in to his wishes. Her whole face seethed with hatred.

'I will spare the woman for now,' she shouted, snapping her fingers.

Tallitha and Tyaas were dragged from the podium and the Helly Dragon was returned spitting to her pouch. Asphodel scrutinised the dishevelled friends in their state of bewilderment, licked her thin savage lips and began.

'Are you going to tell them or shall I?' she asked, teasing Benedict and pushing him with her foot.

'I ... well ... y-you tell them, if you have to,' he said snivelling.

'Of course,' she said savouring the moment, 'I have been waiting a very long time for this.'

She shot her coal-black eyes at Tallitha and her lip curled in a cruel grimace.

'I'm surprised you haven't guessed already. Well have you?' she cried as wicked delight smouldered in her eyes. 'Oh it's too delicious,' she said clutching herself with malicious glee. 'Why,

Benedict is my son and also your cousin,' she said, waving her talons towards Tallitha and Tyaas.

This woman was some kind of enchantress and she had bewitched Benedict. That was it!

Tallitha snorted at the ludicrous lie that tripped off the Queen's tongue.

'That's ridiculous! How can he be our cousin? If he's your son, he can't be related to us as well,' laughed Tallitha.

Asphodel reared up like a serpent, towering over them.

'I'll wipe that smile off your face little girl! He is your cousin, on your mother's side,' Asphodel said with venom visibly pumping through her cold veins. 'Snowdroppe is my little sister!' she screamed.

Tallitha and Tyaas stared in horror as Asphodel delivered her cruel blow. The silence in the room was palpable as the Queen's terrible words struck home. Tallitha faltered and grabbed hold of Tyaas for support.

'You're telling me that you're my aunt?' gasped Tallitha.

'You?' said Tyaas horrified. 'It isn't true!'

Asphodel leapt towards them, throwing her arms in the air.

'Can't you see the resemblance between my sister and me?' she laughed wickedly.

As Tallitha stared into Asphodel's cold black eyes, the resemblance was unmistakable. Asphodel *was* their mother's sister. Tallitha felt physically sick.

'But why have we never met you, or ever heard of you before?' asked Tyaas.

Asphodel bristled and threw Tyaas a vile look.

'Silence, stupid boy! That's not your concern. Benedict has been watching you and making sure we were updated with all your plans. He has been such a good boy, haven't you?'

She stroked Benedict's head as he kept his eyes averted from the Queen.

'When you entered the winding tunnel, he decided he'd had enough of nasty dark, wet places. There's only so much espionage the boy could take. He became bored with your silly adventure and left. I was a teensy bit angry with him, wasn't I, Benedict? Had to reprimand my little soldier, didn't I?' she said pulling his hair a little too hard. Benedict winced. 'But I forgave him because he had told me everything, leaving little notes for my spies to find.'

'Benedict, how could you?' screamed Tallitha in her cousin's face.

Then Tallitha remembered, back in the mausoleum.

'It wasn't my fault. I warned you in the schoolroom, before I told you about Hellstone Tors. But then Aunt Snowdroppe found out and she told M-Mother, and they are very persuasive. I had to do what they said,' he whined.

Tallitha lunged violently at Benedict, but one of the Groats held her firm. Benedict coloured slightly and looked away. Tallitha saw before her a sad, lonely, misplaced boy.

'Ha ha, so sweet,' mocked Asphodel, 'this enduring interest you have in Asenathe after all these years.'

'I hate you!' shouted Tallitha.

But Asphodel carried on playing with her food, feigning

boredom. Then she looked straight at Tallitha.

'You're Agatha's heir and one day you will inherit Winderling Spires and will eventually rule Wycham Elva. That is, until my sister and I help you with your heavy burden.'

'But I don't want to rule anywhere. You can have it!' snapped Tallitha.

Asphodel shot Tallitha a deadly glance.

'Now listen to me Tallitha, and do exactly as I say. I haven't decided whether to keep you here or return you to Wycham Elva for a good ransom. But I'll keep Esmerelda with me, so you do as you are told. If you decide to disobey me, you know what will befall her.'

Tallitha's eyes stung with tears and she shook her head in disbelief.

'I hate you too! I'll get you for this,' screamed Tyaas trying to lash out at Benedict.

Benedict fidgeted uncomfortably at his mother's side.

'I had no choice. You wouldn't listen to me when I said it was too dangerous, so I had to come with you. I knew that Mother and Aunt Snowdroppe would never let you spoil their plans.'

'But what about Great Aunt Agatha, does she know who you are and that Mother is a spy too?' asked Tallitha incredulously.

'Aunt Snowdroppe organised it all. She's very, very clever. I doubt that old woman cares who I am.'

Benedict looked nervously at his mother for approval, and the pair of them smiled at their artful deception. Tallitha knew that their mother was capable of such a scheme and that Great

Aunt Agatha was too preoccupied to notice.

'Anyway, you never bothered to ask where I came from and Essie had her mind on other things. It was much simpler than I thought,' explained Benedict. 'You called me that name too, and I hated it and you kept doing it. I had to get my own back. You were mean to me, weren't they, Mother?'

'Shhhh there, my pet. Yes of course they were, vile and hateful!'

She spat out the words and turned her cold eyes on Tallitha and Tyaas.

'Now run along Benedict, I have business to attend to.'

Without a backward glance, Benedict kissed his mother's bony hand and left. Tallitha watched him leave and a sick feeling gnawed away in the pit of her stomach. She had let this happen. If only she had listened to her brother.

Asphodel summoned one of the Groats. 'Take them to the blue tent and make sure they are firmly bound. Let them have water and food, then tomorrow I'll decide on their fate.'

Asphodel came over to Tallitha and pinched her hard on the arm, staring coldly into her eyes. Tallitha yelped in pain and tried to pull away.

'Remember all that I have said, Tallitha. Disobey me, and you will suffer the full force of my anger.'

With that, Asphodel clicked her fingers and left the tent with the ocelots spitting and snarling about her feet.

Twenty-Five

In the quiet of the tent, securely tethered to each other, they whispered about Benedict's betrayal.

'I'll get him. Someday he'll pay for this,' mumbled Tyaas bitterly. 'I hate to say this, but we didn't know him after all, did we Tallitha?'

Her cheeks flushed a deep pink. She had foolishly ignored her instincts and disregarded her brother's wise words. Tallitha peered out from under her tangled hair.

'I'm sorry, I should have listened to you,' she replied sheepishly.

'Next time, maybe you will, but for now we're in a mess.'

The Skinks were struggling unsuccessfully to untie the ropes.

'How about hypnotising the guard?' suggested Ruker.

'He wouldn't succumb and would alert the others. Perhaps I can make a Death Cap potion,' replied Esmerelda.

'But how will you get him to drink it?' whispered Neeps despondently.

Each one in turn came up with a plan, but their ideas were either too risky or just plain fanciful. This time they were trapped. As night fell, their spirits flagged and they huddled together for warmth, listening to the hooting owls and the noises of the camp settling down. The smell of wood smoke filled the air as the fires were doused and at some point, uncomfortable and exhausted, the prisoners fell asleep.

The night slowly drifted by and the sky was filled with bright stars as two small creatures crept through the wood, sniffing all the interesting smells and plotting their trail. Stealthily, they moved towards the encampment through sodden bracken and over tricking brooks until at last they stood, knives in hand, behind the blue tent. Pester cut a neat hole in the material, tearing it carefully to the floor, and the two Cave-Shroves stepped inside.

It was Tyaas who woke first when a warm dry hand was clasped over his mouth. Ernelle signalled to him to be quiet as Pester busily freed the others. Ruker crept to the entrance of the tent and listened. All she could hear was the fat Groat snoring soundly.

'Come, follow us,' mouthed Pester quietly.

One by one they stepped through the torn fabric, out into the dappled glade and onward through the moon-soaked wood.

*

It was hours before they stopped running, fear coursing

through their bodies, urging them forward, breathless and scared. The strong smell of wet bracken filled their nostrils as they fled past row upon row of fir trees, their heavy branches dripping in the dawn light. They slipped on mossy rocks and fell over twisted roots, too frightened to cry out in case the Groats were following close behind them. Ernelle and Pester were expert trekkers, leaving false trails and leading them swiftly through the wood until they were certain they had put enough distance between themselves and the Groat encampment.

At last, when the sun was rising and the birds had started their early songs, the travellers stepped from the dark forest into the shredded morning light and onto the brow of a hill overlooking the myriad of tiny lakes that made up the glittering expanse of Tear Drop Tarns. A beguiling landscape of sparkling water and undulating hills stretched out before them, wrapped in the rising vapours that hung in misty layers over the twinkling tarns. There in the distance, looming high and proud, stood the unmistakable craggy outcrop with Hellstone Tors erupting from out of its heart like a dark brooding monster, blotting out the sky.

'There's the castle,' cried Esmerelda running to the edge of the hillside. She turned abruptly and her face shone with feverish anticipation. 'Somewhere inside that dark place we'll find Asenathe!'

'At times I doubted we'd make it,' Tallitha replied, staring fearfully at the unwelcoming sight soaring threateningly before her.

Against all the odds they had survived and were in sight of their mysterious destination. They had escaped from the terrifying hounds, made it through the desolate caves and outwitted the underworld creatures and Queen Asphodel. Tallitha felt hot tears running down her cheeks as Esmerelda came up behind her and Tyaas and put her arms lovingly around them.

'I couldn't have done this without you,' Esmerelda added softly, her face glowing at the thought of finding her beloved cousin.

Tallitha, for once, was more circumspect. The castle was an uninviting spectre with a dark past and more uncertain present. She felt the tingling sensation clutch at her stomach.

'What if we've come all this way and we can't find her, or worse?' Tallitha mumbled.

'We'll find her, I'm sure of that. Come, Ernelle wants to get to Melted Water before nightfall,' said Esmerelda pointing to a lake in the north-west, 'but first, let's eat.'

The Skinks were busily tucking into doughy black bread with a reddish filling hanging out the sides. The others were too famished to question the nature of the filling and they fell upon the food.

'I thought we were done for that time,' said Tyaas, hungrily pushing the red stringy meat into his mouth.

'That Groat will be mincemeat once they realise we've escaped,' Neeps chuckled, wiping his mouth on his sleeve and grinning at the thought.

'But how did you get out of the caves without being seen by the Mowl?' asked Ruker.

Pester tapped the side of his nose. 'There's a secret way, only known to Cave-Shroves.'

'We had no choice and had to let you leave without us, in case there were spies about,' explained Ernelle, 'but the Mowl would have soon picked up your trail.'

'We followed the Murk Mowl, who were following you, and bided our time,' replied Pester.

'We knew if they captured you, the Mowl would sell you to the Groats. You're a valuable asset in this wild kingdom,' explained Ernelle.

'We drugged the greedy Groat sitting watch over you. We left food by his bench when he was inside the tent checking on you, and when he came out he gobbled it all up. Know your enemy's weaknesses,' Ernelle sniggered, nodding at Pester.

'If the Groat Captain kept his minions well fed then this wouldn't have happened. They're mean and rotten, are Groats, even to their own kind.'

As they made their way across country, their eyes were irresistibly drawn to the sinister landmark of the blackened Tors, beckoning to the strangers and drawing them closer. Tallitha took Tyaas's hand in hers. What would they find inside? Would she ever see Winderling Spires and her old nurse again?

'It's such a dark place,' she whispered to Tyaas. 'What'll we find in there I wonder?'

But Tyaas had nothing to say.

They made their way down a gully to where a torrid stream flowed into one of the sparkling tarns. The day was warm and as they walked along, Tallitha sidled up to Ernelle.

'W-What's Hellstone Tors really like?' she asked cautiously.

'Oh my, it's a dreadful place,' whispered Ernelle.

'Shush, you'll scare the girl,' snapped Pester.

'How will they survive if they don't know the truth?' replied Ernelle. 'It's a wicked place and …'

Pester nudged Ernelle and she clammed up.

'We'll talk later,' whispered Ernelle into Tallitha's ear.

'We're headed for Raw-Ripple Island', said Pester. 'It's a hideout our traders use when we have to do business with the Tors. We must cover as much ground as we can before nightfall.'

The Cave-Shroves spurred them on, moving through the long grass by the edge of the lakes. For the moment, Tallitha had to curb her curiosity about Hellstone Tors but the gloomy edifice occupied her thoughts.

Sandpipers and curlews waded by the edge of the lakes and waterbirds soared high above them, piercing the air with their plaintive, lonely cries. Tear Drop Tarns was idyllic after the iron-coldness of the caves. Tyaas peered into the shallows at the shoals of fish and threw stones over the water, making skimming ripples across the surface. In the quiet of the desolate tarns, his thoughts turned to Benedict. He almost missed his annoying friend. He felt wounded by what had happened and wished he had seen it coming, but he hadn't. Benedict was an odd one, always had been, but his betrayal had been a complete surprise to Tyaas. It cut him deeply. If truth be told, it made him nervous and unsettled about what was yet to come.

Twenty-Six

By the time the sun was sinking, they reached the shores of Melted Water, one of the larger lakes at the northern edge of Tear Drop Tarns. The Cave-Shroves disappeared into a nearby thicket and after a great deal of huffing and puffing they reappeared, pulling a small canoe behind them.

'There are too many of us, so Ernelle will wait with Ruker and Neeps and I'll take you three over first,' said Pester.

Tallitha, Tyaas and Esmerelda waded out to the canoe and climbed in.

'I'll steer, you take it in turns with the oars, and we'll be there in no time.'

The evening sun glowed warm and the sound of the lapping water on the sides of the boat made an idyllic setting. But Tallitha sat nervously in the stern of the boat. She felt vulnerable out in the middle of the lake in that wildest of wild places. The haunting words of her Great Aunt Agatha came back to her, *'There are some who would take our lands if we let them.'*

Soon they reached the rocky shore of Raw-Ripple Island. Pester steered the canoe into a cove, moored it by the jetty and clambered out.

'These steps lead to the shelter so make haste and I'll go back for the others. They mustn't be out after dark.'

They followed Pester into an earth-floored cabin. At the back there was a storeroom with trunks full of old clothes and a larder with dried provisions.

'Many's the time we've had to struggle through a biting hard winter, hiding out in here. Make yourselves comfortable and I'll be back in the blink of an eye.'

With that, Pester left and they explored the cabin.

'Look! Bunk beds and pillows,' said Esmerelda happily, flopping down and snuggling under a thick quilt. 'Ahhhhhh, bliss! How long since I slept in a bed?' she sighed.

'There's food and root beer,' said Tyaas, already opening a bottle.

They thought about waiting for the others but their intense hunger outweighed their manners. As they ate, their thoughts turned to Hellstone Tors.

'Now we're here it's becoming more real. Have you thought about how we'll find Asenathe without being caught?' asked Tyaas tucking into his food.

Esmerelda had been mulling over the problem. There was only one solution.

'Tallitha must use her powers to locate Asenathe,' said Esmerelda, 'then once inside the castle we can follow Tallitha, she will know the way.'

'I'll try when the others are asleep,' Tallitha replied reluctantly.

She was tired and it had been some time since she had used her gift.

As the evening wore on there was still no sign of the canoe and eventually Esmerelda went out to the jetty. All she could hear was the water lapping against the wooden moorings.

'Any sign?' asked Tallitha coming up behind her.

'They should've been back by now. It's so dark out there,' she yawned.

Tallitha scanned the glistening black water, climbing on the rocks.

'Get some sleep and I'll keep watch. Then you can take over.'

Esmerelda was too tired to argue. She went back inside the shelter, snuck under the quilt and fell into a deep sleep.

Tallitha wrapped a blanket round her shoulders and settled down on the jetty in the cool night air. She relished the quiet time to herself. She was still stinging from Benedict's betrayal and reeling from the revelation about her mother and Queen Asphodel. As the water ebbed and bobbed, something caught Tallitha's eye. A small light twinkled in and out of the rocks, then it suddenly disappeared.

The rhythmical sound of the lapping water was soothing in the otherwise still darkness and Tallitha felt her eyelids grow heavy. She rested her head on her knees and it drooped to one side, closing her eyes for a few sleepy seconds. She was so exhausted she slipped imperceptibly into a dream-like state. As her waking senses deserted her she found herself skimming across the surface of the tarn and taking flight, winding up into the night air, racing on the north wind towards Hellstone Tors.

The castle was shrouded by dark, threatening clouds as Tallitha tripped and bounced round the walls, peering into the lattice windows in the highest turrets. She soon found a lighted window where a large candle flickered in the draught. Inside, the girl was sitting, dressed in a long velvet dress, her hair tumbling about her shoulders, and twisting a talisman between her fingers. She immediately sensed Tallitha outside in the darkness and she came towards the casement and beckoned to her.

'Come inside my sitting room. It's so cold out there in the dark. Don't be afraid,' she said softly as she lifted the latch, whispering mournfully into the chilly night air.

The girl climbed up to the stone window and her thin hand reached out as Tallitha hovered uncertainly in the darkness. Maybe it was something in the girl's glassy expression that made Tallitha tarry by the windowsill but she dared not enter the castle. The girl's icy fingers touched Tallitha's arm, drawing her closer, sucking her further in, as suddenly the face at the window darkened. The young face became much older; the eyes became cold and the once gentle fingers grabbed her, digging their sharp nails into her flesh.

'You're hurting me,' she shouted as the face distorted into an unholy scream.

The room vanished in an instant. Tallitha tumbled back to the island and woke with a start. She rubbed her eyes and felt for the jetty.

'Was that a nightmare?' she mumbled, coming to, 'or my shadow-flight?'

Tallitha shivered in the damp air and pulled the blanket tightly round her.

Then she heard a noise coming towards her through the darkness, the soft splish-splash of oars slicing repetitively through the water. That's what had disturbed her! There was the flashing light again, but this time it was much closer, moving over the surface of the black tarn. Whoever was out there would be at the island within seconds. Tallitha raced back to the cabin and shook Esmerelda.

'Someone's coming. Wake up, Essie.'

'Is it Ruker and the others?' replied a bleary-eyed Esmerelda.

'I don't know, but they'll soon be here.'

'Tyaas, wake up,' said Esmerelda. 'Get in the storeroom. Douse the light.'

They crouched down in the pitch-black earth room and waited. There was someone outside moving about.

'Esmerelda, Tallitha, where are you?'

It was Ruker. She opened the door and shone her lantern inside. Tallitha leapt from behind the door and hugged the Skink.

'What took you so long?' she shouted with relief.

'Groats,' she replied, 'lots of them. They turned up just after Ernelle got back to shore.'

'I thought you'd been captured,' said Tallitha.

'Had Ernelle been any longer she would have been a sitting target out on the lake.'

'Thankfully I wasn't,' said Ernelle, coming in with Pester to greet the others.

Tallitha and Tyaas leapt on the Cave-Shroves with joy.

'Steady on there,' said Pester a little embarrassed.

'How did you escape?' asked Tyaas excitedly.

'There are safe holes all around here. You just have to know where to find them. We snuck into one and waited it out,' said Pester.

'The holes were made by our kinfolk who work around here. It's a dangerous place out on the Tarns. There are often squabbles between the Groats and the Mowl. A Cave-Shrove has to know where to hide when they start to fall out. Now then, what's to eat? I'm starving,' said Ernelle, rummaging in the food bins.

After supper, Tallitha could wait no longer. 'Tell me, what's Hellstone Tors really like?'

'Not now,' said Pester sighing, 'it's too late.'

'But you promised,' she pleaded, squeezing Ernelle's hand.

Pester nodded at Ernelle, remembering the bargain she had made.

'Okay you win,' said Pester and signalled for Ernelle to continue.

'You wouldn't choose to go there, lest you had to. There are many stories,' her voice trailed off mysteriously. 'The castle is built deep into the heart of the Tors and into the sea no doubt.'

Pester tutted and raised her eyebrows at Ernelle.

'Well! I've heard it goes down to a tunnel that only the Swarm know about,' she whispered irritably to Pester.

'Watch the *words* you use,' stressed Pester nervously, motioning towards the door.

Ernelle nodded at her friend. 'There are many floors, secret entrances and towers. The inhabitants from the surrounding villages serve the Thane and his court, mostly Shroves and Grovellers. But those Shroves aren't like us and the Grovellers; they're mean as sin.'

'Tell them about the Bleak Rooms. Given you've started you'd better tell them everything,' urged Pester grouchily.

'The Bleak Rooms are nasty dungeons where prisoners stay for years on end,' explained Ernelle twitching.

'What have they done to deserve that?' asked Tyaas wide-eyed. 'Who are they?'

'Those who 'aven't paid their tithes or 'ave been caught talking about the Morrow Swarm,' mumbled Pester lowering her voice. 'It's a hellhole and that's for sure.'

'There's Cremola Burn, who comes from a village in Wycham Elva,' said Ernelle.

'Don't forget Leticia Trume, who used to serve Queen Asphodel,' said Pester.

'Well she don't serve her no more, does she?' said Ernelle tartly.

'What about the layout of the castle?' asked Esmerelda.

'There's a large courtyard with a marketplace, where the

hawkers sell their wares,' said Ernelle. 'The castle is surrounded on three sides by heavy seas that will dash any boat onto its heartless rocks. The peninsula is home to the Morrow Swarm, who control all the lands round here including the Out-Of-The-Way Mountains.'

'How do we get into the castle?' asked Tallitha.

'As far as I know the only way is through the market square but I've never been inside. This safe hole is the furthest I've been,' said Pester thoughtfully.

'We Cave-Shroves do business with the Tors from a distance. We keep well away,' explained Ernelle. 'Some say there are secret entrances into the castle but only the Swarm know about these.'

'But who are the Morrow Swarm?' asked Tyaas.

'Close the door, Pester,' said Ernelle, 'just to be on the safe side.' She lowered her voice and continued. 'There are thirteen in the Swarm, including the Thane. They serve him and control the borders, exacting tithes from the inhabitants. Far away to the northern reaches they have lands at Stankles Brow and beyond up to Hegglefoot, I've heard tell.'

'What makes them so powerful?' asked Tyaas.

'No one knows. But the Swarm are bound together by a secret pact taken when Edwyn fled Wycham Elva, and remade whenever a new member joins their evil brood.'

'You must have your suspicions about who they are,' said Tyaas inquisitively.

The Cave-Shroves looked furtively at one another.

'It's dangerous to speak about the Swarm. You could end up in the Bleak Rooms. Their spies are everywhere,' whispered Ernelle.

'But you must know. You have to tell us,' pleaded Tallitha.

The Cave-Shroves tried the door to make sure it was firmly bolted. Ernelle and Pester huddled together and beckoned to the others to gather round. Ernelle lowered her voice in the darkened room.

'There can only be thirteen in the Swarm and they must be descended from Edwyn Morrow. How they are chosen, no one can say. As long as the Swarm keep the oath and their pact of secrecy, they can rule. If the oath and the pact are broken, or if there are fewer than thirteen, then their powers will wane, so the legend goes.'

'What do you mean, fewer than thirteen?'

'It's the way of the pact, are you listening?' she tutted. 'There must be thirteen men and women in the Swarm. If one of them dies, or should leave of their own free will, then he or she must be replaced within a year and a month.'

'But how do we fit in to all this?' asked Tallitha, warily looking at Esmerelda.

'I'm not sure, apart from being from the Morrow family,' she said hesitantly.

'Come on, it's late. We can work out a plan in the morning before we leave,' said Pester.

'You're leaving us?' exclaimed Tyaas, glancing quickly at Tallitha.

'We must. This is as far as we can travel without endangering our community,' said Ernelle sadly.

'But what shall we do? Ruker, you'll help us, won't you?' pleaded Tallitha.

'I'm sorry, we can't. There are no Skinks in Hellstone Tors and we would stand out too much.'

Ruker looked crestfallen at letting down her friends.

'We're on our own then,' said Tallitha forlornly.

'We'll be waiting in Ragging Brows Forest, on your return,' said Neeps.

'If we ever return, that is,' said Tallitha and her face crumpled.

Everyone began to share the bunks, sleeping top to tail. In the darkness Esmerelda whispered to Tallitha, 'I can't summon the energy to contact Asenathe tonight.'

'Me neither, I feel too sad. Goodnight, Essie. Maybe things will look better in the morning.'

The thought of their friends leaving was too much to bear.

Once everyone had settled, Ruker crept over to Tallitha and took her hand.

'I hate to leave you to enter the Tors alone, not knowing what you will find ,'she faltered, gripping the girl's hand, 'but I promise, if I haven't heard from you by Middlemass, when the sloe berries fall from the trees, I'll know something is wrong and I'll come and find you, wherever you are.'

Tallitha pressed Ruker's hand next to her damp cheek. The Skink's promise was a shred of hope, something to hold on to if all else failed

Twenty-Seven

When Tallitha woke the next morning, her friends were hanging around in an unsettling way before leaving. Tallitha got dressed under the covers, shook Esmerelda awake, and solemnly sat down to drink a mug of steaming black tea.

'Did you sleep well?' asked Ruker, coming in from loading the boat.

'I dreamt the Mowl were chasing me. I found Asenathe, who only stared at me with cold eyes.'

She absent-mindedly played with some dried fruit, but had no appetite.

'Today we must devise a plan to enter the castle,' said Esmerelda stretching her arms in the air, 'I didn't sleep all that well. I'm much too excited.'

Ruker looked miserable. 'I thought you'd realise we couldn't go inside the castle. A group of seven strangers would attract too much attention, whereas two or three of you might just pull it off.'

'She's right, I'm afraid,' said Esmerelda, 'I've been dreading this day, but I knew we would have to go in alone.'

'Why didn't you say something before?' shouted Tallitha as tears came into her eyes.

She pulled her legs up to her chest and sat back in the chair, turning her head away from the others. Esmerelda touched her lightly on the arm.

'I have the makings of a plan, with your help,' she said couching down next to her cousin. 'We'll disguise ourselves as market traders, and once we're in the courtyard we can take our bearings from there.'

'But where will we stay?' asked Tyaas.

'That's one thing we *can* help you with,' said Pester. 'There's a tavern by the castle walls and the owner will ask no questions. She'll know you're not from these parts, but as long as you pay for your room, no one will bother you. It's called the Castle Keep and her name is Hester Lym.'

'I've a little money and we can sell things in the marketplace,' said Esmerelda brightly.

Tallitha's spirits were as low as they had ever been. Saying farewell was heart-breaking, and Tallitha wept and hid in the storeroom until it was time for the others to leave. After breakfast, Ruker and Neeps packed the boat, hugged their friends and sailed away with the Cave-Shroves in the small canoe. As Tallitha waved them off, she wondered if she would ever see her friends again.

'I will miss them so much,' she said sadly.

Esmerelda tucked a blanket around Tallitha's shoulders. 'Somehow we'll have to carry on without them,' she said trying to make the best of things. 'We can use the old clothes in the storeroom as a disguise, it might be fun.'

Esmerelda began rummaging in the trunks, waving various items in Tallitha's direction.

'Look! These traders' bags are the business. What can we put in them?'

Tyaas and Tallitha sat on the floor, half-heartedly picking clothes out of the trunks.

'I have grown to love our friends too, but we started this search together. We'll see them again when all this is over. I promise.'

'But will we?' sobbed Tallitha, distraught. 'First we lost Benedict, and that was a terrible shock, and now Ruker and the others. I depended on them. How will we do this alone?'

'Do you want to go home without trying?' asked Esmerelda.

'Of course not. It's just so hard saying goodbye, that's all,' said Tyaas brooding about the last time he had seen Benedict.

'I know, and I'm very sorry. We have to believe we're doing the right thing,' said Esmerelda. 'Let's look for the shabbiest clothes we can find,' she said trying to make a game out of it.

They began pulling the musty clothes from the trunk and trying them on.

'Oh no, look at this!' said Esmerelda trying on a feathered hat.

Tyaas fell about in fits of laughter and by the time Ernelle returned, they looked the part, dressed in shabby clothes, resembling poor street hawkers. They packed their belongings and took them down to the canoe.

'So what you going to sell?' asked Ernelle

'Matches, candles and honeycombs,' said Esmerelda

'And these,' said Tyaas excitedly, holding up a selection of odd looking traps.

*

By the time the canoe reached the shore, the Skinks had already left.

'They couldn't face any more goodbyes,' explained Pester, hugging Tallitha and Tyaas and shaking Esmerelda's hand.

'Remember the tavern and take care. The castle is a dangerous place. You'll need your wits about you.'

Tallitha watched the small figures scramble up the hillside. They turned to give a final wave and then they were gone.

Now they were all alone, standing by the water's edge.

Looking down on the three figures tramping by the lakeside it was easy to imagine they were some poor souls trying to eke out a meagre living. Their tattered clothes smelled horribly fusty, like someone had just died in them. Tallitha scratched her arms as the itchy garments rubbed against her skin. On the journey they spoke little, and by the late afternoon they had made good headway up a narrow gulley and out onto a promontory that provided a panoramic view of Hellstone Tors across the bay. It was the first time they had ever seen the sea, and Tallitha was amazed at the roaring rushing waves crashing headlong onto the rocks. Overhead, flocks of seagulls soared way above them, their screeching haunting cries sounding like a warning on the biting wind.

After rounding the headland they came to a settlement of scattered dwellings that fringed the bay, and further along the coastal path was the Castle Keep. As they sat in the tavern eating supper they overheard scattered pieces of conversations, uttered in hushed tones. The travellers sensed that the villagers were in awe of Hellstone Tors. Esmerelda went to the bar and learned from Hester Lym that the market opened early, so they supped their ale and decided to retire for the night. Tyaas was exhausted and fell asleep almost immediately, which gave Esmerelda and Tallitha the opportunity they had been waiting for. They crept behind the painted screen surrounding the wash basin and began whispering.

'When I was keeping watch, I made contact with Asenathe. Either that or it was a bad dream, b-but she tried to pull me into her room,' whispered Tallitha anxiously.

Esmerelda made little of her fears. 'She's only trying to reach out to you. This time, you must go to her, promise me.'

She took the jewelled pendant from her pocket and twisted it back and forth in the moonlight. It sparkled in the darkened room, making fleeting patterns appear on the walls. Diamond, sapphire and topaz lights glittered before Tallitha's eyes. Slowly she began to slide away from her body, like she was being stretched, then *whoosh!* – she had flown to a different place.

The towers pointed menacingly into the blue-black skies with the wind howling fiercely between the turrets, buffeting Tallitha around the walls. She saw the spluttering candle but this time the girl was waiting for her at the casement window. Tallitha steeled herself and stepped into the room. Her cold fingers held Tallitha's hand as she led her along the darkened passageways, higher and higher up into the castle with Tallitha trailing behind her. As the girl climbed the final staircase she turned towards Tallitha with a strange expression on her face. She looked triumphant! Tallitha stepped into a vaulted gallery filled with light. Tallitha knew she had found the Morrow court.

There before her was an ornately carved chair and the girl moved towards it and indicated that Tallitha should be seated. A strange, unsettling feeling began gnawing away inside her. Again something was wrong. The girl's face, once young and pretty, had become much older and dark seeping shadows prowled and twisted around her body. Now the face was etched with lines and her hair, once black and vibrant, was dull and streaked with long grey strands. Her cold dark eyes looked dead. If this wasn't the girl, then who was she? Tallitha's stomach tightened with the old tingling fear. Tallitha hovered for an instant then vanished from the gallery.

She slipped into the grey mist but the way of the shadow-flight was barred to her. She bumped against something and panicked. The brilliance of the silver cord had dimmed. Before her was the silvery timeless face of a woman.

'Leave this place, Tallitha. Go home to the Spires, this is an evil kingdom and harm will befall you if you remain here. Do not enter Hellstone Tors, but if you do, it must be of your own free will. Remember these words and heed me, heed me!' the spirit shrieked.

Then the spirit shattered into a thousand pieces and Tallitha felt herself falling. She cried out as she entered her body.

'What's wrong?' shouted Esmerelda.

Tallitha's face contorted as her whole body jerked uncontrollably.

'Tallitha, Tallitha what is it?' asked Esmerelda, shocked by Tallitha's violent reaction.

Her face was ashen and a dark grey aura crept around her body. Tallitha's head flopped, and her eyes rolled back into her head as she moaned and clung on to Esmerelda, gulping for air. At last Tallitha opened her eyes and looked wildly round the room, making sure she was safe.

'Oh Essie, there's something desperately wrong. We must go home, back to the Spires. Let's leave this dreadful place.'

Esmerelda stepped back from Tallitha as though she had been scalded. 'We can't do that. Not now, not after all we have been through to get here!' she cried.

'Essie, a spirit prevented me returning, she warned me to leave here. Who could that have been?'

Esmerelda shook her head and bit her lip. Her eyes looked haunted.

'Essie, you have to listen to me! Asenathe was different, she was older and her coldness scared me.'

Tallitha gripped hold of Esmerelda's hand. 'Please Essie, you have to believe me!'

A desperate look flitted across Esmerelda's face, just for a second, then she brushed it aside.

'It's just the way of the spirit-walk. Sometimes the process can elicit strange emotions.'

'No Essie, there was something sinister about Asenathe tonight,' said Tallitha. 'The silver spirit tried to warn me.'

'Your path may have become crossed with another spirit walker, it sometimes happens.'

'Essie, I want to go home. Please,' Tallitha begged and began to sob.

'Nonsense, you're overemotional. I'm not going back to the Spires until I find Asenathe. Please don't worry,' said Esmerelda trying to calm Tallitha, 'it will all work out tomorrow. Rest now and get some sleep.'

But Tallitha didn't believe her cousin. Esmerelda hadn't seen those cold dark eyes.

She held her breath as the shadows played across her room. What did it all mean?

In the solitary darkness she wished she had never left the safety of Winderling Spires. Why had she been so headstrong? She hid her head beneath the blankets to blot out the frightening images, but her rapid breathing and her racing heart kept her wide awake, repeatedly pounding, pounding in her ears.

As the seconds passed into minutes and her heart continued beating furiously, Tallitha realised she was absolutely terrified.

Twenty-Eight

Esmerelda was too excited to eat her breakfast, so Tyaas finished it for her. He was too busy wolfing down the eggs and sausage to notice the dark circles under his sister's eyes. Tallitha played with her food, lost in the agony of the night before.

'Do I have to eat yours as well?' he asked as Tallitha pushed her plate to one side.

'If you want to, go ahead,' she said listlessly.

Tyaas polished off the leftovers in a succession of ravenous mouthfuls.

'You okay, sis?' he asked, 'you seem a bit quiet this morning.'

'I'm scared,' she confided, leaning across the table. 'Will we get away with this? I had an awful premonition last night.' Then she stopped abruptly. Esmerelda put her finger to her lips.

'She's fine, Tyaas. She just had a bad dream, that's all. Now let's get into that castle,' she insisted, taking Tallitha's hand and leading her away.

*

As the travellers climbed the steep incline in the shadow of the great castle, the sheer enormity of Hellstone Tors began to unfold before their eyes. The fortification erupted out from the jagged tors like an angry monster, ominous and threatening. Hellstone Tors was an immense edifice, assembled by hundreds of stonemasons over years of back-breaking toil. The dark spiky fingers towered above them, blocking out the sunlight like a twisted crown. Tallitha stumbled, awestruck by the fearsome sight and by the thought of what lurked inside the sombre, impenetrable walls.

'It's so dark and gloomy,' she whispered, taking her brother's hand.

'Come on you two! Stop dawdling,' shouted Esmerelda racing ahead of them.

Between each Tor, the main castle had been forged deep within the bedrock. Carved mullioned windows and fancy iron balustrades covered the grey stone towers, culminating in a spectacle of burnished turrets. The towers coiled upwards to the sky, making the menacing structure look even more nightmarish. *Just like witches' fingers*, thought Tallitha and shuddered.

The path up to the castle drawbridge was covered in mist, a

haunting, damp sea fret sent to unnerve them. Tallitha stepped over the threshold of the castle and the others followed.

The courtyard was a bustling world of hawkers shouting about their wares, haggling for the next deal and trying to entice the passing trade to buy their merchandise. Pots and pans, loaves of bread, linen and silks, musical instruments, herbs, remedies and cures, all these could be bought in the busy marketplace. The quadrangle was thronging with bright, colourful awnings, the smell of freshly baked cakes and the aroma of exotic spices. Tallitha gazed in wonder at the bewildering array of purveyors selling delightful and unusual things as Esmerelda and Tyaas found a small space in the courtyard to spread out their goods.

New sights and smells flooded Tallitha's senses. She wanted to taste the salted nuts and lick the oozing chocolate fondants, listen to the flutes tootling in harmony and touch the velvets and silks draped in splendour over the stalls. The deep array of colours was breathtaking. Shades of crimson reds, simmering blues, violets and greens hummed vibrantly in the morning sunlight, the silks gently flapping in the sea breeze. Entranced, Tallitha wandered over to the fabric stalls and watched as skeins of cotton and silky yarns changed hands, while the women barked orders and heckled one another to make a sale. There were stalls with buttons, bric-a-brac, belts and cotton, and long hanks of wool in so many shades it made her head spin.

In the middle of the courtyard was a round metal grate where the slops and debris of the morning's trade trickled deep under the stained flagstones. Tallitha peered down into the blackened hole. As her eyes became accustomed to the darkness, she could make out a narrow stinking passageway and hear wailing voices coming up from the miserable, dank midden.

'What you after then?' came a rough voice sharply behind her.

'Nothing. Errr, I was just looking down t-there,' she replied nervously, edging backwards.

A fat Groveller stood with her hands on her hips, smoking a pipe and squinting at Tallitha in the brilliant sunshine. Her grey apron was stained with grease and blood, and as she lifted her large arms to shield her eyes from the sun, Tallitha could see the hairy armpits and smell the stench of stale sweat. Tallitha's eyes flickered nervously at the ill-humoured old crone.

'Get out of 'ere, if you know what's good for yer, cos them's the Bleak Rooms down there. You don't want to join them do yer?' cackled the Groveller, picking her brown teeth with a stick and spitting phlegm on the ground.

Tallitha stared at the specimen that lurched uneasily before her, smelling of beer.

'Are there people down there?' she asked, peering into the depressing hole.

'Course! Where else would we keep 'em but in a wet nasty place, to rot and die. Thieving rascals most of 'em,' she sneered eyeing Tallitha curiously. 'What's it to you, anyways?' she barked.

Tallitha made to leave, but something caught her eye. Someone was staring up at her from the pit. There was a flash of mad eyes as three spindly fingers with blackened broken nails poked up through the grate grasping at freedom. Tallitha stepped out of the creature's sight. She could hear the woman moaning in the middens, calling out to her.

'Help me, help me, please, kind lady.'

The old Groveller pushed Tallitha out of the way and stamped on the frail fingers.

'Shut up vermin, or I'll pour a bucket of slops over ya head. Haaaa! That'll teach 'er.'

The bedraggled wretch cried out and shrank from view, back into the miserable hole. Maybe that woman, Cremola Burn, was somewhere down there. What had she done to meet such a punishment? Tallitha slunk backwards from the grate and out of sight of the Groveller.

The marketplace was full of the nasty Shroves, shabbily dressed but remarkably adept at selling, ingratiating themselves with their customers, scampering from one stall to another and counting every last filthy coin into their mean little hands. They reminded Tallitha of Marlin, fawning obsequiously and pretending to be obedient to the Grovellers, who were in charge of all the takings, whilst secretly spying on all the goings-on.

The stall owners got their name from the villages round about; Much Grovell, Small Grovell and Grovell-by-the-Water. Tallitha watched the scene unfold as the Grovellers grabbed their feral children, roughly stuffing doughy food into their ever-open mouths or wiping their runny noses. The horde of dirty bairns ran like a pack of rats across the quadrangle, thieving scraps of food, deftly escaping a clip from their parents to hide, panting beneath one of the stalls. The Grovellers were fatter than they should have been, much louder than was necessary, drunker than was good for them and extremely dirty. They were a scheming lot, motivated by where the next penny was coming from. It was a hideous circus.

Suddenly one of the Grovellers lashed out at a spindly Shrove, sending him flying across the flagstones, squeaking and howling.

'Take that you little runt,' she screamed at the hapless Shrove.

The Grovellers stood in a menacing pack, laughing at the Shrove's miserable plight. Then the Groveller who had spoken sharply to Tallitha caught her watching the spectacle.

'What you lookin' at?' she yelled, baring her teeth.

Tallitha hurriedly averted her eyes hoping to deflect the Groveller's interest. Esmerelda noticed what was happening and dragged Tallitha back to their pitch.

'Come here girl!' she shouted. 'Take that!' and she slapped Tallitha hard on the side of her face.

'Sorry ma'am. We didn't mean no offence', said Esmerelda, dipping her hat.

The Grovellers jeered and spat at the strangers in their midst, deciding whether any sport was to be had at their expense. One of the young Grovellers stepped forward aggressively, but the older Groveller held her back.

'You from these parts then?' asked the ring leader.

'We're travellers, just here for a few days. Then we'll be on our way,' said Esmerelda meekly.

'Keep that girl under control. We don't like strangers, particularly thems that nose about and stare. Thems that think too much of themselves, all high and mighty ain't ya?' The Grovellers laughed at the wary trio.

'Sorry. Right you are,' said Esmerelda lowering her eyes.

She pulled Tallitha close. 'Don't annoy them. They'll have us thrown out.'

'Sorry,' answered Tallitha meekly, rubbing her cheek. 'You didn't need to hit me.'

'We don't want to attract attention, now try and fit in,' snapped Esmerelda, pushing Tallitha roughly to one side.

*

As the day wore on, they sold their wares and wandered around the marketplace looking for a way into the castle. It was Tyaas who found a narrow staircase behind one of the food stalls, a busy hubbub of activity that would give them sufficient cover to disappear when the time was right. By mid afternoon the lazy Grovellers began yawning and drifting off. They had supped enough ale, eaten too many pies, smacked all their horrible brats and were in need of an afternoon nap to sleep off their hangovers.

'It's time, Tyaas, we'll follow when we can,' whispered Esmerelda, making sure the coast was clear.

Tyaas sneaked behind the stalls, darted up the stone staircase and hid in the shadows. Within a few minutes Tallitha joined him. She held her brother's hand in the recess and waited. But Esmerelda was a long time. Seconds ticked by into interminable minutes until Tallitha could wait no longer.

'I'm going to take a look.'

'Be careful,' said Tyaas.

As Tallitha stepped into the corridor she felt the same tingle but stronger this time, a warning deep within her. Suddenly, an enormous gust of wind came rushing towards her down the corridor and the ethereal vision from the night before hovered before Tallitha. Her silver-grey hair floated behind her in tendrils.

'I told you to leave, Tallitha. I warned you. Yet you have chosen to ignore my warning and you have entered Hellstone of your own free will.' As she hovered, her face became grave. 'Then you have made your choice, and the pact is yours to destroy, if you can unlock the secret. But beware the power of the Morrow Swarm.'

The apparition held Tallitha's gaze, looked deep within her eyes, then disappeared as suddenly as she had arrived.

'Tyaas, Tyaas,' Tallitha whispered, 'did you see her?'

'What are you talking about?'

Tallitha caught her breath and turned to see Esmerelda standing behind her.

'Essie, you gave me such a fright. Did you see the apparition?'

'I didn't see anything. Come, we must hurry or someone will find us.'

'But Essie, I saw her, please believe me. She warned me again.'

Esmerelda turned on her heel and began racing down the corridor.

'Come on you two,' was all Esmerelda had to say.

Tallitha instinctively knew the way and took the lead, racing along the passageways and staircases until at last they came to the tower room.

'This is it,' said Tallitha as she stood in front of the wooden door.

Esmerelda stepped over the threshold and immediately a tall girl came towards them.

'Asenathe!' said Tallitha excitedly.

'That's not Asenathe,' replied Esmerelda abruptly.

Tallitha felt her stomach lurch. But this was the same girl she had seen in the shadow-flight. The girl had dark curly hair hanging down her back and she wore the bloodstone at her neck.

'But she has on the necklace!' shouted Tallitha, 'it must be her!'

'She isn't my cousin!' shouted Esmerelda, and shot a desperate glance at Tallitha.

The girl stood framed in the doorway, looking dismissively at the three visitors. She cast her eyes over them, taking in each detail, from their tattered shoes to their dirty clothes.

'I must ask you to follow me,' she said coolly.

'But where are we going?' asked Tallitha.

'Who are you?' asked Esmerelda warily. 'You have the Morrow look about you.'

The girl turned her twisted smile on the visitors. 'You will see soon enough,' she said mysteriously, as she disappeared down the staircase at the back of the room. 'Now keep up and don't get lost, the castle is renowned for its dark places where it's easy to put a foot wrong. Then we may lose you forever.'

Tallitha hesitated and hung back, 'I don't like her, or this dreadful castle. The apparition warned me last night. Essie, will you listen to me, please?'

'Shhh', said Esmerelda, pulling Tallitha behind her. 'There has to be an explanation, and soon we shall find out what it is.'

Tyaas was already halfway down the corridor beckoning to the others.

'Don't just stand there Tallitha,' said Esmerelda, 'otherwise, why have we travelled so far and endured so many dangers?'

'Come on, don't dawdle,' snapped the girl, as they chased after her down the vast, empty corridors.

The castle was indeed a dark, unwelcoming place. It was a colossal fortress, bigger then Winderling Spires and the endless stone staircases were longer and even more tiring. Up and up they went, past hundreds of mullioned windows looking out over the black rocks and grey lashing waves. The girl flounced down the long galleries, up the external staircases and out onto blustery battlements, high up into the complex fortifications of the Tors.

'But who is she,' Tallitha asked, 'if she isn't Asenathe?'

'Beats me,' said Tyaas. 'She's not very friendly.'

The girl stopped in front of a large carved door, standing half-open and waiting for their arrival. Bright light seeped from the room beyond. Then the girl pushed them, one by one into a long gallery filled with people. It was in that moment that Tallitha, Esmerelda and Tyaas stepped into another world.

The gallery was brightly lit with a thousand burning candles arranged on tall plinths, and set into enormous dazzling chandeliers. Around the gallery four huge fires crackled and hissed, throwing a red-golden light across the room. In front of each fireplace a pack of straggly hounds lay snoozing, raising their heads at the strangers' entrance, growling and waiting for the order to attack.

Standing in the middle of the gallery was a group of men and women, members of the royal court. Their clothes and their demeanour oozed wealth and opulence. The court turned and stared at the visitors, but there was no welcome in their eyes. As the girl moved into their midst the court bowed to her. It was then that her eyes smouldered and she stared long and hard at Tallitha.

'My name is Caedryl Morrow, and the Lady Asenathe is my mother,' she said pointing to an older woman sitting passively on a large chair.

Two wizened Shroves stood on either side of Asenathe.

'Asenathe!' cried Esmerelda, beginning to run across the gallery.

But Asenathe's face was like a stone and her blank eyes stared vacantly ahead.

'I don't understand. Have you no welcome for me?' asked Esmerelda, her voice faltering.

Asenathe studied Esmerelda and fleeting recognition flickered across her face, but the response was wanting. Tallitha felt small and vulnerable, exposed in the huge gallery. All the grand people were staring, straight at her, just at her.

'This must be Tallitha,' said Caedryl imperiously. 'Welcome to Breedoor and to Hellstone Tors.' She held out her hand for Tallitha to kiss it.

Tallitha did not move towards the proud girl. She was transfixed by the Swarm. Amongst the grand men and women of the court were the members of the evil Morrow Swarm. Esmerelda noticed the fuzzy vibration begin to surround Tallitha but this time it had a grey-black hue.

'But I saw you. I came to you many times, in my trance,' Tallitha exclaimed, wounded by the girl's hostility.

The girl laughed in Tallitha's face, a haughty, piecing laugh. 'No, you're confused, I'm afraid,' she said pompously. 'It was my mother you saw. At first when she was a young girl, and then as she is now.' She waved her hand in the direction of Asenathe.

'I don't understand,' Tallitha faltered, searching Esmerelda's face for reassurance.

'My mother is the channel not I. But surely Esmerelda knew this?' she smirked nastily from one to the other.

Tallitha swallowed hard as the realisation of her terrible mistake began to sink in. She flicked her eyes desperately at Esmerelda.

'I didn't realise,' cried Esmerelda. 'Your shadow-flight must have taken you back in time.'

'Why didn't you listen?' shouted Tallitha. 'You took too many risks with me,' she wailed and buried her face in her hands. 'I tried to tell you, to warn you there was something wrong!'

'But it's too late now,' a voice shouted from within the group of men and women.

It was then that the court parted to reveal the grandest man in the room. He was tall and thin with sharp angular features. This was the Thane, Frintal Morrow, who was sitting on a grand throne. He had a shocking mass of wild grey hair, randomly plaited with small jewels at the ends. Lord Frintal gesticulated in Tallitha's direction.

'It's taken a long time but you're here at last, and you entered Hellstone of your own accord. Well done!' he laughed wickedly.

Whichever way he looked, the Thane's pointed chin, his high cheek bones, and his sharp aquiline nose reflected the facets of his merciless razor-edged personality. He had the face of an anvil.

The court echoed his laughter and began to circle round Tallitha.

'We've been waiting for you,' said Caedryl, beguilingly.

Tallitha felt her insides grip with revulsion. Esmerelda shook her head as Tallitha's desperate face turned towards her for an explanation. She too, was struggling to comprehend the full meaning of the unfolding drama.

'But how did you know I was coming?' asked Tallitha, finally finding her voice.

'We know everything about you,' said the Thane ominously.

'And what say you, my cousin?' asked Esmerelda walking towards Asenathe. 'Could you not have prevented this? Could you not have protected us?'

'She will not speak to you. She is distressed,' said Caedryl disdainfully, regarding Esmerelda as a worthless being.

'But we came all this way to find you,' cried Tallitha at the silent Asenathe.

'But she wasn't lost,' said Caedryl coldly, patting her mother's arm and pushing the Shroves to one side.

The Thane focussed his black eyes on Tallitha. His jawline shone like a knife blade in the firelight.

'Sit, Tallitha, here next to me. Come, it's your turn now,' he said mysteriously.

'But I don't know you,' she cried, 'I don't want to be in this place.'

The Thane laughed wickedly. 'But you will know me Tallitha! Come, I have someone I want you to meet.'

Lord Frintal ran his cold steel eyes over her face and his lip curled upwards revealing a set of sharp white teeth. They shone in the candlelight as he licked his thin, red lips. Tallitha had seen many wicked smiles in her time, but his was the worst of all evil leers. Shaking and compelled by his powerful gaze, she moved hesitantly across the room and stood before him. The Thane sat back with a victorious expression in his glinting eyes and clicked his fingers twice, click-clack. The long gallery fell silent. Then, from behind the huge throne came a noise. Asenathe's Shroves began to salivate and hop about feverishly.

Damn the Shroves, thought Tallitha, What has this to do with them?

'You can come out now!' shouted the Thane, his lips twisting into a satisfied sneer.

From behind the throne a figure stepped forward. A small twisted body and familiar wizened face appeared before her. It took Tallitha a second of mind-numbing realisation to recognise the weaselly face in the unfamiliar surroundings. It was Marlin who crept from behind the throne and stood beside his Thane. The Shrove motioned to his kinfolk, salivated, rubbed his old hands together, hopped about and gloated at his wicked deception.

'Marlin!' cried Tallitha horrified, 'b-but what are you doing here?'

'Sniffin' you and followin' you,' he growled nastily and chuckled to himself.

'We've been tracking you. All the while you had the Morrow stain upon you,' said the Thane. 'Once the stain touches you, it always leaves its trace.'

'W-what do you mean?' she faltered.

'The dark stain from the Raven's Wing,'tis the blood curse! The birth of our pact, the stain sought you out. The Morrow stain marked you so Asenathe could always find you and bring you to Hellstone Tors.'

It was in that moment that Tallitha understood they had been taken for complete fools. It had been Marlin up on the roof of Winderling Spires. He had lured them to the turret and he had planted the sampler. It had been a grand deception: from her irrepressible curiosity at the beginning, to the end and her downfall in this terrible castle. They had followed like lambs, bewitched by the thought of adventure. They had been spied upon every step of the way.

Tallitha stared desperately around the gallery for an escape route, but each doorway was barred by a Groat. The Thane sprang forward and tightly grabbed her wrist, twisting her arm up her back.

'You're not going anywhere!' he shouted into her terrified face.

'But why me?' she cried.

Tallitha's cries reverberated around the gallery as the Thane held her fast.

It was Esmerelda who understood at last. She screamed and lashed out at Marlin, scratching him across the face, drawing fresh blood. He whelped and wailed, spitting and swearing at her until one of the Groats pulled her off.

'Leave her alone,' shouted Tyaas, bewildered.

He looked at his sister for reassurance, but her wretched face said it all.

'What's going on Tallitha?' he asked quietly, pulling on her sleeve like a lost child.

But Tallitha's face was ashen. Part of her did not want to understand the full horror of their predicament.

Esmerelda struggled against the Groat's strength, watching while the Morrow Swarm took their seats at the table, noticeably leaving three vacant chairs by the Thane's side. Then she put her head in her hands and sobbed.

'What have I done?' she wept. 'I'm sorry, Tallitha. I should have listened to you. I didn't know this would happen.'

'Essie, what is it? Please tell me!' shouted Tallitha clinging to her brother.

But all she could hear was the sound of Esmerelda's inconsolable weeping.

Caedryl moved next to the Thane's throne. Her long dark hair was the same colour as Tallitha's and she swept it over her shoulder in a haughty fashion, looking down her nose at the wretched girl before her.

'We are in black, my mother and I, because we are in deep mourning. My father, Arden Morrow, died this past year.' She paused as the court murmured reverently for the deceased heir of Hellstone Tors. 'We have brought you here because it's your turn now, Tallitha. You must take your place with the Morrow Swarm.'

The nasty smile played on her lips and pure wickedness filled her eyes. Tallitha stared at the girl and heard her words but it seemed as though everything was happening to someone else.

'Essie, tell me this isn't true!'

She screamed at the grimacing faces of the Morrow Swarm crowding around her, their pawing, clutching fingers touching her, embracing her and sucking her into their evil world.

'Get away from me!' she shouted.

The Thane waved his arms and his face glowed with devilish triumph.

'You are the thirteenth!' said Lord Frintal exultantly. 'We have you in good time. We had but a year and a month to bring you here. "*Get the thirteenth in thirteen months*" the sacred pact decrees and here you are. You came of your own free will!'

The Thane's sharp features twisted in the candlelight.

'But I can't be part of this!' Tallitha cried desperately, searching their evil faces.

The room spun before her eyes. The Swarm's wicked intention filled every corner of the huge gallery and leeched out of their cruel faces.

'Indeed you *are* part of this, Tallitha,' said the Thane.

He took out a large jewel and dangled it in front of Tallitha's face. It was identical to the one they had seen in the Jewel Room. The Swarm gathered around and sighed longingly at the sparkling gemstone as it twisted in the firelight. Horrified, Tallitha watched them encircling her, their faces enthralled and in awe of the stone. Suddenly an array of sparkling colours sliced the room as they had done all those weeks before in Winderling Spires. Tallitha's head began to ache.

'This is yours, Tallitha. Put it round your neck,' demanded Lord Frintal as he handed the jewel stone to Tallitha.

'Never!' she cried and flung it across the room.

It clattered against the fireplace as the Swarm let out a cry, and ran to retrieve it.

'You're wrong. You're lying. I'm not part of this pact nor the dreadful Edwyn Morrow!' she screamed.

But as she said the words, the familiar gut-wrenching feeling gripped her in the pit of her stomach. She couldn't be part of this evil brood, the brood whose faces bore a terrifying resemblance

370

to those ghostly spectres she had seen in the Raven's Wing!

The Thane stamped his foot, his eyes lit up like the devil and he pointed towards the huge oak door at the far end of the gallery. The room was swimming before her and she felt as though her head was about to explode.

'Look over there, Tallitha. See who's coming through the door,' the Thane chortled malevolently.

Tallitha did not want to look. She screwed up her eyes and hid her face. She was afraid she would see what she feared the most. But the Thane would not let the moment pass. Tallitha must witness the entrance he had so carefully arranged. He gripped Tallitha's face in his wretched fingers, and forced her to lift up her head.

'Open your eyes! Look Tallitha, over there, LOOK at my beautiful daughters!' he shouted as he stood up to greet his children.

Through the entrance, draped in silken dresses of red and gold, Snowdroppe and Asphodel entered the gallery and regally took their seats at the grand table.

'The last seat is yours, Tallitha! Now we are the thirteen!' shouted the Thane.

The Morrow Swarm and their entourage clapped their hands in delight and shouted with whoops of pleasure.

'Let it begin! The Swarm will be complete!'

The Thane shouted ecstatically as the baying cacophony of the jubilant Morrow Swarm filled the long gallery.

Tallitha screamed and screamed.

This could not be happening.

It must be a nightmare.

'Let me go!' she yelled, struggling to get free, 'I won't be part of this.'

Marlin held her tightly, his eyes glinting as he hopped about, saliva running down his whiskery chin.

Her mother's ecstatic face beamed at her from across the table.

Tallitha gasped. She was trapped in this evil, wretched place.

She tried to wrench herself free, but it was no use.

They were all trapped in the evil clutches of the Morrow Swarm in the depths of Hellstone Tors.

She was doomed if she stayed in the Swarm's lair.

How would she ever get free?

But somehow, someday she had to find a way.

And that is the end of this story and the beginning of another one.